THE WOMEN OF WILD COVE

J. KELLAND PERRY

The future has an ancient heart.

— CARLO LEVI

How I wish that somewhere there existed an island for those who are wise and of good will.

— ALBERT EINSTEIN

Change is coming whether you like it or not.

— GRETA THUNBERG

To all the strong, brave women I have known and loved.

CHAPTER ONE

EARLY SEPTEMBER 2203

The rabbit lay dead in the snare, its soft pelt gilded in morning dew. Kat frowned at the animal at her feet. Her bucket brimmed with dark red raspberries, sweet-scented and ripe to bursting, and the woven pouch clipped to her belt bulged with medicinal herbs. But among the snares she'd set yesterday, this was her only capture: a rust-brown hare, and a leveret at that. She'd crept off to Black Spruce Forest at sunrise for a rare hour alone, well before Shyla's usual wake-up time so she wouldn't need to take her along.

When she bent to loosen the puny carcass from its slip, branches rustled behind her. She stiffened. By reflex, her hand grazed the bone knife tucked into a loop of twine at her hip. She straightened up by inches and turned around, wary of a confrontation with a predator. A coyote or lynx, maybe. Duty-bound and distracted with recent changes, she'd forgotten to keep an eye out for any danger lurking nearby.

The rustling ceased. Peering through the tangle of brush, she found the source—a man she'd never seen before.

He lay on his back in a scrubby glade, little more than a stone's throw away. She held her breath and studied his profile, caught in flecks of sunlight through the canopy of leaves. Thick lashes fanned on a sunburned cheek. She stared at the curious length of his hair, stringy and unkempt. Patchy, stubbled jaw, yet youthful in slumber. Her eyes flitted over his foreign clothes. His charcoal pants were heavily stitched with ragged patch pockets on the thighs. The front of his torn shirt and rolled-up sleeves looked gritty with sand and muck. Scuffed leather boots stood rigid next to his outstretched legs.

She knew at once that he was not one of the men managed by her island's female elders. He was not dressed in the familiar clothing of the indoctrinated village labourers, the peons. And he certainly wasn't dressed in the apparel of the refined consorts she'd seen from time to time at the clinic, the males used in the matriarchy's breeding program.

Everything about his appearance told her he was not one of the peons or consorts from Wild Cove, or from any of their island villages.

The man stirred. He curved his arms over his head, yawned, and shifted his bulk on a crude bed of dead spruce boughs.

Kat ducked behind an overgrown thicket of raspberry bushes. She crouched and waited, still as a tree stump. Her heart thudded like a campfire drum. Even this early, the slanting sun beamed hot on her neck through the flickering gaps in the trees. A black and yellow hornet droned nearby. It buzzed closer, pitched on her bare thigh for a moment, then flew off.

She knew she must report this man-creature to the others, but she couldn't risk detection. For now, she could only observe. Her thin tank top clung to her back. She smelled her sweat as it trickled under her arms and down her chest. What would he do if he saw her?

Spotting this stranger carried her back to her fifteenth year, to the day she and Harper had discovered the wreck of a long liner on Five Mile Beach. Keen to be the first to reveal their spectacular find, they'd raced each other to the elders' house. Kat had quickly outpaced her friend and spilled the news to Ms. Eleanor. As fast as her short, chunky legs could carry her, the elder had bustled through the cove to alert the other villagers and send word to the peon quarters.

They didn't discover the body aboard the forty-foot wreck until later. A band of her people dragged the enormous vessel over the kelp onto dry sand. When three armed and brawny peons had completed the search inside for invaders, the rest of them clambered aboard. They found two brass-bound trunks inside the lower deck, intact among a jumble of debris. Bryce, a senior peon, broke the rusted padlocks while Kat and the others watched. One trunk brimmed with knives, rifles, ammunition and other weaponry, a practical and valuable acquisition. In the other, an abundance of medical supplies.

A gruesome stench led them to the battered hold, where they'd discovered the dead man under a tarpaulin and a moldy snarl of fishing nets. The peons had relieved him of the binoculars looped around his neck, the same pair she'd brought with her today. Reminded of them, she resumed her surveillance of the stranger through the bushes with the help of magnification.

They'd burned the wreckage, with the corpse, in an enormous bonfire on the beach where they'd found it. The old women of the village had whispered of similar occurrences years before. Kat watched the rogue stir on his pallet of branches. If he hadn't come by boat, what other means explained his presence?

Her legs in their crouched position started to cramp. She shifted and knelt in a sponge of green moss. She didn't see the brittle sprig of deadwood underneath.

A sharp crack pierced the silence and pushed her heart into her throat. She gasped and ducked lower behind the raspberry canes.

Too late.

The man leapt to his feet and whirled in her direction.

Through the thorny brambles, his startled gaze locked onto her face. For one suspended instant they were both prisoners, caught in each other's eyes.

The corners of his mouth tugged upwards into a hesitant grin. But Kat took his implied friendliness as a ruse. When he lunged for his boots, a jolt of adrenaline shot through her.

Leaving the snared hare and bucket of raspberries where she'd dropped them, she bolted through the trees. She didn't bother to check if the stranger gave chase—she would know soon enough. She flew like a hurricane gale through the underbrush, flushing waxwings and thrushes from their woodland nests and driving rodents to scurry to the safety of their burrows. She leaped over shrubs, exposed tree roots and rocks. Her binoculars bounced on her chest as she fled.

Though an excellent runner, she had more at stake this time. This was not the benign race she signed up for each fall at Harvest Festival, where the fittest among them competed in a 400-metre dash for the coveted prize of a free day of their choice. Nor did she liken it to the hunt of an animal as a much-needed food source. If the animal outran you, you acknowledged the loss and hauled your sorry ass home. Her gut warned her the outcome of this race could mean the difference between life or death, or an even worse consequence.

In spite of her speed, the stranger gained ground, closing the gap between them. The crunch of his footfalls and his laboured breaths grew louder and louder as he hurtled after her through the trees.

She stole a backward glance when she broke out onto the barrens. When he, too, cleared the woods, she saw a twist of pain on his face and a pronounced limp on his left side. Her chance to gain ground. Even so, his determination to keep on her tail with every stride of his long legs rattled her.

She remembered a nearby hiding place.

When she came to a downward slope at the end of the barrens and bog, she squeezed herself into a tight ball with chin to chest and rolled. She knew the area well. She'd played here as a child with Wren and the others in games of hide and seek and foraged for foodstuffs with Shyla now that she'd grown older. She counted on her familiarity with each veiled nook and secret cranny of the landscape to save her.

At the bottom of the grass-covered hill, she sprang up and veered left behind a wall of granite boulders. She grabbed deep lungfuls of air as she pressed on through a stand of dogberry trees and dark, leafy alder bushes. Beside a knoll behind the alders, she nudged aside a mass of dead brushwood to expose the low opening to a root cellar, dug out of the side of the hillock centuries ago.

The abandoned cellar's sunken, three-foot-high entrance was surrounded by a half-moon wall of tightly-layered slate rock and topped with a roof of packed soil and sod. It no longer had a door like the cellars her village still used. Over the years, she'd kept the sloped entryway packed with forest debris and its interior tidy for her own use.

She pulled out the knot of debris stuffed in the opening. Before she stooped and descended to safety, from the inside she hauled the dead brushwood back over the entrance to obscure it. The lack of light inside didn't matter. She knew its dimensions from memory: one hundred square feet of floor space, mortared stone walls, and a boarded ceiling ten inches above her head to keep it from caving in. Two square, wooden produce bins stood against its side walls, filled with items of food and other odds and ends she'd collected.

She would stay perfectly silent and wait until the stranger gave up his hunt. Pawing through the produce bin, she plunged her hand under a bag of moose jerky she'd stowed there and grabbed a pile of dusty, hemp-woven potato sacks. She spread some of them on the dank floor of packed earth and squatted on top of them.

Acute pain stabbed her. She clamped a hand over her mouth to smother a cry. Something razor-sharp had pierced her right thigh. She felt wetness on her leg. In the darkness of the cellar, she found the slender blade of her bone knife stuck in her thigh. Her elbow had dislodged it from the loop on her hip in her haste to crouch. She pulled it out. Warm blood streamed over her hand. Laying the thin knife aside, she pulled off her tank top to compress the wound and threw an armful of potato sacks over herself in a shroud.

The crackle of twigs and branches intensified as the stranger's footfalls approached the stand of alders. Then, silence. She strained to listen. Maybe he'd given up. She recoiled when she heard him grumble to himself outside the cellar entrance.

"Jeez! Where the hell did she go?"

Rooted to the spot, she held her breath, determined not to give herself away again. She gripped the hilt of the bloody bone knife in one hand and felt around in the darkness with the other. Her hand closed around a hefty stone that had come loose and fallen from the mortared wall.

After a harrowing wait, the sound of heavy footsteps resumed, then retreated until she couldn't hear them anymore.

And still she waited. An eerie sensation of déjà vu engulfed her, of hiding from someone in this cellar a long time ago. How old had she been? Ten? Eleven? She wasn't sure.

A fuzzy memory flashed. Another man, running through the forest, carrying her over his shoulder. She'd screamed out for help to her sister-guide, but the man had kept running.

She suddenly remembered how she'd stiffened and curled her body to wrench herself off him. He'd held on tighter. She'd twisted her head around, rammed her open mouth into his bulging arm, and sank her teeth into his upper bicep. The coppery taste of blood. He yowled and swore and threw her off him with a solid whack to the side of her head.

He must have been a rogue too. Wren had told her to hide. A

surge of fondness welled up for her sister-guide, swiftly devoured by a wave of self-loathing. And as always, the sting of rejection.

No. Hardly the time to stew over Wren.

She listened and sat in silence a little longer. Her assailant must have left.

The children would not get away from him as easily as she had. She needed to go back to the cove and warn the others before he threatened anyone else. The elders would organize search parties to find, capture, and bring him in.

She crawled out of the cellar. She made no attempt to go back and retrieve the hare or the berries she'd picked. As much as they needed other sustenance to supplement their farm-grown fare and seafood catch of the day, she couldn't hazard another encounter with the outsider. And her thigh bled profusely. She redonned her blood-soaked top to cover her nakedness, plugged the entrance and concealed the cellar again with brushwood, and then ran across the rocky barrens to home.

CHAPTER TWO

All the way back to the cove, Kat stole frequent backward glimpses to make sure the strange man hadn't followed her.

The rear of the yellow saltbox house came into view as she crossed the cow pasture. Panting, she skirted around the lofty weeping willow to the front where Ms. Bee and Ms. Naomi sat in conversation on the veranda.

"Katrena!" shouted Ms. Bee. "What has happened? What's wrong?" The silver-haired woman jumped from the porch swing and hurried down the steps to meet her with the junior elder close behind.

Breathless from the run, Kat wiped her dripping forehead and upper lip with the back of her arm. "I'm the finest kind now. He almost caught me, but I escaped."

Ms. Naomi smothered a gasp. "What almost caught you—a bear? There's blood on your clothes. And your leg is bleeding! Is that how you got hurt?" She pulled a square of cloth from the pocket of her cargo shorts and held it out.

The old woman appraised Kat with open suspicion. Her aged face, an intricate symmetry of deep seams and wrinkles carved by time, closed in. "Well? Was it a bear or some other animal? And you dodged your mentoring duty again this morning. Miss Shyla searched high and low for you!"

"I didn't see the harm in checking my slips and picking a few berries before I collected her. But never mind that now, I'm trying to tell you it wasn't—"

"Do I need to remind you she's the second sister-ward you're about to alienate? What are we going to do with you? Your disobedience and your lack of accountability has become a major headache for us."

"But I was only gone an hour or so..." She paused, stung by the harsh reprimand. She didn't deserve this. A worm of defiance gnawed at her insides. It held her back from buckling under the chief senior elder's interrogation. She admitted nothing—she had to think this through. Though nobody knew it, she'd seen firsthand what could happen to a rogue among them. A childhood memory of that nature wasn't easily buried. If she told Ms. Bee about her discovery this morning, would the peons capture him too? Would they kill him at once and ask questions later?

"Answer your elder, Kat," Ms. Naomi said. "Was it a bear or not?"

The lace of one of her hiking boots had come loose. She weighed her reply as she bent to retie it. Maybe he posed no threat to anyone. Maybe he was harmless and needed their help. "I—I'm not sure. It might've been a wolf or lynx, or just a coyote—not like I had time to stick around and take notes. When I heard something move through the trees, I dropped my berries and ran, but I tripped and, stunned-like, stuck myself with my knife." She patted her hip for the bone knife she'd made weeks ago, but it wasn't there. In her haste, she'd lost it while she ran or had left it behind in the cellar.

"Well, whatever it was, it must've changed its mind and went back to the woods." Ms. Naomi tucked her wheat-coloured, shoulder-length hair behind her ears. "You're safe, that's the main thing, and it may have been providence that Miss Shyla hadn't gone with you today. Go on in the house and take care of that wound. There's a first aid kit in the cupboard above the range, and you'll find a clean tank top in my bedroom." She turned to her colleague. "We should discuss setting out more traps at this evening's meeting."

Kat started to go into the house, but Ms. Bee seized her wrist, her bony fingers clamped on like eagle talons. Head lowered, Kat focused on the pronounced blue veins and constellation of liver spots on the back of the elder's hand.

"You know you must tell the truth, Katrena. And shirking your responsibilities comes with a price. As of today, you are on notice as a sister-guide. If I hear of one more infraction, your morning privileges will be revoked. And if that doesn't keep you in line, we will reassess your ranch placement."

Kat blotted her weeping wound with the cloth and avoided the senior elder's penetrating glare. She dipped her head in a half-nod but stayed silent, fighting an overwhelming impulse to pull away.

Ms. Naomi gave her a stern look. "I'm sure she will do better going forward."

At last, the old woman released her grip. "Away with you, then. As per your schedule, report to the nursery as soon as you've cleaned up. You're already late."

"This won't take long." She scooted inside the elders' house. Within minutes, she had her leg washed and bandaged and her top switched to a fresh one.

"Shyla is finishing her book report on *The Call of the Wild*," the junior elder said when she reappeared. "She's in your dorm, I believe. Make sure you fetch her!"

"Will do, Ms. Naomi." She dashed off across the cow pasture, taking the shortcut through the elders' gated alleyway and passed the horse paddock to the main road. She didn't slow down until she was well out of their sight.

For the first time ever, she gave thanks for nursery duty. Even the brain-numbing routine of baby care trumped the humiliation of Ms. Bee's disapproval. Defying the rules had become damn near impossible. And she needed to think some more about the outsider and what to do about him.

Over the past six weeks, life in Wild Cove for her and her peers had undergone a drastic shift. And the way she saw it, not for the better. From the time she was big enough to gather herbs, pick berries, mend a gillnet and rig a trouting pole, her outdoor jaunts to the woods and on the water had filled most of her days. Now, between the responsibility of mentorship and the addition of domestic chores, her life no longer felt like her own.

As she passed by the cottages that dotted both sides of the road, Ms. Bee's warning replayed in her head. Dragging her feet, she curved left onto the pebbled path to the nursery. The thought of losing her half-morning outdoors irked her. Doubtlessly to shut her up, the elders had granted her that one compromise—the freedom to trap, fish, forage or tend to the horses in the early hours—as long as she took her ward along. She'd try to watch her step. She would not jeopardize her Western Path education for anything.

The year of her twelfth birthday, she spent the entire summer at work on the southwest coast's thriving livestock ranch. Her assistance with the birthing of calves and breaking in of new foals during one busy fortnight in May was all it took to demonstrate her knack for the work. With the head rancher's permission, she'd sent a fervent plea to Bianca—or Ms. Bee, as she preferred to be called by her underlings—to let her stay on. Ms. Eleanor told Kat later that because it might ease the ache of Wren's departure, the elders had agreed to extend her junior apprenticeship at Western Path to September.

But stints with ranch orientation were offered to all teens since it opened, so she had no choice but to wait until her graduation from regular school to move there. The elders had signed off on her chosen vocation and her permanent installation would commence late in the fall, after harvest. Provided she didn't screw it up and evade Shyla again. Not to mention her keeping mum about the rogue.

A modest but sprawling bungalow with scaling wood clapboard and shuttered windows served as the village nursery facility. As an outdoor extension of the toddler/preschool playroom, a yard had been attached on the side. Over the whitewashed picket fence, Kat spotted Grace, the assigned attendant, and Harper's sister-ward, Alice. Small heads bobbed up and down in the swing and seesaw area. The buzz of childish voices and squeals of laughter filled the air.

Inside, she kicked off her boots and entered the spacious main room of the nursery. Eight wooden cribs lined the left wall, four cribs and two low cradles lined the right. Three change tables flanked the rear wall next to a counter, a biofuel cooler and a wood range. In the center of the room, five ladderback rocking chairs curled in a crescent on a multicoloured, braided rug. A slipcovered futon, mainly used for the teen attendants' night-time catnaps, faced the rockers.

Falon and Ruby rocked infants while Harper hovered over a baby boy at a change table. Like their supervisor, the attendants wore identical, mauve uniform dresses.

What a miracle! No babies were crying—a rare occasion indeed. "They saved their yammering for my ears, I s'pose," she said in a contemptuous tone.

The rosy-cheeked girl gave her a knowing wink. Harper removed the soiled diaper, cleaned the little one's bottom and tossed the cloth in a nearby laundry hamper. She and Kat were the same age. "It has been peaceful, but now that you're here...maybe not so much." She laughed, high ponytail bouncing as she pulled a fresh diaper from the shelf under the change table.

Kat sidled by the others, careful to hide the bandage on her thigh. "I wouldn't doubt it in the least."

Across the room, a stout young woman carried a baby in a bath towel. She placed her on the table next to Harper and clucked her tongue. "For your information, ladies, children often sense a caregiver's hostility." She slipped the gurgling tot into a clean onesie and combed her damp, red curls into a crown of ringlets.

Kat brushed by her supervisor. "Them's the breaks, Yvonne. I can't fake enjoyment."

She hurried down the hall that led to the preschoolers' bedrooms to change her clothes in the supply room. She sighed. She knew what to expect since last week's labour-intensive orientation—five long days and nights filled with non-stop feeding, changing, and rocking of the twelve babies in their charge. With five other apprentices around her age, Kat worked her shifts under managerial check-ins from Senior Nursery Practitioner Nola, and under the constant supervision of Junior Practitioner Yvonne.

She took off her top and shorts and pulled on the ill-fitting uniform over her head. She detested the baggy dress with its sickly, mauve colour almost as much as the work, but at least it covered the bandage on her leg. As she slipped her feet into leather sandals, she made a face. She thought of the coddling, the endless baths, the countless strolls, and the attempted naps grabbed in between. Twice on nightshifts, she'd fallen asleep with a babe in arms, unused to the demands of a squalling, selfish infant.

Yvonne acted as if nursery work was of the highest calling, caring for the fussy brats with their constant gas and spit-ups and shitty diapers, and their incessant wailing all hours of the day and night. The infant Kat had fed at orientation last week projectile-vomited over her, and after she'd cleaned up and rocked him for a while, the little fiend had exploded in diarrhea over her lap.

Unlike her, the other apprentices weren't bothered by the new order. Content with the added responsibilities, few of them voiced any real complaints. Why did she feel so utterly out of place?

When she re-entered the main room, her supervisor stood in wait.

"Here. Have a spell with Red." She dropped the red-haired little one into Kat's arms. The children received their official names from the elders at three months, so the staff used temporary nicknames until then.

The tiny child peered up at her and stiffened. She screwed up her delicate rosebud of a mouth and bawled as if her world had been shattered. Taken aback by the volume of her lusty cries, Kat tried to comfort her by bouncing her against her chest.

"What did I tell you? Think she's hungry?"

"She might be." Yvonne pushed back coiled tendrils that had escaped her messy bun. She reached into a wooden cradle for an infant who had started wailing at the sound of the other baby's sudden shrieks. Her wide hips stretched against the fabric of her dress as she leaned over.

"She could probably do with a few sucks and a cuddle. Give it a chance. It won't kill you to be nice, you know."

Kat stuck her tongue out at Yvonne's back. With the squirming bundle held in one arm, she drew a bottle of breast milk from the freshly stocked cooler. She warmed the bottle in a pan of simmering water on the wood stove and plunked herself in the rocker next to Harper, joining the intimate semicircle of teenage girls feeding and rocking babies.

Yvonne, twenty-three, had been granted the supervisory job last month after her three-year attempt to conceive within the breeding program failed. As a consolation and a way for her to still contribute to the program, the elders had awarded her the new live-in position. At the time of the young woman's placement, Kat couldn't decide which role was worse. But Yvonne appeared to relish her new status and had taken it in stride as her permanent profession.

Kat and many of the other teens knew, despite her fruitless

efforts at reproduction, Yvonne still craved sex. She nipped out regularly to spend her off-duty nights with her current fellow-of-the-month. And not with a consort either, with their procreation-class stamp of approval. She had a penchant for the more youthful peons of their village.

Kat came to realize the elders knew of her supervisor's night-time sex-capades. She'd even hinted how several women visited certain peons purely for sexual purposes. So, why wouldn't she?

On occasion, Yvonne went AWOL for an hour during the day to meet a peon. Everyone knew the elders wouldn't approve of her stealing off when she was supposed to be in charge of the nursery. And Kat could not erase from her memory the orchard incident last year, when she'd happened upon Yvonne and Ruby with their hands full. Not with apples, but with a ripe-for-the-picking, newly minted peon. She couldn't forget the sounds either. The rhythmic smacks of skin on skin—the first hint something other than apple-picking was in progress. On Ms. Jaleena's insistence, she'd gone to help the girls wrap up their chore before supper and instead, uncovered the trio in a sweaty ménage among the ladders and bushels of fragrant fruit. Shameless Yvonne hadn't had the decency to cover her stark nudity, though Kat recalled how Ruby had jumped quick as a bunny back into her sundress, and how the peon blazed scarlet as a Red Delicious before he fled the scene.

Yvonne fetched a bottle from the cooler and settled in the last available rocker. She cooed at the infant in her arms. "Now, my wee one, it's time for your last drop of milk in Wild Cove. Some lucky village will get to take you in today, my sweet."

"When is the transfer taxi coming?" Harper asked as she rocked her charge for the morning.

"Due to arrive shortly. I don't know if we'll get an exchange today or not."

Kat struggled to feed Red. "I swear this one despises me." The baby's cries filled the nursery as she rejected the offered milk.

Yvonne snickered. "Takes a bit of time to get the hang of it, tough girl." She waved her hand as if to dismiss her complaint. "You're not the first to suffer these growing pains, and you won't be the last."

Her supervisor was right on that point. To maintain the status quo, someone had to care for the babies and small children until their school enrollment and transfer to their respective segregated dorms at four years of age. Long before the teens took on the new chores, the parameters of It Takes A Village had taken precedence. Once delivered from the womb and before the birth mother formed an attachment, each newborn was transferred via water taxi to another island village nursery for care and guardianship. No offspring belonged to any one parent; rather, they belonged to the island as everyone's responsibility.

Harper's ward, Alice, stuck her head in from the adjoining playroom. "Shyla here yet? One of the boys won't share the blocks, and he won't pay me no heed! Should I drive him out to play in the yard with Grace again?"

"I'm on my way." Harper stood up and leaned toward Kat. "Where's your new ward? Have you forgotten her again?"

"Crap!" She groaned in dismay. "Yes, again. I'll go get her."

Her charge's ear-popping screams continued. She tried to soothe her, but her efforts had no effect. Determined to fight her, the baby twisted her little body as if to free herself. Kat put the untouched milk back in the cooler.

"How about a little ride then, Red?" She grated the words through her teeth as she strode to the door. Outside, she found a baby carriage by the fence. The sun was broiling hot, so she'd made sure to follow protocol. She'd quickly dressed the tiny girl in a romper and bonnet and pulled the carriage's woven hood over her to prevent sunburn and heat stroke.

The updated domestic work schedule included nursery and kitchen service, with laundry and sanitation duties everywhere in between. Kat's month-long assignment of kitchen service had ended and her stint with infant care had begun. She hated the second assignment even more and sorely missed her independence. Except for the early half-morning excursions and activities with her sister-ward, the rest of the day belonged to the babies, the chores and again with Shyla when the younger teen finished her afternoon humanities classes with Ms. Naomi.

She steered the carriage south toward the girls' dormitory, which housed the female wards and their guides. Truth be told, she didn't care for mentoring and its imposition on her time any more than the dreary domestic duties. She had barely adjusted to having the girl around, shadowing her daily activities, stuck to her like a burr, when the new dictates were forced upon her.

At least she had glorious November to look forward to, when the animals of Western Path would rescue her from this daily grind of human interdependence. She only had to tough it out, and stay out of trouble, until then.

Her stomach contracted with hunger. While she bumped the carriage past the Gathering House, the child's cries mercifully subsided, but she wished she could forget about Shyla and run into the mess hall for a snack to tide her over until lunch.

She approached the stark, L-shaped building. Her ward ran out the door, her raven mane flying behind her. She was a natural beauty with high cheekbones, startling dark eyes, and a pleasant demeanor. Before her arrival from Battle Cove, one of the sister-ship's coastal Labrador villages, she had already passed through puberty. She'd developed a trim but feminine figure early for her age, a ripening which had bypassed Kat's own maturity and her sinewy-strong, boyish frame.

After her escape from the strange man, the run-in with "Queen Bee," and the cranky baby rubbing on her last nerve, she had no desire for the thirteen-year-old's perky company. And she knew her face exemplified it. She saw the girl's bright grin falter and fade.

"You're punctual as usual," Shyla said as she brushed hair from her eyes.

The rebuke rolled off Kat like water. "Tell me something I don't know. Anyway, I'm here now. Come on if you're coming."

The elders had assigned the girl to her as her sister-ward two weeks ago, due to her and Shyla's sudden disruptions within the mentorship project. Little Quinn, her first assignee, begged the elders to remove her from Kat's mentorship last spring. Such an incident rarely occurred. As for Shyla, Kat had acquired her at an advanced age after the loss of the girl's former mentor to a hunting trip accident.

In the months leading up to her original sister-guide enrollment, Kat had griped about its encroachment on her solitary pursuits. She'd asked the elders to make an exception for her, but they rejected her request. No special concessions were ever granted when it came to mentorship, Ms. Bee had said. She'd reminded her that when she moved to the ranch, she'd be obliged to mentor a girl there as well.

A flurry of whispered questions and innuendos arose over Quinn's hasty removal in April after three short weeks, but she refused to offer any explanation. Bianca, on the other hand, knew the score. Kat had been called to report to the elders' house for a thorough lecture and a sharp reprimand.

"Whatever happened to the cooperative young girl we used to know?" the senior elder had asked. "You're mean now, Katrena. And to an innocent child! Miss Quinn told us how you treated her and what you did at Timber Pond that last day, and it is inexcusable. We realize you prefer to march to the beat of your own drum, which is fine. We respect your individuality and independence. But we never imagined you'd turn it into disdain for a child or take it to such a dangerous extreme." Ms. Bee's icy-blue eyes had glittered with condemnation. "Where does it come from? Or are you being difficult for its own sake?"

Kat had defended herself, insisting Quinn's high-strung tendencies had blown the incident out of proportion. She'd brushed off the interrogation, though deep down she knew her actions had been at fault. Finally, she agreed to write a note of apology to the little girl. A water taxi delivered the note the same day.

For months, no other young girls were available for her to mentor, which suited her fine. Then Miss Shyla barged into her life.

"Ooh, hurray! Nursery duties. I can't even contain my pleasure." Shyla's words drew her back to the present. "What are you supposed to teach me about our darling cherubs today?" With an elaborate shudder, she made a wry face.

Kat smirked at her ward's unexpected show of sarcasm. "I don't know if you can handle the oodles of fun I have planned for you. Stinky diaper changes, colicky screeching, getting peed on—oh, and don't forget the puke, kiddo. There's no end to the excitement we have in store."

"Yippee! I'm counting the seconds."

Circling back to the nursery, they approached the Gathering House, a repurposed brick courthouse from a bygone era. Situated in the center of Wild Cove, the ancient but sturdy relic accommodated the sistership's central kitchen, mess hall, assembly hall and community room.

"I'm famished. Here, you ride the squirt around a bit while I run in and grab some food to inhale."

"Sure. But when we finish our chores, can we do something fun before I go to class?" Shyla let go of the carriage and clasped her hands together in a symbol of prayer. "Some of the girls are off for a swim at the pond. Can we go too?"

"Not today." A swim at Timber Pond was the one pastime she felt least inclined to share with her new ward.

"Well, could you take me out for a ride on Joy like you promised?"

"The horses are busy with the harvest. You know that."

"Oh, right. Well, we could bait muskrat or coyote traps. Gumming the new canoe is insane fun compared to this." She gave Kat a sidelong glance. "Jeepers, even cleaning horseshit out of the stalls would be an improvement. Domestic work is so bloody tiresome!"

Kat grinned to herself as she hurried to the mess hall entrance at the rear of the Gathering House. Though she wiggled out of mentor duty every chance she could, she thought it ironic she and her new ward were at least like-minded in one regard.

CHAPTER THREE

TWO DAYS EARLIER

The conical shape of a gleaming white lighthouse came into view three miles out of the mouth of the wide blue bay. It loomed up from a crest of rock near the coastline, standing in stark contrast to the panoramic backdrop of a dark, majestic mountain range.

The beacon took the young sailor by surprise, hidden from his field of vision until he'd sailed around an overhanging cliff of steep headland that jutted out into the strait. It appeared deserted. Unaware of how much life he would find on the island, he hadn't expected such a blatant sign of long-established civilization, still intact.

Frantic to avoid possible detection, he dropped the tattered sail of his skiff as fast as humanly possible. He ripped off his bright orange life vest and shoved it out of sight under the sail. He rowed the oars in earnest and strained against the wind, veering off to glide behind a meandering reef of jagged, black rocks. He prayed his boat didn't run aground or break up on any hidden shoals.

Half a mile from shore, he thought he was safe from what laid beneath the water's surface. He breathed easier. Seconds later— abrupt impact. With the splintering crack of the hull against submerged rock, his world tilted. His body pitched forward from the violent collision and he fell headlong into the belly of the craft. Cool seawater gushed into his ruined vessel and everywhere around him.

He grabbed the tilted port side and pulled himself up until his head was above water. Coughing up brine, he scanned the remains of his skiff, its gunwales wedged in a cleft of the reef. He poked around the broken boards and rubble in the foaming current for his fishing gear, life vest and other supplies, but he saw them nowhere. A string of curses ripped from his mouth, followed by a gasp when he spied his knapsack under the same plank that had pinned his leg. A dagger of pain knifed through his left ankle as he pulled both free and set out to swim to safety.

He plunged into the rolling breakers, ignoring the twinges that shot up through his shin. He arched his arms in long, steady strokes until he made it to shore. On his hands and knees, he scrabbled inland over the sandy beach until he came to the foot of a steep, grassy incline. With a quick glance around, he scaled the hill. He crossed a shrub-covered marsh with faltering steps, his eye on the burnished horizon and a grove of trees a quarter-mile away.

Farther from the coastline now and feeling less vulnerable in a thick stand of birch and maple, he threw down his soaked knapsack and fell, panting, near the trunk of a tree. Leaning back on the rough bark, he rested long enough to get his bearings and for his wild breathing to return to normal. His twisted ankle ached and had visibly swollen, but he sensed no other injuries.

Twenty minutes later, he'd recovered a semblance of his depleted strength. Despite his injury, he knew he should hide the wreckage of his boat before nightfall, and more importantly, before anyone spotted it. He shrugged off his pain and retraced his steps to the shore.

Once more, he plunged into the pounding surf which, by this time, had freed what was left of his skiff from the cleft of rock. He willed it not to float out of reach and swam to the floundering wreckage as fast as he could. By slow, agonizing inches, he hauled the bulk of it through the water and onto the wet sand. He tried to camouflage it under a tangled heap of brown sea kelp, though he didn't spend too much time with it. Hiding himself came before all else.

Drenched and stinking of brine and rotten kelp, he stumbled across the stretch of beach.

His passage across the strait to the island had taken longer than he'd expected. From consulting an outdated map among his meager possessions, he'd miscalculated the distance from the mainland. Rising sea levels had flooded coastlines and had left him unprepared for how much of the island's Northern Peninsula now lay underwater. But the wind speed and direction had been favourable and steady and the water relatively calm for navigation. He did make excellent time, even if it took the entire day.

He'd exhausted his supply of drinking water early, running out about halfway across the wide strait. Throat sore and parched, he retreated to the safe shelter of the grove. He heard the gurgle of water, hit upon a stream and dunked his face into it, gulping mouthfuls of the cool water until he quenched his fiery thirst. Deep hunger gnawed at his insides and made his head ache, but food would have to wait. The furious row, the swim, and hiding of the wreck had drained the last drop of his physical fortitude.

Well before he detected any signs of life beyond the caw-caw of crows overhead and the trill of songbirds in the maples, he realized he'd found a unique and magical place. He marvelled at his new environment as the sun faded and twilight settled in. The terrain was green and lush, the wind warm but not dry, the air heavy with the late-summer scent of flowers and fruit.

The island of Newfoundland? Shrunken in size, maybe, but somehow its plant life had escaped the ravages of ecological ruin. Did it mean he would find other animals besides birds, and the rumours of human life here were indeed true? The island bore such limited resemblance to any place he'd ever been, he thought it might be all a dream.

Not that he'd travelled much before he struck out alone on this crazy expedition, leaving his family behind. Newfoundland and Labrador had left Canada's confederation of provinces and territories more than a hundred and fifty years ago, yet his mother's homeschooling had taught him how its citizens had enlisted alongside Canadians in the devastating North American wars. Those wars, the global collapse, and the cataclysmic aftermath had wiped out much of the continent's population and must have decimated the island's along with it. Curled up under a shelter of juniper and birch with his head rested on the coolness of his sodden knapsack, the young man willed himself to relax. He needed to rest and recover if he expected to fulfill his crucial mission.

His wild pulse gradually slowed to normal, but his head pounded and his ankle throbbed until sleep overtook him.

* * *

He cradled the tiny sleeping boy in his arms. With a gentle touch he brushed back coiled wisps of hair from his damp brow and hugged the light heft of his body to his chest.

It grieved him to accept the validity of his brother's words: the child was not thriving. Since he fell ill with fever and cough ten days ago, he'd taken on a familiar sickly pallor and had even begun to lose weight. Three years old, and Hudson's brief life had come to this.

He thought of other recent losses to the illness and prayed it wouldn't claim his son as its next victim.

Tenderly, he pressed his lips to the boy's burning forehead, laid him back on his cot, and covered him with a light blanket. "I don't care what Trent says," he murmured. "You will be spared. You must get better."

As he left the boy, he drew a sudden breath. A slender young woman stood in the doorway. Her coppery, sun-bleached hair tumbled over her shoulders in gentle curls.

"Ava," he whispered to the child's mother.

A tender smile illuminated her face as she walked toward him.

He awoke with a jerk. Pitch blackness surrounded him. At first, he had no clue where he was. When he felt the unforgiving ground beneath him and heard the lonesome hoot of an owl overhead, cruel memories flooded back. With a hoarse moan, he dropped his head into his hands.

It had only been a dream, one of many that had visited him over recent weeks.

Wide awake, he brushed wetness from his cheeks and stood up. Night-time or not, he could not sleep again until he filled his empty stomach with something—anything—edible.

With hands extended to feel the trees that popped up in front of him, he groped his way out of the darkness of the grove into the direction of faint light. He reached a small, moonlit clearing. He pawed through nearby shrubbery, hoping to find berries to at least take the edge off his great hunger.

When he'd almost given up his search, his hands fell on tall bushes, sharp and prickly. He flinched and pulled back his fingers, but his nostrils filled with the sweet, heady smell of sweet juice.

Raspberries.

No longer caring how much the thorns stabbed and stung, he pulled the fat, over-ripe berries from their brambles and shovelled them into his mouth by the handfuls. In his haste to relieve his appetite, he hadn't counted on the squirm of insect life as it slid past his tongue and tickled his throat as he swallowed. He chuckled in the darkness. A few bugs were no big deal and added much-needed protein.

His initial hunger satisfied, drowsiness overtook him again. Instead of retreating to the grove he'd slept in earlier, he passed the berry brambles and entered a darkened evergreen forest. He made a pallet of dead branches from a fallen spruce tree in an inner clearing, stretched out on his side with a groan, and made a wish this time for Ava and the dreams to leave him alone. In an instant, he fell back to sleep.

CHAPTER FOUR

The elders were seated on the stage when Kat filed into the Gathering House assembly hall with the rest of the stragglers. She spotted the bobbing ponytail in the third row. Quickly, she slipped into the chair Harper had saved for her.

Ms. Naomi glided forward, the hem of her simple hemp skirt sweeping the elevated pine platform beneath the podium. The thick red binder lay open on the desk behind her, ready for the meeting. "Good evening, my sisters," she said with a gracious smile.

From the platform, the elder focused on the front row of her audience where the sister-wards sat. "To begin, we have a major announcement. To ensure our more youthful sisters become initiated in the quickest amount of time, we've promoted them to the role of journal readers, effective immediately. Let's give them a warm welcome!"

The room filled with applause and a buzz of conversation. No one beyond the elders had known a sister-ward would read tonight; up to now, the readers had been eighteen and over. This shift had come so quickly on the heels of the additional chores, Kat accepted it as another adjustment in policy. She thought about how Shyla would conduct herself when her turn came. Already a proficient reader at thirteen, the girl rarely appeared self-conscious. Not-so-shy Shyla would likely do well.

Ms. Naomi smiled at a girl in the front row. "Miss Alice, you shall be our fledgling. We have selected an entry from the Childhood Memories Anthology for you. This anthology, as our older girls know, is one of four volumes from our Old World Archives on Domestic Abuse. Come up, dear."

A rumble of conversation erupted from the audience as Alice ascended the three steps at the right of the stage and walked swiftly to the podium. Head bowed, she peeked out from under her long bangs at her mentor, Harper, in the third row and over the rest of the assemblage. Naomi placed a footstool next to the podium to compensate for the nine-year-old's height.

Meanwhile, Ms. Bianca flipped through the heavy binder behind them. When she made her selection and popped the laminated sheet from its rings, she handed it to the youngster with a flourish and trundled back to her seat beside Ms. Eleanor.

"If you aren't familiar with any of the words," Naomi said, "let me know and I'll help you." She gave Alice's shoulder an encouraging squeeze and retreated a step behind her.

After a short pause, Alice started to read from the laminated sheet.

"A Memory of My Father at, um, Chris..." She peeked over her shoulder at the elder. "I don't know this word, Ms. Naomi."

A few titters erupted from the front row, which Ms. Bee shushed at once.

"Christmas," the junior elder said. "You younger girls probably haven't heard or read much about Christmas. Allow me to explain in brief. Christmas was a long-ago annual pagan festival which became combined with a religious holiday. This holiday commemorated the birth of Jesus Christ, a spiritual figure, and was celebrated in many countries around the world. People who practiced this faith, Christianity, were called Christians. Kids were told a fairy tale about an elf in a red suit named Santa Claus, who rode in a sleigh pulled by flying reindeer—or caribou, as we know them—down from the North Pole to give toys and other presents to the well-behaved children."

A much louder burst of giggles prompted another loud shush and a stern frown from Ms. Bee.

"You do know what the word Father means, correct?" Naomi asked.

"Yes, Ms. Naomi," Alice assured her. "We've already learned about family unit culture and how people used to live with a mother and a father."

"Then you may carry on."

Faint and shaky starting off, her voice grew steadier and more confident as she read:

"A Memory of Father at Christmas. Recorded February 2, 1978.

"My name is Laura, I am nineteen years old, and I'm from the town of Harbour Grace, Newfoundland. In 1967, the Christmas I was eight years old, Santa brought me a newborn baby doll named Thumbelina. Never had I owned such a pint-sized, gorgeous and perfect doll. I treasured her as soon as I tore off the gift wrap. She had a painted face with blue eyes, silky golden curls, and her soft little body was dressed in a powder blue dress with a gauzy overlay. Her finest feature, though? When I pulled the string in her back, she wiggled like a real live baby! That same year my big brother Jake got his first guitar, with a fancy strap and a 12-pack of guitar picks. I'm sure he adored his present as much as I adored my new doll.

"We played with our new gifts for most of the day. Mama cooked a huge turkey with all the trimmings and a yummy dessert of chocolate cream pie, my absolute favourite. She and Daddy acted happier than usual, and it pleased me because they didn't argue that day, not even once.

"After we ate Christmas dinner, Mama put away the leftovers and washed the dishes. Our next-door neighbours visited. Daddy opened a bottle of rum and made drinks for them. The neighbours had one drink each and didn't stay long, but our father kept on drinking the rum until the last drop had been drunk. When he lunged for the cupboard and pulled out another bottle, Mama said she thought he'd had enough already.

"Our peaceful day came to an end then, and the horrible fighting took over. Again.

"Daddy slammed his fist on the table. It made our mother jump. He told her there wouldn't be any turkey or presents for any of us if it wasn't for him and how hard he worked, and why didn't she shut up for once. My brother Jake and I watched helplessly as he grew angrier and angrier and his voice got louder and louder.

"This time, though, Daddy didn't hit Mama the way he usually did. He called her ugly names and swore a lot, but he didn't smack her or hit her or kick her or anything. Instead, he went after my brother and me. We brought it on ourselves, though, because we shouldn't have spoken up. We should have hidden upstairs. It happened because Jake and I begged him to leave our mother alone.

"Petrified, I watched him walk toward me. I knew how mad he could get when he drank his rum. I'd seen it too many times before.

"Mama said, 'Frank, please don't,' but he came at me and grabbed my brand-new dolly, Thumbelina, out of my arms.

"With horror, I watched as he yanked on the string in her back until it broke. Then he tore off my cherished dolly's head. Through silent tears, I saw him go for Jake's new guitar under the Christmas tree. My brother tried to stop him but Daddy forced him out of his way. He picked up the guitar, swung it over his head, and brought it down with a crack across the woodstove. Pieces of it flew across the room. Our father stood there with nothing but the neck of the guitar in his hands, then he gathered up the pieces of my torn-up doll and Jake's broken guitar and rammed it all into the burning woodstove.

"Too terrified to say another word, Jake and I fled to our bedrooms and stayed there until the next morning. I remember I cried into my pillow for hours before I fell asleep.

"That Christmas, I learned how vicious our father could be. I'd grown up with the belief that lots of families were like ours. Fights on a regular basis, the calm covering up of bruises, the hiding of broken possessions. When I saw my uncle smack my aunt upside the head one night, it only reaffirmed my belief. I didn't take into account until later how my uncle and my father were brothers cut from the same dysfunctional cloth.

"Daddy didn't beat Jake or me—I guess he thought he was above that, at least—but he ruined many days and nights for us, and special occasions were no exception. Those hateful remembrances are seared into my brain forever.

"I didn't blame the booze like Mama did. That year, I also stopped believing in Santa Claus. Mama stayed with our father for six more years before she finally wised up, but I can't fathom how she'd lived that way. How could anyone put up with such abuse? I suppose she believed she'd sacrificed her happiness for us, but she didn't realize the emotional scars her staying had inflicted on us all.

"I am sure of one fact. At no time in my life will I allow a man to put his hands on me or hurt my children in any way—not without consequences.

"I will not be like my mother.

"The End."

The entire assembly had listened with rapt attention to the story. The silence gave way to light applause as Alice returned the sheet to Ms. Naomi's outstretched hand, left the stage and scurried to her seat.

Kat noticed Harper and other listeners brush away tears. Most of the older women in the back of the room sniffled into handkerchiefs and shook their heads. Many of the stories had this effect on them, even though the senior girls and the women, young and old, had already heard them. The elders, Kat knew, were aware of the impact these cautionary readings had on the girls, thus the reason for their frequency.

She sat dry-eyed as usual. However troubling the story, she had been struck most by young Alice's delivery of the reading. Harper's ward had related the passages clearly and with remarkable eloquence.

Ms. Naomi stepped back to the podium. "Thank you, Miss Alice. You did an exceptional job. My compliments to your teacher, Ms. Lynn, and to your mentor. It is apparent they have served you well."

In her seat next to Kat, Harper blushed as all heads swivelled in her direction. A swell of renewed applause filled the room.

Naomi took her seat and Ms. Bianca stepped to the podium.

"Hello, my dear sisters. For the youngest of our girls tonight and before we touch on other issues, I wish to take this opportunity to thank you. We are immensely proud of your cooperation and diligence as contributing citizens of Wild Cove and of our island as a whole.

"Our passage to independence has been fraught with a host of challenges too numerous to mention here. But with careful planning, courage, and vision over the decades since the Great Collapse, together with our sister villages we have created a life that has afforded us self-sufficiency. Under my co-management of fisheries and agriculture with Ms. Jaleena, and along with the abundant gifts nature provides, we've maintained our farms, orchards, and greenhouses. For basic power needs, our island citizens continue to operate and maintain our biomass plants, generators, and solar energy systems left to us by our predecessors, and we are working to use these tools for more complex applications.

"This year, as you know, has ushered in essential modifications. Population growth remains our principal goal. To build on our populace more expeditiously, we've reduced free days from once weekly to once monthly and have reassigned many daily chores to our younger citizens. This way, each fertile woman twenty and over can devote her time exclusively to bearing children, to take pride and draw joy from it as an honourable and highly esteemed pursuit.

"As for our diminished stock of Immunity-2 extract both here and in Labrador, we are optimistic we will find more of the spiked sage orchid, the wildflower which provides it, and subsequently cultivate it for our sustained protection from viral and bacterial disease.

"We have thrived these past decades," the senior elder went on, "because of two realities. Number one: we work in synergy with our natural environment. Against extraordinary odds, our home-land hasn't merely survived, but flourished, with an ecosystem and climate more desirable than it has ever been. While restoring balance to our island with self-sustained management of our foraging, fishing, and agricultural practices, we have proven this is the proper way to live, to the benefit of our natural world and every creature that lives here. We reject the old ways outright. How can we succeed as a society or as a planet if we operate on outdated methods and ideologies?

"Number two: the world, or what is left of it, appears largely ignorant of our existence. Any survivors on the continent have plenty of cause to presume it is as mean and uninhabitable here as it is there, unaware our island has survived the worst ravages of global ruin. In spite of the increasing intensity of hurricane systems, flooded coastlines and peninsulas and severe loss of land mass, it has endured as a sweet spot and a fantastic quirk of nature. Back in 2049, when Newfoundland left confederation..."

The elder's voice rambled on. Bored by political talk and distracted by her own thoughts, Kat's eye wandered over the assemblage. She spotted Shyla in profile at the end of the front row, who appeared to listen intently to Ms. Bee's words.

The girl had come a long way in the short space of time since Kat had taken over as her mentor. When she'd arrived from Battle Cove, Shyla had still been grief-stricken over Daisy, her original guide. The young woman had gone on a group caribou hunt, and while scanning for the herd at the brink of a cliff, she'd slipped on loose gravel and had fallen to her death. It was natural their first days together had been unsettled and problematic. Immersed in her own reservations about mentorship at the time, she'd done zilch to assuage the girl's sorrow. She realized now how swiftly Shyla had rallied—no thanks to her.

When the meeting ended, Kat funnelled out of the assembly hall behind the others. She thought again of young Quinn. At the time of her abrupt discharge from her care, the other Wild Cove girls of age already had wards, therefore Quinn had been reassigned to Little Greenland, a distant village on the island's northeast coast. Kat's face burned and her insides twisted when she remembered the last day she'd mentored the girl.

It wouldn't bode well if the second ward entrusted to her requested a transfer. Another disruption would undoubtedly threaten her career aspirations and prompt the elders to rescind her ranch apprenticeship altogether. For the sake of her future, she would try harder to curb her self-absorption from now on.

And the kid deserved at least that much.

CHAPTER FIVE

The man leaned against the weathered corral fence that surrounded the plot of land. An acreage of bright green and gold sprawled in front of him in tall, uniform rows. The ripe ears of corn swayed in the humid breeze, tantalizing him. His insides growled in protest and his mouth watered at the thrill of tasting new food.

He had to steal some. It was crucial to keep up his energy, and the drive to quell his hunger was too powerful to ignore. Careful not to aggravate his injury, he climbed over the fence.

It had been years since he'd tasted the sweetness of fresh-picked corn. A bittersweet childhood memory glimmered and warmed his heart. As boys growing up in Quebec, he and his brother had eaten as much as they wanted of the crop on their grandparents' farm, the yield so abundant their grandmother had canned dozens of jars of pickled corn relish with the surplus for each winter. She'd done the same with the excess of tomatoes and cucumbers she'd grown. Along with sweet corn, they had farmed grain corn to feed their cows and grind into meal. Times had been tough in those days too, but at least they'd never gone to bed with empty stomachs.

He waited. He checked the landscape. Seeing no one around, he slipped in between the stalks of towering vegetation. The rich, familiar scent, so green and fresh, surrounded him.

He remembered the ease of picking the ripe ears, even with his immature strength at the age of nine when he, his brother, and his grandfather had helped his father with the harvest. His hand grasped one of the plump green husks topped with dry, reddish-brown silk. He pulled down and twisted until it plucked from its high stalk. He repeated the quick plucks, satisfied when he'd picked a half-dozen more.

With the ears poked inside his knapsack, he fled from the field. He climbed back over the fence and waded through a meadow of tall, swaying grass to hide in a grove of junipers.

As he staggered back into the shelter of the woods, distant female voices broke the silence with shouts of alarm. He didn't dare stop to see who the voices belonged to as he disappeared through the trees.

In the evening, he leaned against a massive granite rockface at the north end of the beach and scanned the ocean horizon with tired eyes. From his vantage point he couldn't see the lighthouse perched above him near the overhang of a cliff, so he assumed if a keeper were there, he could not see him either.

Out of nowhere a quarter-mile from the shoals, a long, open watercraft glided by in near silence, cutting through the waves at a nice clip with the help of its two expert oarsmen. Both shirtless, their muscles rippled in their sinewy arms and shoulders as they rowed. A bold, black number 5 stood out on the white vessel's starboard side.

He scrambled for cover nearby. He dipped low behind a thicket of tall beach grass, his belly in the sand. Slowly, he raised his head and watched the boat cruise southeast beyond the beach until it faded from view.

He liked this spot on the beach to the lee side of the granite wall but needed to find something to sleep on before it grew too dark. He scaled back over the dunes and ducked into a stand of balsam fir trees to collect boughs. The healthy evergreen branches were too hard and sturdy to tear off with his bare hands. By the time he'd collected enough deadwood strewn about the ground and returned to the beach, his body quivered with fatigue.

The intense heat of the day had dwindled significantly. He'd eaten the stolen corn raw, but it had tasted sweet, crisp, and delicious. His hunger satisfied for now, he tried to relax for a fresh start in the morning.

A seagull swooped down, pitched on the sand close by, and gave him the side-eye. It observed him with mild curiosity, then hopped over to a tide pool that lay between a granite plateau extension of the rockface and the shore. The man watched the sea bird take to wing and hover over the pool for a moment before it made a quick plunge-dive and caught a small crab in its beak. Wings outstretched, the gull lifted upward on the breeze. From forty feet in the air, it dropped the crab on the rocky plateau, breaking open its shell to expose its meaty flesh. While the gull pecked at its meal, the man readjusted himself on his russet pile of branches behind the tufts of grass. Once more, he rested on his side and used his knapsack as a pillow.

The northwestern sky swirled with the colours of a painter's palette, its gossamer clouds of coral, burnt orange and magenta curdled against a tableau of azure blue. The undulating waves on the water shimmered like liquid gold. The dazzling seascape taunted him and only magnified his troubles. How could such splendour exist when his own world lay in ruins?

The man brooded on the wasteland home he'd left behind. Though filled with gut-wrenching memories, it held its share of treasured moments too. It was where he and Ava had met and started a family.

When he slept, vivid dreams hounded him. A coping mechanism, conceivably. A way for him to keep putting one foot in front of the other and not give in to the desolation that threatened to swallow his soul. Most of the dreams were wishful and pleasant, filled with his wife and son in happier times. His little family is healthy, serene, and as joyful as the day he and Ava met.

He was still mourning the death of his aunt, one of the earliest victims of the illness four years ago, when Ava came into his life. She and her mother had showed up one summer afternoon from a nearby camp in a critical search for food. When he saw their canoe cut across the lake, he'd been wary at first. And when the two women requested his help, he was polite but noncommittal. Their tiny hamlet didn't have enough food for themselves, let alone any to share with visitors.

But Ava won him over before the full moon rose that night. He couldn't explain it at the time, but he knew he wanted her to stay and had told her so. The warm smile reserved for him alone, the way her gentle voice soothed his spirit—she restored in him the courage he needed to go on. Trent had moved in with his girlfriend recently. How could he refuse the same for his younger brother?

As expected, Trent had tried to talk him out of it. They had enough mouths to feed already. And women? They needed hardy, healthy males, not more females to care for. When Marcus explained how they needed women to bear children and were doomed without them, Trent finally saw reason and caved.

"All I pray is they aren't full of disease. Women or not, Marc, we can't handle more of it. Babies riddled with illness is the last trouble we need."

In the early blush of love, nothing had mattered as long as they were together. But eventually the conditions of their existence—the dry, sweltering climate, the scarcity of food, the sickness and failing health—took their toll. The endless slog to find nourishment alone had worn them down. And when they managed to find an edible food source, constant vigilance against attacks from thieves and plunderers was a must.

They'd tried hard not to lose faith in the future with each new threat or calamity that struck. He couldn't blame his wife for growing more and more depressed. She reached her breaking point last summer when their infant girl arrived in the middle of the night, two months premature and stillborn. Reduced to a pale shadow of herself, Ava had given up. They still had their son, but he had feared she would never be the same again.

And now his son was back there, fighting for his life.

Guilt washed over him, leaving him dizzy and weak. When the boy fell ill, he'd promised Ava he would do everything he could to save him, and he'd meant it. He hoped Hudson somehow understood why his father had deserted him in his time of great need. What could he do, but seek a solution to their hellish plight?

Since the initial outbreak of illness five years ago, the population of their hamlet had dwindled drastically. It took the elderly among them first. Next to succumb were the very young and sickly. The same year Hudson came into the world, the infant twins of his cousin left it, dying within days of each other. Since then, about half of the children had perished.

They had no means to prevent or fight the epidemic. Vaccines were nonexistent, and production and distribution of antibiotics had ceased decades ago. When the rumour of a cure circulated, how could he not leave to try and find it? Wouldn't any devoted father and decent man do the same?

He imagined his return with the life-saving medicine and his reunion with his son. He envisioned him strong and energetic again, his health restored. But even if Hudson survived, he knew a continued existence in the impoverished region would be bleak.

He took his fervent wishes one step further. He pictured

bringing the boy to this peaceful island haven to grow and thrive and set down roots. If he managed to find enough of the reported cure, he could save the lives of the others in his settlement. When they had healed and regained their strength, he'd bring them here to this sublime anomaly, this island oasis in the middle of a new temperate zone of the North Atlantic.

His son might meet a girl here and raise his own family when he became of age. More than that, he imagined a life where the boy would not need to worry about lack of food or bear any of the atrocities he and Ava had endured for far too long.

He didn't want to intrude on the girl or her people, but the island had to be large enough for them to coexist in peace.

Or was it?

He'd followed the strange girl yesterday. He'd hoped she might give him the answers to his urgent questions, but she'd given him the slip. He would have preferred to get the necessary information from her, rather than chance a confrontation with a gang of islanders who may or may not be friendly, or even approachable. God only knew how the men here would react to a mainlander. He'd seen enough aggression in his twenty-four years to be wary of just about anything on two legs.

With any luck, he'd see the girl again. He'd searched for her again today but had been too weary and in too much pain to stay on his ankle for long. When he got spooked stealing the corn, he decided to rest his leg one more night and try to find help from one of the islanders tomorrow.

He pictured the girl as he rested. Her darting eyes and tawny skin. Her close-cropped hair spiked with sweat. The skimpy, mud-green clothes she wore which had helped camouflage her among the bushes. The long purple scar that snaked around her lower right leg. Her coltish frame, spare of size but shaped with lean, sculpted muscle.

At first he'd taken her for a prepubescent boy. Granted, she acted unlike any girl he had ever known. Wild, and with an autonomy he found intriguing. Naturally, she'd fled from him, no doubt out of fear for her safety, yet she had an air of tenacity he'd seldom witnessed in the opposite sex.

Then again, she probably hadn't experienced any life other than what she was used to on this island. How would she have ended up if she'd lived the life he'd faced?

The sunset had faded to swaths of violet and dove-grey and the deepening shadows of late dusk closed in. The protective cloak of darkness helped him breathe easier and as he yawned and turned over on his back, the buildup of tension and strain ebbed away through the boughs and into the sand beneath his weary bones. Grateful for the safety of the oncoming night, a heavy lethargy overtook him.

The crescent moon lifted and the stars winked down at him. He closed his eyes. He listened to the gentle lap and pull of waves on the lonely beach. Would the dreams revisit him tonight? Would they prey on him with the tearful faces of his dwindling family?

CHAPTER SIX

While Baby Red napped, Kat and Shyla gathered up the overflowing hamper baskets placed in convenient locations around the facility and carried them out through the back door. They piled the soiled crib sheets, towels, onesies and other tiny articles of clothing on the floor of the immense covered porch built onto the rear of the nursery.

Kat brought the empty baskets back inside and returned to Shyla, lugging a pail of presoaked dirty diapers. "Come on," she said wearily. "Let's get this done."

Two bicycle washing machines stood on the porch, attached with pipes to a pair of industrial steel tubs atop sturdy metal stands. The peons had completed their tasks for the domestic workers hours ago. They had filled the tubs with well water and lit fires beneath them at the break of dawn. With their own laundry finished, the domestics had refilled the tubs and refueled the fires to heat the water for the nursery workers.

At last month's meeting, the elders reported the consort team of systems technicians, overseen by women, were building electric washing machines and water heaters with central plumbing, their latest project to make domestic life easier. The project aimed to bring the dorms, schools and other village facilities up to a standard already maintained at the elders' residences and the Origin Suites. The clinic would also get an upgrade, sure to greatly please Ms. Eleanor, their community health coordinator. Kat could not imagine such luxury.

Adjacent to the porch, six parallel clotheslines extended from tree to tree, lined off with the domestics' laundry. Dormitory towels, sheets and pillowcases bobbed and flapped in the warm breeze.

Shyla peeped up at them through shiny black bangs. "Where will we pin our wet clothes? All the lines are chock-full."

Kat touched the billowing sheets at the end. "These are practically dry. When we're done, we'll take them down and pin up ours."

Shyla tossed laundry into the wash tubs attached to the front wheels of the bikes. Kat opened the spigots on the water pipes and told her ward to drop in the soap while they waited for the tubs to fill. She complied, throwing in two bars of the aromatic soap the domestics made, kept in ample stock on the porch shelf. They both sat in their bike seats and started to pedal to agitate the wash.

"Hope I get an A on my sociology test," Shyla said, pumping her legs hard.

"You've already scored high marks in the course, haven't you?"

"Yeah, mostly." She peered sidelong at her sister-guide. "Ms. Naomi says I'm a wicked fast learner." The girl prattled on about school, her teacher, and her classmates.

Kat gave a little snort. Fast learner. The same words the junior elder had used to encourage a cooperative attitude when she was Shyla's age. Their teachers had always known what to say to make them work hard and eager to please. The proof was in the pickles right here, sure. All for one and one for all, or some such foolishness. At times, though, she missed the afternoon humanities classes

Ms. Naomi taught. She sighed and leaned into the pedals, cycling faster.

"Ms. Naomi taught us how a long time ago, lots of men and women used to live together as couples and raise children as a family, as they did in last night's journal reading. Yikes! Can you picture living in the same house with a man?"

"I don't really care to picture it, Shyla." Kat hopped down off her seat. "Did you know many of the First Peoples in Labrador still live in such a way?"

"I heard about it back in Battle Cove. My sister-guide told me a man and woman would enter into a marriage and have children." Shyla curled her lip. "But imagine my shock when I learned most of the world used to live that way. Sure hope most of those babies had better fathers than that girl Laura. Oh, but didn't little Alice read beautifully?"

"Indeed she did." Beads of perspiration trickled down Kat's neck, back and chest as she opened the lower spigots to drain the washers, readying the laundry for rinse water. A cloud of mosquitoes nipped at her arms and buzzed in her ears with their high-pitched whines. She tried in vain to swat and shoo them away. "Fly to hell, nippers!"

Shyla giggled. About to rip out a far more colourful term, Kat bit her tongue when their senior elder appeared from around the corner.

"Special emergency Sundown Circle this evening, girls, immediately after your self-defence classes. Make sure to tell the rest of the staff, please."

Kat gave a curt nod as she opened the pipes to refill the washers.

"Will do, Ms. Bee," Shyla said to the old woman's retreating back.

An emergency Circle was out of the ordinary, particularly since they'd held their monthly meeting just last night. Had anyone else spotted the outsider? She mulled over her sighting of the mysterious man yesterday. It gave her an uneasy jolt. She hadn't yet told a soul about him, which in itself was more than unusual.

They finished the laundry and were hanging the last few diapers on the line when the lunch bell rang.

"You go on and I'll catch up in a bit." Though ravenous, Kat had to go back inside to feed Baby Red her bottle.

She managed to get six ounces of the milk into Red before the child pushed the bottle away with stubby fingers. Stomach rumbling, she bundled her into a woven carrier-basket, swung her around to hang from her back, and jogged to the mess hall.

Chef Jaleena's lunch menu of the day consisted of scrambled duck eggs and toutons fried in churned butter, served with sliced tomatoes and sprinkles of fresh-picked basil from one of the greenhouses. Wooden bowls of fruit lined the centre of the long mess-table, stacked high with apples, plums, and pears.

Full plate of food in hand, Kat slid in next to Shyla with Falon and little Patti to her left. Baby Red, lodged between her shoulder blades, babbled over the cloth doll Kat had poked in with her and tied to the carrier with a piece of twine.

Harper and Alice sat across from them, their meals already half-eaten. A baby also sat secured in a carrier-basket on Harper's back. Above the din of girlish voices and clatter of forks on plates, the tiny boy's squeals rang out. His chubby fist shook a wooden rattle in the shape of a squirrel. Harper had carved and polished it for him out of a piece of pine.

Kat noticed Falon steal a glance at her.

"You know, you're smart to cut your hair super-short. Babies can't grab a hold of it, styled like that. One of the little monsters practically tore mine out from the roots this morning." Falon's own hair, sun-bleached to a pale blond, fell long and straight to her waist.

Kat reached for the pitcher of water in front of her and snorted.

"Chop it off, then." When her own hair started getting in the way at nine years old and no longer seemed worth the bother, she had her teacher Ms. Lynn cut it short for her. She'd kept it shorn tight to her head ever since.

"Or put it in braids, same as mine!" tiny Patti chimed in.

"Keep it up in a ponytail like me," Harper said. "Or perhaps a bun."

Falon handed an apple to Patti. "Ugh! I don't know. A bun is far too Yvonne-esque."

Harper chuckled. "Good point."

Kat, beyond famished, dove into the mound of food on her plate.

"...Yes, Yvonne heard about him too," Harper said.

Kat's ears pricked up. "Who are you talking about?" She tore into a touton, warm butter dribbling down her chin from the chewy fried dough.

Harper leaned across the table. "A rogue! Somebody saw him steal a few ears from the cornfield earlier today. They thought the farmers had put up a new scarecrow—until they saw it jump over the fence."

"How did he get here?" Alice asked as she bit into a pear.

Kat didn't answer. She stabbed at her plate and scooped a forkful of egg into her mouth.

"Doesn't this bother you?" Falon's eyes were as wide and as blue as the ocean on a clear day, yet they did not rise to meet Kat's. The teen tended to fix her gaze on the chest region of whomever she spoke to, her timid way of avoiding direct eye contact. "What if there are more of them? You're the toughest girl I know, Kat, but aren't you the least bit worried?"

"Well, it's news to me." She sipped her water and chose her words carefully. "Worried? S'pose I should be. Did he threaten anyone, Harper? Did they give a description?"

"That's all I heard. Yvonne thinks it's why they called the emergency meeting, and I bet she's right."

When they gathered at the south end of Five Mile Beach at dusk and hunkered around the Sundown Circle bonfire, their suspicions were confirmed. Ms. Bianca stood on a knoll closer to the blaze, apart from the girls, women, and the other elders. The golden hue of firelight accentuated the grooves and hollows of her ancient face as she spoke.

"My sisters," she began. Her voice rang out above the crackle and hiss of the fire. "Please be forewarned, but don't be alarmed. A stranger has landed in our midst."

An audible gasp swelled as one voice from their gathering. Shyla sat with a group of her schoolmates on the opposite side of the fire. Kat saw their faces cloud with worry.

"Where is he?" Yvonne asked.

"We're not sure, but we'll plan a search. Two of our women spotted him stealing corn from our cornfield. This is only the second time an outsider has walked among us in the last half-dozen years. We don't know where this man came from or why he is here. A search for a more habitable place to settle is an appropriate assumption. We have no idea how serious a problem he poses for us, or if he poses one at all."

The Assimilation and Refinement Solution had its introduction more than seventy years ago, according to the speeches and stories Kat had heard throughout her life. The collective distrust of the male species had been dealt with and put to rest at last, once the island elders designed a means to subdue the diminished population of men among them, and those who were born since, for practical use. As Ms. Bee often intoned in her lectures, eradicating the "alpha-male" and systemic misogyny did not mean the matriarchy didn't recognize their worth and necessity for many areas of employment around the island, particularly heavy manual labour. And, of course, reproduction.

The venerable woman paused over the sweep of upturned faces. The dance of campfire flames gave her an ethereal glow. "Does this outsider represent a new threat? Does he act alone, or is he leading the way for others? I wish we knew the answers. Word has been sent to our sister villages both here and in Labrador to warn them to practise extra vigilance. And this is where you come in. It is imperative each of us is on her guard until this man is arrested and subdued. Please stay the course with your mixed martial arts and self-defence training and remember to practice your skills as often as your schedules permit. If you are alone and the stranger attacks you, you will need to use those skills to save yourself.

"If we capture him and integration is not an option, he will be destroyed. We'll do whatever it takes to prevent this interloper or any others of his kind from threatening what we have worked with sheer determination to build. Are we in agreement?"

A brisk cheer sprang from their group as everyone scrambled to their feet and began to chant. The voices of the young and the old blended together as their fists punched in unison at the twilight sky.

"Mother of Nature, come what may
    we are strong and here to stay
    each of us is but a spark
    together we outshine the dark
    the patriarchal age has passed
    in sistership we rule at last!"

Swept up in the rousing chant, Kat fell in line as, one by one, they congregated closer to the campfire and placed their palms over their hearts. The intonation grew louder and gathered intensity as the black gloom of night descended around their warm halo of light.

The chant carried on for ten repetitions. Ms. Naomi raised her hand for silence, the cue that the business portion of Sundown Circle had ended. Without a word, the women and girls linked hands with one another.

With Naomi's signal to begin, Ruby's ward, ten-year-old June, sang "Island in the Sun," a favourite among their campfire songs. Her youthful voice, faintly audible above the snap and pop of the fire, grew louder as her solo progressed, each note clear and sweet. When she completed the final chorus, her audience burst into earnest applause.

Ms. Eleanor threw another log on the blaze, shooting orange-red sparks and a plume of grey smoke skyward. The others joined in on the next song, with Grace on bongo drums, Yvonne on flute, and Ms. Jaleena and her kitchen assistant on ukuleles. The bonkity-bonk of the bongos kept the tempo smooth, while the bright timbre of the flute played the melody and the ukuleles plunked the bouncy rhythm. The smell of woodsmoke mingled with tangy wafts of sea spray and warm, wet sand. A handful of the older women coaxed the little girls up onto their feet to join in a spirited hand-clapping dance around the fire.

Kat edged back from the heat of the blaze, preferring the cool night air. In spite of the jubilant music, the songs, and the warm camaraderie around her, she remained stuck in her head. If the others had any hint of the concerns spinning around in there since yesterday, they would have been shocked.

When Circle ended and they'd gone their separate ways, images of the strange man dogged her. He had looked peculiar to her, but not particularly dangerous. Yes, he'd followed her, and her instinct to run and hide to protect herself had kicked in, but in retrospect she had the clear impression he was not a threat.

She wondered if he had come from a town or settlement on the mainland, and if life there was as awful as she had been taught in school. He might have lost his way during his explorations from goodness knows where and simply needed food and shelter.

Earlier, while she and the other workers gave the infants their baths, Yvonne guessed he might have come from upper Canada by way of the Strait of Belle Isle, or from the St. Lawrence Seaway and Gulf in a boat or canoe. Harper thought it possible he'd traveled up from Eastern America. But hadn't geography class taught them the entire eastern seaboard of that country had flooded ages ago and lay under water ever since, as had happened with parts of their own coastline? The rogue couldn't have come from anywhere much farther south either. Their earliest lessons on global collapse explained how more than half the planet had been rendered unfit for human habitation for well over a century.

Once she'd said goodnight to Shyla in the wards' wing of their dormitory, Kat readied for bed herself. She stripped off her smoky clothes from the bonfire and stepped into the shower in her wing's shared washroom, welcoming the cool water as it sluiced over her skin. She peeled the bandage from her thigh and inspected the puncture wound. It had scabbed over well enough not to require another dressing.

Though it could mean trouble if the trespasser were one of many, her curiosity had been weirdly galvanized. Was it the novelty of him, an interest in his personal history, or could it be more?

Shaking her head, she turned off the shower and grabbed her towel from its hook. She must be bonkers. Why did she half-hope to see him again? She pushed the foolish notion aside while she dried herself off. No matter how much the idea of a newcomer helped combat her crushing boredom, no matter how much the secret of him fed her inner rebellion, she had to remember what she'd been taught about outsiders. What had been drilled into all of their brains since they were mature enough to understand. The welfare of her people was always top priority.

By the time she ate a snack of mixed berries and yogurt in the mess hall and retired to her bedroom, her bunkmates were already asleep. She put on a clean nightshirt and crawled into her bunk next to the window. She pulled her feather pillow over her head to block out the rattle of snores. With five single beds lined off in one cramped room for her, Falon and Harper, and with Grace and Ruby as regular snorers, she usually tried to get to sleep before they did. But tonight, sleep would not come easily anyway.

As she lay awake, she wandered back through memories of her childhood. Like the others, she'd been assigned as a ward to an older girl. Her constant ally for four years, Wren had been the epitome of the person her younger self imagined becoming. Sturdy and brave, funny and kind, Wren had taught her numerous skills under her tutelage, and Kat had tried to emulate her in every way. She'd shown her how to trap with stealth and fish with cunning, and how to track and outsmart even the wiliest of prey. She'd taught her how to swim and dive for mollusks and other hidden treasures from the ocean floor and tidal pools. In their last year together, she gave her preliminary lessons in canoeing the rapids on Blue Mountain River, a skill few village females dared to attempt.

Wren had also tended to young Kat's personal care. She'd made sure she received her necessary meds and proper nutrition, combed the knots from her hair each night after her shower, and tucked her in bed in the children's wing promptly at nine. She'd seen to it that her ward attended school, finished her homework, didn't miss curfew, and made it to each meeting and Sundown Circle.

Then one April morning, Wren didn't show up for breakfast at the mess hall. Twelve-year-old Kat had asked the other wards and their sister-guides if they'd seen her. None of them knew of her whereabouts. But when she complained to the elders, Ms. Bee told her Wren had gone to live in another village and they would assign her a replacement guide in a day or two.

Besieged with hurt and anger on that dark day, she'd refused to eat her porridge or anything else. In class, she couldn't concentrate on her schoolwork. As she wound up for a full-scale tantrum, Ms. Naomi had taken her by the hand and brought her around to the back of the schoolhouse. They'd sat alone together at the picnic table where the girls usually ate their recess snacks.

"Kat," she'd said, "Wren has been sent to another village to live and work."

"But why? Why did you send her away? Why couldn't she stay here?"

"We reassigned her to one of our Labrador villages which needed her expertise. You know all those useful skills she taught you? Well, their school needed a teacher like her. She relocated there to help train their girls to become as skilled and capable as you are."

Kat didn't know how she toughed it out that spring. She'd refused to give in to tears, but her heart felt as if it had been trampled into a thousand pieces. She couldn't comprehend why they hadn't let her go with Wren. She didn't even get a chance to say good-bye to her, but Ms. Bee told her it was for the best. And, as expected, no one would tell her which Labrador village Wren now lived in.

"Be careful not to get too attached to one person."

"No one is more important than anyone else."

"We must learn to adapt to new situations and duties."

"This is the way of life if we hope to flourish in this world."

"We do this for the good of the village and for the sake of our future."

"Nothing is as vital as the welfare of our people."

They had grown up on these maxims. They'd heard them repeatedly until they were a part of them, ingrained into their psyches. But Kat had never gotten used to the Wren-shaped void in her life no other sister-guide could fill.

Her alternate guide Mack had tried, but their relationship had been doomed from the start. Kat's disobedience had tested the older girl's patience and frequently the elders had to intervene. But no matter how many times they'd chastised her or stripped her of her privileges, she hadn't warmed to her new guide and avoided her at every opportunity.

Sometimes on cooler days, she'd sneak off by way of old logging roads to a secluded inner pond with her trouting pole, or to random beaches at low tide to collect driftwood, shells, and sea glass. Other times she would take refuge in the abandoned root cellar, a hideaway Mack and the elders knew nothing about. Back then, she'd squirreled away a stash of snacks, apple cider, or berry juice in the cellar for those days that had particularly taxed her and she needed time alone to recharge. She'd grown fond of the coolness of the cellar on a stifling-hot day and the smell of layers of dirt, hundreds of years old, that permeated its interior. She remembered the spring she'd brought the barn cat and her litter of kittens inside, a safe haven for them from coyotes and hawks, and the perfect place for Kat to have them to herself until they'd been weaned.

Perhaps the maxims were right. Forging new attachments was pointless. They only ended in pain and loss anyway. She knew Mack had shed no tears this past February when Kat reached the age of eighteen and was no longer her worry or responsibility.

The volume of Ruby's snores kicked into high gear. Muttering, Kat flipped over on her back and kicked off her quilt. She stretched up to the windowsill above her bed for the miniature pine-wood horse she kept there. Lying back down, she held the five-inch carving and stroked its smooth, tiny muzzle. When she moved back from her summer stint at Western Path six years ago and gushed to her dorm mates about the beautiful horses and ponies she'd worked with, Harper had whittled it with her pocketknife as a welcome-home gift.

When the elders had told her another village needed Wren, somehow their words hadn't rung true. Had she let Wren down and that was why she left? Had her over-attachment or petulant ways played a part?

Perhaps she'd grown weary of the millstone her ward represented. Kat knew she'd been a trifle difficult and out of control at times. Wren must have had her fill of her and needed a change. Deep down inside, a tiny voice whispered: if Wren didn't care enough to stick around, who would? She made up her mind she was better off relying on no one.

But she couldn't set a trap, rig a snare, or bait a hook without thinking of Wren. And despite the doubts, despite the passage of time, she secretly fantasized of their reunion one day. After all, youngsters were often disobedient and unlovable, and she had matured a great deal since their separation. Taking this into account, she held onto the hope her beloved mentor had already forgiven her.

CHAPTER SEVEN

His stomach clenched again, with a hunger he could no longer satisfy with berries, corn and the like. He needed to find meat or another source of protein.

He thought of the river that flowed through the forest a few yards from his pallet of boughs, his source of drinking water since he'd arrived. Might it be a source of food? Perhaps he'd catch a trout or two there. Or a fat, pink salmon.

He could fashion a pole from a tree branch, but he had no line or hook. As teenagers when they'd lived in a near-deserted township near the Quebec-Labrador border, he and his brother often built a dam of sorts from old brush or with a scavenged window screen, a weir to catch fish in the shriveled river which ran through the township. But the stream, like many in the area, had dried up. Then the real hunger kicked in. With the ever-increasing heat and degraded, dusty soil, they could no longer grow the vegetables they'd relied on for sustenance.

They'd pulled up stakes and travelled east into southern Labrador, where they found a thinly populated hamlet whose citizens agreed to let them stay. For years, life was manageable again.

But the yield from their potato crop for the last three summers had been abysmal, and the few livestock they'd managed to keep but could no longer feed had long since been butchered and eaten. The oppressive climate had killed off cold-water species of freshwater fish and had created a dead zone in the lake, exhausted of oxygen and incapable of supporting life. Their drinking water stank and their once-ample fish supply had essentially vanished.

It had also become harder to hunt any creature worth eating. He imagined whatever wildlife remained had migrated farther north. Many of the locals from their settlement had left to trek north too, willing to brave the consequences of trespassing on the territory of the Indigenous Peoples.

On his wounded leg, he skirted back to the woods and through the tangle of underbrush until he made it to the bank of the river. If he had a net ....

He pulled off his shirt. It might work as a net of sorts, and heaven knew it could do with a wash. Winding the sleeves around his wrists, he knelt at the water's edge and dipped the shirt into the lathering current. The river was deep here. With enough patience, it could work.

What did he have to lose? More weight? He had zero of that to spare. Ava had told him she was frightened by how much he'd lost and how gaunt he'd become. But how could he eat when he barely had enough for his wife and child? How could a man take food from the hungry mouths dependent on him?

"Please, Marc," she'd whispered one night beside the fire. Hudson had already eaten, curled in his father's lap, drifting off against his chest. He had managed to get two spoonfuls of the jack pike and lichen stew into him before he'd shoved the bowl away. She'd nudged the half-eaten meal of stew toward him. "You eat the rest. You need to stay strong too, sweetheart."

He'd shaken his head and nudged it back. He remembered

wishing she would stifle her pleas so as not to rouse and upset the boy. "I'll get a bite to eat later. Don't worry."

"When was the... last time you ate with us? Listen, if you refuse to eat, I will too."

She'd said this to him between shallow fits of coughing, a recent and troubling development. Over the past months, those who had fallen ill and died had been afflicted with the same racking cough.

"You will not." The stern words had sprung from his lips, faintly audible above the boy's head. "You'll eat every last drop of this stew if I have to force-feed it to you."

With reluctance, Ava had complied. But as the days and weeks crawled by, her appetite waned, her cough became more persistent, and flecks of blood showed up in her sputum. She, too, grew pale and rail thin.

The young man's attempts to keep his family healthy had become all-consuming. There had been no pharmacies or stores of any kind for decades, and hospitals and clinics had long since shut-tered their doors. Joel, the older man who lived in a shack next to his, had suggested he make tea from wintergreen leaves to help with the fever and aches.

He'd tramped to neighbouring centers which were essentially ghost towns. He'd trekked to tiny camps and backwaters on a desperate quest for answers and medical advice. Following other suggestions of the folk he talked to, he gathered chickweed to eat and clover to dry. He used the dried clover heads to make another medicinal tea for his wife. Admittedly, any positive effects proved minuscule. A couple of strangers in a nearby camp had suspected Ava, like many others, had contracted tuberculosis, and without the proper antibiotics she wouldn't survive.

An elderly physician had advised him to go east. He'd heard about a wildflower that grew there. Its extract reportedly saved lives. The Inuit people of Labrador had developed the extract during a severe tuberculosis epidemic many years prior, and as far as he knew they still used it as a key remedy in their arsenal of natural medicines. The doctor had also heard a rumour the Inuit had shared it with a small population of survivors on the island of Newfoundland.

He had little desire to journey north and trespass on indigenous land, but Newfoundland struck him as a viable option. This meant going by way of the sea, and the trip could be treacherous. Could he find the mysterious wildflower, or its extract, and make it home in time to make a difference?

Along with others of his hamlet, he'd trapped squirrels and the occasional rabbit or muskrat when he could. He blanched at the thought of the protein resource he and the remaining citizens had fallen back on—mice and rats. He'd cooked and served them to Ava and Hudson without divulging what they were, passing them off as scrawny chipmunks or weasels. Fish catches of any kind were harder and harder to come by. The last time he'd tried, the brook and lake trout had been as tiny as minnows and the pike were puny and scarce.

He remembered the day before he left Minipi Lake, each minute detail razor-sharp in his mind. Up to then, he and his brother hadn't settled on who should go east to search for the medicine, or if it was prudent to take such a trip at all.

He'd rocked his son in his arms that evening as he paced the floor of their two-room shack. The boy hadn't eaten more than a spoonful of supper and his fever had spiked again. Marcus had hurried to the shallow water hole behind their shack and scooped up brown water with an old well bucket. When he returned, he wrung up a cloth in the cool water next to his son and sponged his forehead, cheeks and neck. His desperation peaked as he tried to soothe his flaming skin and lower his temperature. The child's cries had become weaker in the past two days, as if he sensed tears were pointless. But as frail as he was, his coughing fits didn't let up for hours, even after his father grew frustrated and brought him back to

THE WOMEN OF WILD COVE

his bed. At long last, the feeble whimpers diminished as the child slipped into the merciful release of sleep.

He watched the boy's thin chest rise and fall, and as his vision blurred, he feared the worst: with no medication to treat the disease, the end was imminent. Did it herald the end of humankind as well?

One solution remained: to leave on the expedition as he'd proposed.

As he got ready to turn in for the night, he'd broached the subject to his brother again. He told Trent he'd made his decision.

"I'm leaving at dawn tomorrow. I can no longer sit back and do nothing."

"Is it a wise move, though, to chase down this rumour?" his brother had countered. "All well and good for the rest of us if we find it, Marcus, but you can't guarantee it will save the boy at this point."

"It could be his only chance, and ours too. If there are easterners left and they have the plant source or the medicine, or if it's in the hands of the northerners, we have to find out!"

"But why do some sicken and die," Trent said, "while others, such as you and me, have resistance to this disease? If it's contagious, we would have been sick or dead by now for sure."

"Maybe our immune systems are healthier. And there's the dormancy factor, according to the old doc I talked to. If it is TB, we might be latent carriers for the rest of our lives. Or it's just a matter of time before it becomes active and we too fall sick."

"Job's comforter." Trent gulped the last of his birch tea and banged his mug down on the wooden table. "Alright, you've convinced me it's worth the trip. If anyone goes, it should be the two of us. We're the strongest and fittest of the bunch."

Marcus fell silent, deep in thought. All that remained of the Atlantic provinces was a portion of Nova Scotia, an archipelago and a stretch of reefs where New Brunswick once existed, and the shrunken island of Newfoundland. The entirety of Prince Edward Island lay under water. At least that's what a motley gang of transients told his people when they came back from the east coast three summers ago.

"We can't both go. Someone has to stay here with the others and keep them safe. Hudson is still doing poorly, and I don't—"

"I should go. Say the word and I'm out of here." Trent grabbed his hunting knife from the cluttered counter. He touched the blade to his thumb and examined its edge.

Marcus crossed his arms. Kin or not, his brother wasn't known for his unblemished character, a fact he had to bear in mind. His track record and his hot-headed, violent streak spoke for itself.

Growing up, Trent had been a punk, a bully, and a troublemaker, the wayward youngster who landed himself in one scrape after another. He'd brawled with other boys and taunted his little brother relentlessly, much to the chagrin of their parents. Five years older than Marcus, Trent had been their mother's son by another man before she met Marcus's father. On one occasion their mother had forced him to apologize to a teenage girl's family for his overt and uninvited sexual advances. The victim had been his buddy's younger sister. In the wake of that episode, he'd revealed to his kid brother that he found girls more of a kick if they put up a fight. Marcus had questioned with disgust how the two could have any of the same blood flowing through their veins.

And who had more to lose here? Trent's pregnant girlfriend had succumbed to the disease last year, leaving him more hardened than ever. Understandable, but his attitude often disturbed Marcus, particularly his coarse talk around the few women who remained in their hamlet. Who's to say if ol' Trent tracked down a better place to settle, he would bother coming back at all? His brother might be the more self-assured between the two of them, but he was also more reckless.

He made a judgment call. "No, I'm the one who should go.

And I'd rather cross the strait and check with what's left of Newfoundland, to begin with. The healing extract could be there."

He preferred to leave the indigenous Labrador northerners out of it for now. Earlier efforts to build a relationship with them had failed and had prompted repeated warnings to the people of his hamlet to be left alone. The warring migrants had made them loath to any communications with strangers. Would another attempt make any difference? A hunt for a cure up there was a last resort, and only if his exploration of the island and of Nova Scotia, if needed, came up empty.

"At least you have the cougar meat. It should last until you or Joel or one of the others manage to kill something else. Try to get some into Hudson." Marcus downed his own tea and stared into the empty mug. "And please keep close guard over the others as usual. Still have the 12 gauge?"

Trent cleaned the dirt from under his fingernails with the point of his knife. "No damn good without ammo. I used the last shell on the cougar."

"Anyone who threatens you won't know that. The sight of a gun might be enough to scare them off. And it's been almost a year since that last scuffle with drifters. You probably have nothing to worry about anyway."

"Here's hoping. I'd feel a whole lot better if you had a firearm to take with you."

"I told you I don't want a gun."

"Make sure you pack your buck knife with your supplies. And take that old life jacket too." Trent stood up abruptly. "I'll go make splits for tomorrow morning."

Marcus nodded. "Hang on a sec—along with the others, you must swear to me you will oversee Hudson's care. I'd take him with me, but he's too ill for a trip such as this. He is the most vulnerable here, which makes him priority number one. Understood?" Marcus pushed back from the table and drew himself up his brother's height. "Keep him as cool as possible, get him to eat, and keep giving him the wintergreen tea. It helps his symptoms, at least a bit."

"Still think I should go instead," his brother said. He combed his fingers through his wiry beard. "But if you believe it's better this way, so be it."

"I do. Can Hudson and I count on you to step up?"

"I'll do whatever I can for my nephew. But if you're not back here in three weeks, I'll get Joel's old sailboat and come looking for you."

Marcus had agreed, and they'd shaken hands on it.

At first light the next day, he'd packed his supplies and he and Trent had portaged their lightweight skiff across the stretch of lakes, ponds, and rivers to the Strait of Belle Isle.

After he'd donned his life vest, he waved good-bye to his brother and took the oars. He'd prayed for the courage—and a supreme dose of sheer luck—to bring his undertaking to a successful end. He knew it was a long shot, but he'd refused to consider any other outcome.

*　*　*

After twenty minutes of fruitless waiting and scooping with his shirt, he took a break. Were there any fish left in these Newfoundland rivers to catch, or had climate change obliterated the freshwater ecosystem here too? Doubtful, what with the fertile richness of the region. Drops of moisture popped out on his neck and forehead as the blaze of the sun burned his shoulders. He edged his way along the riverbank where the waterway narrowed, until he stepped into a shaded area under a dense cover of pine and balsam fir. He welcomed the coolness as it settled on his clammy skin.

Lightheaded from hunger, he bent to dip his shirt again. At last, his persistence paid off. He swung his shirt from the rushing water.

The trout twitched and thrashed until he grabbed it by the tail and ended its life with a sharp whack of its head on a nearby boulder. He retrieved his knapsack from the ground to put his catch inside.

As he straightened up, he had a clear sense he was no longer alone. Someone was watching him. His body tensed, ready to flee and hide. He spied a flutter of movement from behind an enormous pine tree.

That girl again!

CHAPTER EIGHT

Kat spotted the rogue the next morning on the southern boundary of Black Spruce Forest, not far from where she'd encountered him two days before. He knelt on the bank of a cascading river that flowed from the Long Range Mountains, where the waterway tapered to a stream. He'd taken off his shirt and dipped it repeatedly with both hands into the gushing water. Angling for breakfast, she surmised.

She'd given Shyla the slip early, taking off for the woods at daybreak, with the intent to make it back before anyone missed her. Her growing impudence even surprised herself, but she didn't see any real harm in it. Plenty of time remained for an activity with her ward before nursery duty. As usual, she'd checked her snares for rabbits, and was hitching two of the dead animals onto her belt with twine when she spotted him. To play it safe, she hid behind a massive pine tree and spied on him through her small binoculars.

She guessed his age at somewhere between twenty and twenty-five. His hair, lank and glossy with sweat, hung over his shoulders, longer than she'd ever seen on a man. His face in profile was attractive and his skin deeply tanned with touches of sunburn, but what grabbed her attention was his physique. He looked thinner than any of the peons she knew. More angular and haggard. Due to prolonged undernourishment, she guessed. She focused on the muscles in his back and arms, glistening in the sun. Lean, young and vigorous, he brought to her mind a certain underdog Roman gladiator she'd read about in the school library last winter.

As she studied him, an unexpected surge of frustration flooded through her. She needed to remember no matter how harmless he appeared, no matter how distracting the package, she could not trust an unassimilated man. And yet a part of her longed to find out more about him. Where did he come from? How did he injure his leg? Was he all alone in the world?

Mindful of the stranger's presence, she'd taken better measures to protect herself before she ventured out at daybreak. She'd taken along the binoculars again. And from now on, a makeshift bone knife would not do. She patted the encased spear-point survival knife on her right hip.

The man stood and walked farther along the riverbank in her direction. He stepped into an area shaded by balsam and pine. Again, Kat noticed a hitch in his gait. Shortly after, his efforts were rewarded. He pulled a foot-long rainbow trout from the stream with his shirt-turned-fishing net and smacked its head on a rock. When he picked up his knapsack and checked the area, he caught her spying on him.

She froze.

"Hello again," he called out. "What's your name?"

She detected a slight accent. "My name is no concern of yours. Where'd you come from and what do you want?"

He took tentative steps towards her. Yes, his left leg had a decided limp. She shrank behind the pine tree. She checked the footpath where she would flee if necessary and pulled her knife from its caribou-leather sheath.

"You think I mean to hurt you? I won't come any closer, alright?"

"For your own good, you better mean it. I asked where you're from."

"North of here."

"From Labrador, or—?"

"Yes. I trekked to the coast and sailed across the strait."

She puzzled about this. The tip of the Northern Peninsula had been designated as a lookout site, as did every major point of land around the island. Why hadn't the lighthouse personnel spotted this outsider and ordered the peons to seize him? Perhaps they'd grown lax lately due to inactivity and had left the scope unattended. She ought to report this too.

As if in answer to her unasked question, he spoke again. "I avoided detection when I crossed, I guess, but my boat hit some shoals and broke apart. I swam ashore and hid in the woods."

"How long have you been here?"

"A few days, foraging for food and searching for people who might have other ideas besides killing me. Most of my supplies were lost with the skiff. I only have this knapsack. I lost my knife and fishing gear, and I don't have anything to light a fire with to cook this trout. Can you help me?"

"Listen up, stranger. I have enough problems to worry about, and none of yours make the list."

"So you won't help."

Kat pressed her lips together in a tight line. "Why should I? You're not welcome here, and if I don't inform our elders about you, someone else sure will."

"Your elders? As in church elders?"

"No, and again, no business of yours."

The man stepped closer. "How many of you live on this island?"

She made a firm decision not to furnish him with any more

information. "You don't need to know that either. But know this: you could lose your freedom or even your life if you stick around."

"I'll die anyway if I don't eat soon. If I had a weapon to hunt with...."

She felt an unwelcome twinge of sympathy but quashed it at once. "I've given you fair notice. Leave the island and I won't tell the others I saw you."

"But how can I possibly leave, for God's sake? Swim?"

She saw his point, though she was at a loss as to what to say or do next. She imagined the peons overpowering and arresting this young man. It gave her no gratification. The thought of him subjected to punitive measures—or worse—turned her stomach. "You still haven't answered my question! Why did you leave your home in Labrador to come here?"

His mouth twitched. "Labrador wasn't always my home. My people hailed from Quebec, back when Canada was a unified country. We were forced to live elsewhere when American immigrants drove us off our property."

"Where did you settle?"

"Near the border, but I migrated farther east with family and finally settled in the Minipi Lake region. Farther north would've been better, but the Innu and Inuit people are territorial about their land and don't appreciate any encroachment either. But who can blame them for protecting their livelihood, to prevent what had already happened to us?"

Who could blame them indeed? She'd been taught how the Indigenous Peoples had their land and their hunting grounds taken from them in the Old World. Having reclaimed what was rightfully theirs, they weren't about to let history repeat itself.

"All we want is a way of life that can sustain us. We've toughed it out for years now. We've lived off the land, trapping and hunting. But it's gotten much hotter lately and more barren. It's a job to keep body and soul together."

What he described was reminiscent of the stories her teachers had shared. "Are there others, aside from your family?" Family. The word sounded foreign on her tongue.

"Yes, we moved into a hamlet there. Mostly men, besides my brother's girlfriend's three sisters and their children, and..." He mopped his brow with his soaked shirt. "If I tell you about it, you'll know why I came all this way."

His eyes bore such profound sadness, Kat had to turn away.

"How far from here do you live?"

"That's something else you don't need to know." She had an idea. With halting steps, she emerged from behind the pine tree. She made sure he saw her knife. Its five-inch steel blade glinted in the sun. "Follow me from a safe distance and I'll show you where you can take shelter to hide and rest. There's a mini stove there to cook your trout too."

He brightened. "You're a lifesaver! I'm more than grateful."

Don't shower me with gratitude yet, stranger.

"Please tell me your name."

"Kat. With a K. Yours?"

"Marcus. But you can call me Marc." A trace of amusement played around his lips.

When his gaze swept over the length of her and met her narrowed eyes, her skin prickled all over as if she'd stepped in an ant nest. She hastily turned her back to him.

She slowed after one step. Had she gone soft in the head? Trusting him to walk behind her? "Better yet, go in front of me. It's a bit of a trek to get there, but it's well-hidden." She waved the tip of the knife toward the footpath.

He submitted without a word and shuffled ahead of her.

As she followed him on the path, she deliberated over what to do. What would her elders and the others think of her actions? Was she helping him or setting him up?

How dreadful his life sounded! The bleakness, the hunger, the struggle for subsistence. He had nowhere to go. Why would he have fled from his home and his people to come here if he didn't have just cause?

If she helped him only this once....

Deeper and deeper into the forest they hiked. She gave the man directions from time to time, but beyond this, not a word passed between them. Shyla and the nursery staff expected her back by now, but at this point, what could she do? The rogue was walking as fast as his bum leg allowed, at a steady pace but painfully slow all the same.

The woodland became tougher to pass through and the mountains loomed closer the farther they trudged. The density of coniferous trees, the uneven ground, and the overgrowth of thick grasses and shrubbery impeded their progress. But within the hour, they arrived at their destination.

"Here it is." She pointed at a side path to her left.

The man stopped pressing through the trees and vegetation and circled back. A sheen of perspiration gleamed off his forehead as he joined her on the path.

Six yards through the foliage peeked the rear outline of an ancient travel trailer, its tiny back window covered in mosquito netting. The windowsill and the rest of its visible surface and edges were caked in thick green moss.

"Come on." Again, Kat directed him with her knife.

When they cleared the shrubbery and stepped into the hidden glade, she pointed at the side door of the eighteen-foot trailer, also grown over with patches of moss and spots of rust. She told him to take a gander inside. "There's a portable stove with biofuel in there. I know it still works because I used it a couple of weeks ago. It has a sink but no running water. Right over there behind the trailer is a stream." She pointed to a stout wooden bucket near its rear wheel. "There's a bunk inside." She untied one of the rabbits from her belt and threw it at his feet. "Something to go with your trout. You'll find a frying pan and other utensils in the cabinet."

"Thank you, Kat." His words were cordial, but his contorted expression alluded to the pain he suffered. "You're very kind."

He entered the trailer and she shadowed him, still brandishing her weapon.

"Plenty of fruit around," she told him. "You'll find apple trees beyond the stream. Many of the apples in this way are green, but they're edible. And loads of raspberries and blackberries are growing over there behind those pink rosebushes."

"That will be helpful." He tugged a red-checked handkerchief from one of the side pockets of his pants and rubbed it over his dripping face. He sat at the table, squinting through the screened window at the diffused sunshine that filtered through the trees. "I can't wrap my head around how vibrant everything is here on your island. Hot, but not too dry that plants can't grow. So green and flourishing, like an oasis in the middle of a proverbial desert. It's a Shangri-La." He dropped his head. "Not at all like where I live."

"Your home is more inland, so it's naturally warmer than here on the coast. Plus, we get plenty of rain. But even here, the temperatures are rising from year to year. Our teachers say in the future our seasons will be even less distinguishable from one another, with spring as scorching as summer, and winter much the same as a mild fall."

"It sounds as if the whole planet is heating up." With both hands, he lifted his left leg under the fold-out table and rested it on the edge of the seat opposite him. He rubbed his shin and winced.

"And I wouldn't call it a Shangri-La. We work hard to survive here. Another downside is the fall hurricanes are expected to worsen. What happened to your leg?"

"Twisted my ankle when my boat broke up on the rocks. At least I think it's only a sprain." He gestured to her right leg well below the scabbed cut, where an angry purple trench ran down her shin and around the calf. "Quite the scar. A story there, for sure."

"Black bear attack as a kid. He didn't fare as well as I." If it hadn't been for good old Bryce and Caleb, she would have been the bear's supper that day. She strode to the door.

"Wait! What's your hurry?"

"I have to get back to my chores and my ward."

"Your ward? Do you mean you're his guardian?"

"Hers, and in a way, yes."

"How does that work?"

"When eighteen-year-olds graduate from school, they're assigned eight-year-olds to mentor. The child's classroom hours are cut back to afternoons at that age, for them to learn more about practical skills not taught in schoolbooks."

"Makes sense, I guess. How long does the mentorship last?"

"Usually until the ward turns eighteen and graduates to mentorship herself."

"The parents must appreciate the extra help."

She gave him a smirk. "I really have to go."

"I will see you again, right?"

She paused, her hand on the trailer door latch. "I'll try to secure a boat so you can get off the island. Like I said, if you stay, your life could be in peril."

He sat motionless, staring at the tabletop as if chewing over an important decision. "I'll stay around here until you come back."

"Don't draw attention to yourself." She thought it doubtful anyone would uncover him here, a fair distance from Wild Cove, their farmland, and their usual hunting grounds. The trailer had served as Yvonne's secret boudoir a few years ago. Kat heard she'd entertained her sexual partners here until others found out and Yvonne caught them spying on her through the window. Ruby told her she'd ditched the trailer in favour of other hiding places closer to the peon quarters.

"With any luck, no one will find you. I'll try to come back in a day or two, though it might take longer. You must be patient."

She waved a good-bye and left. Once she cleared the deepest part of the forest and located the main footpath again, she stepped up her speed. She was already late for the nursery. She needed an excuse for her tardiness that would sound half-way plausible.

Was she truly going through with her hairbrained scheme to help this fellow escape? And why the devil did she volunteer information about mentoring?

As she cut through the trees, it dawned on her what she should do—what her upbringing had taught her to do. Now she knew exactly where to lead the peon corps to pick him up. She'd take them to the trailer and have him arrested for trespassing and for what he might be plotting against them. She would, and she should.

She had no reason on earth to place any confidence in him. She knew what his kind were capable of. She'd heard horror story on top of horror story at their monthly meetings, ever since she was old enough to grasp the concepts of patriarchy, oppression, abuse and mortal danger.

No matter how sad a tale he told or how harmless he represented himself, it didn't erase the fact he was a man. And an unnaturalized one to boot.

Why had she ever entertained the crazy notion of helping him?

CHAPTER NINE

By the time she arrived at the nursery, she had her version of the truth concocted.

Falon, Harper and Yvonne, all rocking infants, bobbed their heads up when she walked in. Grace, working her usual shift with the young children, nodded a hello as she pulled a pitcher of milk and a basket of strawberries from the cooler for the children's midmorning snack.

Yvonne pursed her lips. "Look who finally decided to honour us with her presence. You're two hours late. We had to feed your charges and cover your turn at laundry. Better not skip out on your overnight shift with Nola this evening, missy."

Falon's forehead wrinkled.

"What happened?"

"I checked my snares earlier than usual. I didn't sleep well last night, and when I rested under a tree, I dozed off."

Yvonne huffed and sputtered to herself, shaking her head.

Kat shifted into her mauve uniform and rejoined the others. "Shyla already here?"

"She's helping in the playroom with Alice and Tansy," Grace said as she poured milk into child-size cups she'd set on a tray.

She went to check on her ward in the playroom, but the girl had gone outside to push the tots on the swings.

Yvonne rose from her rocker and laid the sleeping infant she held back in its wooden crib. "Ah, the charmed life you lead. You're lucky an elder didn't drop in and discover your absence. In fact, you're lucky if I don't march over to Ms. Bee right this minute and report your tardy ass for dereliction of duty!"

Kat stomped over to her and seized her wrist. "Go ahead. I dare you. But remember, report me and I'll tell 'em what you've been up to with the peons during work hours!"

Yvonne yanked her arm free. "Fly to hell," she hissed, reddening. "You have no proof of any infraction."

"And neither do you. Who said I didn't get here on time? Falon will vouch for me. Right, Falon?"

Falon squirmed under her expectant stare but nodded. "Of course," she mumbled.

Harper burped a plump baby boy against her shoulder. "You still play with peons during the day, Yvonne?"

"If I am, what of it?" she snapped. "That's my business, not yours." She glared once more at Kat. "In the meantime, Miss Privileged here thinks she's above the rest of us, getting special favours while we toe the line and do whatever we're told. What's wrong with this picture?"

"Special favours, my ass. If you're whining about my transfer this fall, I've waited years for this, and they need me there."

"You're right, Kat," Grace put in. "Some help with baby cows and horses, some with baby humans. Growing the animal population is vital to the island too." Humming a tune, she withdrew to the playroom with the snacks.

Miss Privileged indeed. And what did Yvonne have to complain about anyway? Hadn't she been pleased with her appointment as junior practitioner of the nursery? Sure, she'd been disappointed when she learned of her sterility, but she survived, and this way she could stay on baby duty for the rest of her working life.

Yvonne barreled toward her with a tiny bundle. "Well, animals or not, you're needed here now."

Kat took the mewling infant thrust into her arms. She gasped at its size and weightlessness. "And who, pray tell, is this poor little scrap of humanity?"

"Our new preemie, born last night. He's due to be fed but needs a diaper change too." She gathered up the empty milk bottles scattered around the room and brought them to the sink to wash. "Get a few ounces into him at least. He threw up what he drank a couple of hours ago."

Kat changed the preemie's diaper, warmed a bottle, and sat with him to nurse. Because he wasn't feeding well yet, the newborn would stay a bit longer before he was shipped off to a village in Labrador or on the other side of the island.

While the newborn sucked down the milk, she rejoiced in the knowledge this drudgery would soon be behind her. She dreamed of Western Path almost nightly now, her anticipation rising to a fever pitch.

Why work in infant care—or even worse, breed—when a more fitting role awaited her? Now that her wish to become a horse-woman and ranch hand would soon be a reality, she secretly hoped her skill set would excuse her from the expected interval of procreation duty on her twentieth birthday. Though such exceptions were rare, Ms. Naomi told her Dr. Olivia's significant medical expertise had exempted her from the breeding program. And at supper last night, Ms. Jaleena had announced that her gifted protégé, Vicky, had earned herself an exemption upon her graduation to chef this week. The young apprentice would take control of the kitchen at the same time the aging elder stepped back full time into her managerial role and hung up her apron for good.

The notion of mating and giving birth like a prized mare for the benefit of the island held no appeal for a young woman like Kat. Nor did the idea of expressing milk for other babies while the one she birthed was whisked away. She appreciated the women who wanted to help grow the human population. It *was* a noble and meaningful endeavor. But for all its virtue, she had no desire to be a part of it.

She speculated sometimes about where she'd been born. What woman had given birth to her and where did she live? But no one born here in the past twenty years ever learned about their bloodlines. It Takes a Village, as the elders intoned ad nauseam at almost every meeting. None of them knew about attachments, relatives, or family units, beyond what they heard at journal readings, learned in social studies and history class, and read about in their school's library of classic and historical literature. These were concepts that had no purpose anymore and were only brought up these days as models of living which no longer worked.

The door whooshed open. Her colleague Ruby breezed in with a fat little cherub of four or five months she'd taken for a stroll. Her sister-ward June trailed behind and without being told, dashed to the playroom to help Grace and the other wards.

Ruby, freckled, tall and full-figured, sat in the rocker next to her workmate. "Holy moly," she said, eyes wide. "He's minuscule!"

Kat gave the infant a break from the bottle and burped him. Resting him on her lap, she rewrapped him more snugly in the light blanket. "Ever see one this premature?"

"I caught a glimpse of a smaller stillbirth from the Origin Suites last month, but he's the scrawniest I've seen alive. Think he'll make it?"

Kat coaxed him to suckle some more. "If he doesn't take the

milk better soon, he won't. Hmm, what can I nickname this puny runt?"

"How about Humongous?" Ruby said, which prompted a giggle from Falon.

"Humongous it is—but Hugh for short." She prodded at his tiny mouth with the bottle's nipple. He gagged.

"Ewww!" She glared down at the infant. He'd vomited the milk he'd managed to drink over himself and his blanket. When she fetched a clean onesie from a stack of fresh laundry on the counter, she overheard Ruby speak of the rogue to Harper.

"What about the rogue, Ruby?"

"The peons found the wreck of a small boat under a pile of kelp on our beach's north end. That means he must still be here. The elders have the organized search in place now. Our peons, along with those from our villages on the north shore from the peninsula to Cape Baie Verte, will set out at dawn tomorrow."

Back in the rocking chair, Kat made motions of fussing over the preemie as she swaddled him in a clean blanket. She hoped her face didn't betray herself as she mulled over this piece of news. It shouldn't have rattled her. She'd expected it. And he wouldn't elude them for long on that twisted ankle.

"Anyone know where the hunt begins?" she asked.

"The peninsula lighthouse, I believe. They'll work inland from there through the mountain passages. If that doesn't uncover him, they'll search Black Spruce and Poplar Forest and the rest of the peninsula. And if necessary, as far as Grand Lake, Ms. Bee said. The east and south coast villages are getting ready too in case we need search parties there as well."

A rush of self-reproach flooded through her. She knew she should quit her dilly-dallying and hand him over to the peons at once. The entire day ahead would be a test of her loyalty.

For the good of the village.

For the welfare of our people.

For the sake of our future.

Little Hugh lay sound asleep in her arms. He didn't drink anymore once he'd regurgitated and had slipped too easily back into slumber.

At lunchtime, she tucked him in his cradle and trooped out with the others to the mess hall. Today, Falon took her shift to stay behind with the junior and senior practitioners. Kat sighed. The preemie's wellbeing troubled her somewhat, but the bulk of her ruminations centered on her surrender of Marcus. She had to do right by her elders and expose him. She resolved to tell Ms. Bee as soon as lunch was over.

But when the time came, she vacillated for an entirely different rationale that hadn't occurred to her earlier. As a consequence of exposing the newcomer, he might reveal to his captors how she had helped him up to this point. And what punishment would she receive for such a reckless transgression?

Knowing her elders as well as she did, particularly the imperious Ms. Bee, she suspected she would pay a dear price if they uncovered her deception. Without a doubt, a misstep such as this would put her ranch career on the line.

If she intended to go ahead with her plan, she'd better act soon. But she remained stuck with the babies, so her search for a boat this afternoon was impossible. She couldn't dodge all of her duties without arousing major suspicion and gambling with her career plans.

No, she would not divulge the man's whereabouts. She had to help him now, though self-preservation only accounted for part of her decision. Rogue or not, all she could see was Marcus's hopeful face. All she could hear was his voice, begging her for help.

* * *

The next morning, the sun peeked over the watery horizon as her overnight shift ended. The search for Marcus would begin today at the tip of the peninsula. He would be safe for a while yet, so she'd have time to get him out of the trailer and to the wharf within the next few hours, long before the peons had concluded the opening phase of their search.

She walked to the dormitory to collect her ward, but one of her bunkmates told her Shyla had gotten up early to spend some quiet time with the horses.

Kat scooted to the outbuildings behind the dorm and the Gathering House. She passed the weather-beaten storage shed with its exterior of soft driftwood-grey. The shed housed the sistership's tools, hunting supplies, and weaponry. A dozen yards beyond it stood the modest, red-ochre horse stable.

When she flung open the wide swinging doors, the three horses inside their stalls whinnied and snorted with delight. Sure enough, Shyla was there, putting down fresh hay from the overhead loft. She told her mentor she had already cleaned out the stalls, so watering the animals was the only chore left.

Kat watched her as she spread an armful of hay in the last stall. "Not your first time tackling stable duty."

The girl snorted. "Hardly."

Together, they dumped the horses' buckets, cleaned them out with scrub cloths, then brought them to the well behind the stable to rinse and refill them.

"The farmers have granted the horses a break from harvest work for the day," Kat said as they brought back the water.

"Ooh! Can we take them for an early ride, then?"

Though preoccupied with enabling Marcus's escape, she didn't want to brush off her ward again. The girl had gotten a jump on the stable chores, so she agreed. And unbeknownst to Shyla, she could still check out the boat situation.

She pulled a carrot from the pocket of her shorts and

approached the stall of Thunder, the eldest horse. He gave a soft snicker in greeting. "Maybe you can come next time, my sweet." The dapple-grey gelding plucked the carrot from her hand with nimble lips and munched on the treat. "Ms. Naomi might take you for a short ride later."

Pippa, Ms. Bee's quarter horse, bobbed her noble head and stamped her hooves in anticipation. Kat bridled the animal for herself and Ms. Jaleena's brown Morgan, Joy, for Shyla. Together they straddled their warm bare backs and rode them out of the village to stretch their legs.

Kat remembered simpler times when she'd blazed through entire afternoons riding Pippa wherever her fancy took her. Years ago, she'd trained herself to handle the animal with the correct leg, seat and hand techniques, which held her in good stead during the summer at the ranch. Since then, Pippa and the other two horses had become her stand-in for the work she missed at Western Path.

Side by side, they trotted smoothly along the curved dirt road that led out of Wild Cove. The early sunshine had dissipated, blotted out by a blanket of leaden clouds rolling in on a brisk wind from the east.

"Don't you adore Pippa's colour?" Shyla cried out. Her dark-eyed gaze swept over Kat's mount. "What I wouldn't give to have a horse to call my own!"

You and me both, kiddo. She glanced over her shoulder at the quarter horse's chestnut flank and honey-coloured tail. "She's a beauty alright. You mentioned a horse in Battle Cove the other day. You didn't own it?" By the style in which Shyla held the reins and the skill she displayed as she switched gaits, Kat could tell she also knew her way around a horse.

"No, Icarus was a gorgeous pinto that belonged to my sister-guide, Daisy. I cared for him and helped break him for riding. After that, I used to take him for runs whenever I got the chance." She dipped her head. "Those were the happiest days of my life."

Kat caught the shadow that flickered over the teen's face. "If the ranch produces the horseflesh they're hoping for, I dare say you'll see plenty of riders with their own horses or ponies one day."

"Yeah. One day." Shyla reached down and stroked Joy's glossy black mane, remarkably similar to her own hair. "You're such a lucky duck, going there to live. Ms. Bee told me I'll have a stint at junior apprenticeship later on, but not until your training is over. P'raps I'll get to go next summer."

"You're right, they only accept one newbie at a time."

"But you've already spent a summer there. I heard about it from Ms. Naomi. She told us in class yesterday how you not only helped with the foals and other livestock, but you also rescued animals too."

Kat did a double take. "She did?"

"Yep. She mentioned an eaglet?"

"One day I saw a murder of crows mob and attack a juvenile bald eagle." Kat grinned as she warmed to the topic. "When it fell to the ground, I brought it to the barn loft and fed it mice and water until its bruised wing healed."

"She said you also helped an injured fox?"

"That's right. I found the critter caught in a wire fence. Its paw had been punctured and it was half-starved. I nursed him back to health and re-released him to the wild."

"What a cool thing to do."

"I would think anyone who cares about animals at all would've done the same."

As they broke into an easy canter along the wide, well-worn trail that spanned the east side of Black Spruce Forest, a squirrel darted in front of them from the meadow, gave a perplexed chirp, and sprinted across the trail into the woods.

"I served as a junior apprentice that summer," she explained. "There's much more involved as a senior trainee. Besides horses, I will learn how to raise cows, sheep, goats, and pigs. Did you know they've acquired Newfoundland ponies from a hobby farm near Avalon Shoals and plan to breed them too? And there's brood-mare handling, training as a farrier, a shot at a veterinary career—"

A smile lit up Shyla's face. "Hey, then if I get picked next year, you might be the professional who trains me!"

When they came to the fenced graveyard at the northern edge of the forest, they wheeled the horses and cantered back toward the cove. Kat nodded and returned the smile. "I suppose it's possible. Come on, let's give them a decent run." She leaned forward and applied pressure with her thighs, prompting Pippa to pick up her pace.

They took off in a gallop, with the elder female a couple of lengths ahead until the ocean came into view. Riding past the outer perimeter of the village core, they neared the harbour wharf. Kat decreased her speed and scanned the familiar fleet of fishing dories that rocked in the cove under a pewter sky. No one had jigged or checked their nets for days because of relentless high winds and choppy seas over the past week.

Shyla squeezed back on the reins. "But I thought we weren't finished horseback riding! Why are we here? You already taught me how to bait hooks and jig for squid and sea bass. Are we fishing with gill nets?"

"No new lesson today. We're here to check on the fleet, and then we'll go to the nursery."

They dismounted and tethered the horses to a fence post. Shyla crinkled her nose in distaste at the mention of the nursery. Exactly how Kat felt.

Obviously, she couldn't tell her ward the real purpose for coming here. She tried to guess which dory would be the least missed, yet sturdy enough to cross the Strait of Belle Isle. And when its absence was discovered, would the fishers assume it had sunk or slipped its moorings and floated away?

Her eyes lit on a sturdy punt moored to the wharf. The

Serendipity. Old, in need of minor repairs, but she was a durable little vessel Kat often used. She'd have no trouble taking Marcus to safety once the turbulent waters settled down. He could skirt along the coast of the peninsula until he met the strait, then go back to where he came from without anyone learning of the part she'd played.

She walked down onto the narrow wood and stone slipway. "Can you help me with this?" She beckoned to the punt.

"Help how?" Her ward inched to the edge of the slipway where the waves slapped, curled and dissolved into white froth. Buffeting winds whipped her black hair around her head and neck and lashed it across her mouth.

"She's taken on a bit of water. We need to bail her out."

"Alright, show me what to do."

Kat hopped aboard the rocking punt, reached into the bilge, and picked up the square, wooden hand bailer. She made a few sample bails to give her ward the idea.

After they switched places, she hurried to the nearby stage head and climbed up its cribbing. She entered the red-ochre shed to collect a few items for the rogue's voyage: a large life-vest; a blanket in its waterproof sack; two four-litre water jugs which she filled from a nearby running hose; a jigging line and hooks; a small tub of bait; and a coil of rope. As an afterthought, she grabbed a compass from a shelf on the shed wall. She found a sack, stuffed the supplies inside, and carefully concealed it behind a fish barrel in the corner of the shed. She climbed down the cribbing and returned to the water's edge.

The sky had grown darker. Giant splatters of rain started to pelt her face, but the waves had settled down somewhat since their arrival. Marcus could leave this afternoon! She would run the risk of punishment again if she expected to send him on his way today. As soon as she arrived at the nursery, she'd figure out a way to sneak off to the trailer—risk be damned.

"Let's go before we get too soaked. That's fine for now."

Shyla groaned but jumped out of the vessel and onto the slipway without protest.

They scaled over the rocks to the grass-covered bank. "How about you teach the toddlers a clapping game when we get back? Try 'Four White Horses' or 'A Sailor Went Down to Sea.' Or you could play 'Teensy-weensy Rock Crab' with them."

"Ah, the untold bliss," the girl said as they untied the horses. She grabbed Joy by the mane and vaulted herself effortlessly up onto her back. Kat followed suit. "How ever will I come down to earth after all the gobs of fun and frolic? It's enough to put a person in a coma." She put her arm to her forehead and faked a faint as they trotted back along the trail.

"You'll survive. Come on, let's race each other to get ahead of the rain. I'll give you a head start."

"You're on!" She gave a short click with her tongue. Without delay, the Morgan stepped up her gait to a lope, overtaking Pippa across the field of clover. Both animals broke into spirited gallops. Their hooves thumped in rhythm under their riders.

The wind and rain freshened as they rode. Before long, Kat spotted two of their elders approaching from across the open field, their bodies leaning into the gale. It lashed at their clothes and dampened the hem of Ms. Eleanor's long skirt.

"We hoped to find you," Ms. Naomi called out.

The girls brought the horses to a standstill.

The junior elder squinted up at them through the teeming rain, her forehead creased. "Nola found a newborn dead in his cradle, and we thought you should hear it from us."

Kat clutched the reins tighter. "Was it Hugh? I mean...the new preemie?" Had she done something wrong with the infant last night?

"Yes, it was. This makes four newborns we've lost this year."

"Yikes!" Shyla said.

"Were the four of them premature?" Kat asked.

Ms. Eleanor still panted from exertion and her sodden grey hair frizzed like lichen around her ruddy cheeks. "One had a serious aortic valve defect, the autopsy found. She survived less than an hour. But the other three were preemies. Our track record on healthy births hasn't been the greatest these last few years."

"Another of your duties is care of the deceased and disposal of the remains," Ms. Naomi said.

"You're telling me to cremate him? Why must I do it?" An odd emptiness engulfed her as she thought of the tiny boy she'd held and fussed over. It wasn't because of any real attachment she felt for him, though she ruminated on the futility of his short life and what it meant for her people.

"No one cares for a chore such as this, dear." Ms. Naomi's words were gentle, almost imperceptible above the wind. "But it's customarily the obligation of the last nursery attendant who cared for him. This goes for apprentices and practitioners alike."

In silence, the girls rode their mounts back to the stable. When they reached their stalls, Shyla offered to brush down the wet horses and blanket them in her mentor's absence.

Kat resigned herself to the grim task. It was true. She had been the little boy's last attendee during her overnight shift. She had coaxed the final few ounces he would ever drink. The infants woke up at regular intervals around the clock for their feedings, but she realized Hugh had slept through without as much as a stir. Now she knew why.

Helping Marcus had to wait until she'd finished with the cremation, and by then the water might have calmed completely and the wharf could be teeming with fishing activity. As much as this upset her, she had no alternative.

She found the still infant in his cradle, wrapped in the same light blanket she'd swaddled him in the previous night. Ms. Naomi told her she'd accompany her for this cremation, as it was her first. Kat gratefully accepted.

The rain had dissipated to a soupy haze. She and the elder took the tiny body behind the peon and consort dormitories to Puffin Bight, a narrow inlet hidden beneath an outcropping of cliff topped with a snarl of tuckamore. Naomi brought along a yaffle of dry tinder, matches, and a basket with a baby blanket in it, saturated in a mixture of fish oil and linseed oil.

On the pebbled beach, Kat wrapped the body in the oil-soaked blanket, laid it on the pile of tinder, and surrounded it with beach rocks. She lit the fire. A bundle of wood the peons had collected waited beside her.

"I'll come back and clean up when the fire goes out," Naomi told her.

Together, they fed more wood to the fire and fanned the flames with the basket. Her elder reiterated their belief that the fire and smoke carried the child's soul back to nature. Kat had been taught at an early age about this custom of last rites for babies and children, but she'd never witnessed it, let alone taken part in it.

"To ash their earthly remains are committed," their primary teacher had taught them, "and to the sky their spirits shall rejoin Our Mother of Nature. A short life is still of value, and why we hasten its re-entry into the cosmos on a column of smoke and flame. In this way it gets another chance for birth into a new life."

Kat reserved judgment on this precept. She couldn't see how the fire did anything but reduce the wee child into a lifeless mound of ash.

When their funerary duties were completed, they left Puffin Bight. "You did well," Naomi said.

"Then why do I feel like crap?"

"Because he was under your charge."

"I should have checked on him more often, but I fell asleep on the futon around three o'clock. If only I had—"

"Don't take this on as something you did or didn't do. Sudden infant death happens for any number of reasons. And he was premature, remember."

"That's true." She exhaled a heavy breath as they skirted the men's quarters.

"Oh, I meant to tell you—we're holding our Meeting of the Harvest Moon earlier than usual. It's tomorrow night. Would you please notify the nursery staff for me?"

"Will do. But why so soon? It's not even October yet, and we had a meeting just a few days ago, and then we had the emergency Circle—"

"Something has come up that requires full attendance. There'll be a special announcement that pertains to you and the other girls your age."

"Oh really! Let me guess. You're not about to give me a heads up, are you?"

"You know I can't. I will say, though, you better brace yourself." She squeezed Kat's shoulder.

She would sneak off to the trailer as soon as the elder left. Mixed with her concern for Marcus, a new disquiet took root. How did tomorrow night's meeting relate to her? Hadn't they endured enough change? Whatever the nature of the announcement, she had a strong intuition she would be far from enthused about it.

Ms. Naomi threw her an anxious look. Now she knew it for a fact.

CHAPTER TEN

Half of the morning had slipped away before the steady drum of rain on the roof of the trailer stirred Marcus from sleep. He scolded himself, though he realized how much his body needed the extra rest. The long portage with his brother, the furious row across the strait, the hikes over rough and unfamiliar terrain, the avoidance of detection ever since his arrival. The constant travelling and perpetual hypervigilance had sapped his usual stamina.

He swore as he rolled out of the bunk. None of that meant anything to a sick three-year-old.

He thought about lighting the stove to boil the kettle but decided to wait until he had something to cook. He pulled on his clothes and boots, then snatched up his knapsack and an old dip net. He'd come across the dip net in the storage locker yesterday while scrounging around the trailer for items he could use or repurpose.

He set out for the woods that surrounded his rude quarters. The heavy downpour had diminished, replaced by a misty drizzle that clung to everything. The gale had lightened to a soft breeze but the mugginess was still extreme. The air smelled of moss, berry grounds, black earth, and wet leaves.

By the time he found the gurgling stream he'd used yesterday, he was slick with drizzle. It dripped from his long hair and his swollen ankle pulsated in pain. After he emptied his bladder in the bushes, knelt at the stream and splashed water over his head and face, he got busy fishing for his breakfast.

Marcus followed the meandering course through the forest for half a mile until he reached its end. With great care, he positioned the dip net at its mouth where the water emptied into a wide but shallow pond covered in brilliant green lily pads. He wedged the net tightly between rocks, took a deep breath, and waited. "Come to me, fishies," he whispered as he watched over the sinuous trail of water.

The penetrating mist had dwindled to a warm fog. He thought about Kat again. He needed an ally, an islander to help him accomplish his objective. And who better than the person who had already helped him? She might be the one who would lead him to the alleged medicine in her people's possession.

But why would she agree to give up any amount of drug crucial to their wellbeing? If the rumours were true, how much had the northerners given them? Could they afford to hand over any amount to a random stranger?

When he'd talked to the girl, he'd tossed around the idea of revealing his entire situation. He came close to telling her about the epidemic, and about Hudson and Ava. Instead, he'd thought better of it and edited them out of his narrative. No, he couldn't tell her his true motive for coming here, at least not until he'd ingratiated himself with her more and had won her sympathy and friendship. And he would not leave on any boat she found for him yet.

His wait was a short one. The dip net bulged with not one or two brook trout, but four. He killed the trout and threw them in his knapsack. His mouth watered in anticipation on his way back to the trailer.

Half an hour later, he had his meal ready. The speckled trout were so large he'd only cleaned and fried two, saving the rest for his hunger later. He twisted the knob on the tabletop stove to the off position and stuck a fork into the plump pinkness. The smell that steamed up from the skillet was pure heaven, and strong enough to overpower the musty stink of the antiquated trailer. He grabbed a chipped plate from the overhead shelf, plopped the fragrant fish onto it, and sat down to eat.

Halfway through his meal, he realized he'd forgotten to bring back water for tea. Wolfing down the rest, he snatched up the wooden bucket and hobbled back to the stream. When he got back to the trailer, he pulled the door open with a loud squawk from its rusty hinges and stepped inside.

He came face to face with the girl.

"Hello again, Kat-with-a-K," he said with a grin. His body eclipsed the meager light from the window as he towered over her.

She stood near the counter where the few dishes he'd used yesterday lay drying on a wood-slab cutting board. Visibly shaken by his sudden entry, she backed away at once. She collided into a pair of wet towels he'd hung from an improvised clothesline.

"Sorry, didn't mean to spook you." Marcus strode to the stove with the bucket and sloshed water into the kettle. He pointed at the uncooked trout curled in the tiny sink. "Great catch, huh? How about I fry you some?" Might be one way to get on her good side.

With scant inches between them inside the close confines of the trailer, he drew in the youthful woman's scent: wild, woodsy, unfamiliar. Her sweat smelled of fear. She retreated another step, her rear hip bouncing off the edge of the table. Her gaze veered to the tabletop and fell on the advanced game of solitaire he'd abandoned last night. Her discomfort was palpable, but Marcus could tell she tried hard not to show it.

Her chin jutted out, challenging him as she unsheathed her survival knife.

"Hey, put that away! I have no desire to hurt you—when will you get it through your head?" He tried another tack. "Maybe you could clean the fish, seeing your knife is ready and waiting. I'm sure it's sharper than that one." He gestured to the ancient filleting knife on the cutting board.

"There's no time," she said, her words clipped. "Take your trout with you. You have to leave the island at once!"

He stared down at her. "Why?"

"Did you know they saw you steal corn the other day? And they recovered the wreck of your skiff? They've launched an organized search for you this morning. We have no time to waste."

His heart lurched. "You've found a boat for me?"

"Done. Gather up your stuff and say good-bye to this place. It's better if we act quickly. Come on."

Without another word, Marcus hurried around his cramped quarters, jamming his few possessions back into his knapsack. He took one last sweep of the trailer. "Let's go."

Something had caught the woman's eye. She stepped to the end of the counter and picked up a furry paw, the foot Marcus had saved from the hare she'd given him yesterday. She tossed it to him.

"Here, you might want to hang onto this. I'm not superstitious, but you'll need all the help you can get."

He scoffed at the idea but poked it down in his boot anyway.

"I realize it's a lot to ask, expecting you to trust a stranger."

Funny thing, he did trust her. His instincts told him trusting her was his best option. Perhaps his only one. And yet to leave prematurely and empty-handed discouraged him greatly. To quit the island, and with it, any prayer of saving his son was unthinkable. A cold pall of failure enveloped him.

"Hang on a sec...."

"Yes?"

"If I surrendered peacefully to your people, would they accept me as a friend? Not as an enemy? Wouldn't they try to help me?"

"Not a chance."

"But why not? What are these superiors of yours all about? Why can't we meet and talk with them? I'm sure they'll listen to logic, won't they?"

"It's obvious our society is a far cry from the one you're familiar with. Men are not our equals here. The men who live here do have essential uses but governing our people isn't one of them. We no longer have faith in men to lead, after the mess you've made of our earth. Our elders are women. None of them are men."

"You mean—you've created a matriarchal government?" He gaped at her, incredulous. "Wait. Yes, I remember hearing about this a long time ago. Because of the loss of so many men to the wars, women had taken over isolated pockets of surviving administrations. But I hadn't realized it had happened here, or it still survived to this day."

"If you don't care to become another sad statistic around here, I suggest we get a move on. Or do you prefer capture and assimilation? Or worse, death?"

"Assimilation? What do you mean?"

"I'm not certain it would work in your case, because indoctrination of males usually starts at birth to ensure perfect compliance. If you'd been born here, I'd say you would have been adapted as a peon. They are our workhorses. The consorts are much fewer, and their refinement is more intensive and involved, but they are key to our survival too."

"Peons...as workhorses?" This new information prompted more questions. "And consorts? What do they do? Or need I ask?"

"I'm not telling you anything else because we have to go. Now!" She stormed from the trailer, leaving the door agape.

He had no choice but to cooperate. He believed her, and a dead or captured father was useless to Hudson. He had to find another way. The Labrador northerners and with any luck, their good will, were back on the agenda. If that too failed, Nova Scotia remained.

He'd never felt so weary in his life.

As before, the girl had him walk ahead of her through the woods. The fog had thickened once more into light rain. As they trudged along, their feet squished in the warm, wet earth. It was slow going because, bad ankle or not, walking over the uneven boggy ground cover of deep moss felt akin to walking on a giant, bloated sponge.

When they reached the muddy fringe of the forest and stepped out into the open air, something alerted the girl. She stopped walking. "Shh!"

Marcus strained to listen. Voices grew more audible, talking back and forth. In the distance, he spied two heads crest the soggy horizon and bob across the rocky barrens toward them.

They doubled back toward the forest. Too late. He was sure they had been spotted.

"Who's there?" called a female voice. "Speak!"

Damn it! Marcus receded into the dark shadows of the woods.

"Quick," Kat whispered, "I know a hiding place!"

He stumbled after her. They cut back through the shelter of trees and crept in a diagonal line inside the periphery of the forest.

Each step on his injured ankle shot a spasm of pain up through his leg. When he thought he couldn't go on any longer, they broke out of the woods onto rocky barrens scattered with russet patches of marshland. He remembered this area—it was where he'd lost track of the girl when he pursued her a few days ago.

With her finger to her lips, she beckoned for him to follow. He gritted his teeth and shadowed her across the open terrain until they made it to the embankment. They scrambled down over the grass together.

"Here." She waved him over to a cluster of dogberry trees. He trailed after her, skirting tall boulders and a dense stand of bushes. Hauling aside a heap of dead brush, she fell to her knees and pulled out a clump of woody debris wedged in a low rock wall. "It's an old root cellar. Don't worry, it's abandoned. Hardly anyone knows about it. You'll find potato sacks to lie on as soon as you go in. Stay there until I come back. Hurry!"

Marcus nodded, ducked low, and crawled into the hole. Darkness surrounded him when Kat plugged the hole again and replaced the pile of brush over the narrow entrance. He listened as her footsteps faded away.

He pawed around the cellar and breathed in its cool, earthy air. He found the potato sacks right away. He'd dodged detection again, but how long until his luck finally ran out? Dropping his knapsack, he buried his face in his hands. Forget luck.

How long until time ran out for Hudson?

* * *

She had told him not to leave the root cellar, but when morning came his thirst prevailed. He couldn't go back to the trailer for fear of being seen or captured, nor light a fire to cook his trout for the same reason. But he had to find water.

Before he left the cellar, he pulled his bright, red-checked handkerchief from his pants pocket and tied it to a high branch of a large bush near the entrance. It would make it easier to find when he doubled back.

He topped the hill to the marshy barrens. The temperature and humidity had soared early with a sunless haze. Dark clouds were beginning to form. They scudded in from the horizon, changing the overcast sky to a weighty dome of gun-metal grey. The scent on the southern breeze hinted of more rain. In the woods across the barrens, he drank his fill of water from the river and picked and ate enough apples and blackberries to quell the hunger pangs. Reluctant to go back to the gloom of the cellar, he thought a quick dip might help clear the cobwebs from his brain.

A short while later, he flopped on the riverbank, refreshed. The swim had invigorated his body and mind, and his muddied instincts were now revitalized and focused on the job at hand. He wriggled his wet legs into his cargos and gathered up his boots and shirt.

"Where the hell are you, Kat?" He hated waiting and wasting valuable time, but it would take extreme ingenuity to elude the islanders *and* fool the girl.

An ancient quote came to him: When something is important enough, you do it even if the odds are not in your favour. He'd resolved last night not to leave until he'd ferreted out what he came for. It wouldn't be easy prying information out of Kat, but he had to find a way to enlist her help. Even if it meant telling her the truth.

He figured her village was not far, what with her comings and goings since she'd found him. But even if he knew of its location and where they kept their medical provisions, he couldn't simply barge in and grab it. To say it would be a challenge getting his hands on a cure and escaping, unseen, had to be the understatement of the year.

He needed the girl. He'd go back to the cellar and wait for her as agreed. Most likely she'd show up before long, and he'd reveal to her why he couldn't leave yet. If she knew how desperately his son needed help, surely she'd understand.

He pulled on his boots. Keeping most of his bulk off his injured leg, he crawled up from the riverbank and back through the woods as the first spatters of rain trickled off the spruce branches.

A half-dozen yards in, a startled shout reverberated in his ears. His head snapped up. Directly in his path, two teenage boys stood among the trees.

"There he is!" shouted the tall boy, pointing at him. "Quick, Caleb! Rory! Over here!"

The teenager at his side stood spellbound, his mouth gaped open like a fish.

Ignoring the throb in his ankle, Marcus fled.

Journal Reading #2

Old World Anthology - Adult Memories Archives of Physical &
Sexual Abuse
Volume 3: Domestic Violence
Entry recorded: May 29, 1991

MY ACCOUNT OF SPOUSAL DOMESTIC VIOLENCE

My name is Diane, I am forty-two years old and I live in Conception Bay South, Newfoundland. This is some of what happened in my late twenties during my tumultuous marriage to my ex-husband, Philip.

I worked at home throughout my married life. I'd hoped to make a name for myself as a visual artist, though my earliest bid at an artistic career had been as a singer-songwriter back in my twenties. I'd played guitar in a pop-rock band and we toured Ontario, Atlantic Canada, and the Eastern United States. Six years later we disbanded, but I scored critical and financial success with one of the songs I had written. A wildly popular American sit-com TV show picked it up as their theme song, and when the show was sold into syndication, I lived comfortably off the song's royalties for years, and I still do.

The cushion of income allowed me to pursue my first love: painting. When Philip and I married, he worked as an insurance salesman. I soon found out he was a moody sort, a trait he'd kept hidden during our brief courtship. (A piece of advice I'd heard and neglected to follow: don't commit to anyone until you've weathered at least four seasons with him.) We bought a house, and my husband let me take the master bedroom as an art studio. I got underway, creating in earnest. Despite my husband's occasional fits of anger for whatever perceived action of mine he found fault with, most of the time life was OK. I was exhibiting and selling my work.

Then the day before our fifth wedding anniversary, Philip lost his job.

When he couldn't find work, he applied for and collected unemployment insurance. When it ran out, our relationship went from bad to worse. Philip's behaviour became routinely unpleasant and negative. Before long, I was no stranger to his rage and didn't know when he would explode into another of his vicious tirades, sometimes striking out with little or no provocation.

I became depressed from tiptoeing around his temper, the arguments, his fists, and worry over money. My royalty income and my art sales were stretched to the limit, and we had to remortgage our house. My doctor prescribed Lexapro to help me cope.

The worst side effect of the pills? They impinged on my artistic ability. My creative muse vanished, and with a new exhibit of my work scheduled in six months, I was tearing my hair out. I decided to wean myself off the meds, so I could paint with unrestrained passion. My own mood took a downward turn, but my impressive new collection of acrylic and watercolor artwork grew.

Then I made a grave error. I told Philip I'd given up the meds, and why. Unsurprisingly, he used it against me. He blamed our arguments on my fluctuating emotions to justify his hostility.

On this particular Saturday night, he was in his usual bad temper. We had argued about money or lack thereof, a constant concern. I tried to lighten the tension by suggesting we go out for a drink at the nearby pool hall. It would neither make us nor break us, and he could play a game of pool with the regulars while I chatted with their wives and girlfriends.

But he was too cantankerous to even entertain the suggestion. What's got into you, eager to go out all of a sudden? he barked. I get bored in the house, I told him. Day in and day out I'm in my studio, and I do the housework and the cooking. It would be nice to get out for a couple hours, at least. He ignored me and flicked on the television to watch a hockey game.

I gave up on my attempts to convince him. Instead, I told him I'd go down to the pool hall by myself for an hour to chat with friends.

Well, he let me have it. Why? he asked. You hope to find a date? Some stranger to fuck around with? But who in the hell would have you? he shouted. I'm the only one silly enough to get tangled up with the likes of you.

Not waiting to see if he'd resort to violence, I went to find my shoes. I'll get out of your way until you cool down, I told him. I was pulling my jacket from the back door closet when he cornered me. He held a full mug of black coffee. Blocking the doorway, he grabbed the jacket from me with one hand and threw the hot coffee at me with the other.

I screamed and ran to the sink. I fumbled for the cold-water tap and managed to splash water on my neck and chest to lessen the scalding pain. He grabbed my arm, spun me around and held me by the chin. This wasn't the first time he'd knocked me around, but the wild hatred in his eyes convinced me he could do serious damage this time. In the next second, he hit me with both of his open hands on either side of my head, clocking me on both ears. Picture him clapping his hands together, hard, with my head between them. This was how he usually beat me. He'd hit me in places that wouldn't leave a mark. He was clever enough not to give me black eyes or bruises I couldn't hide.

As soon as the ringing in my ears diminished, I knew something was wrong. The hearing in my right ear was muffled, as if sound echoed back to me from the end of a long tunnel. I fled upstairs to the ensuite bathroom and locked myself inside. I cried and cried, though thankful he didn't bother me anymore that night.

The next day, my ear was no better. I thought he might have broken my eardrum. Too afraid to go to the doctor, I prayed it would heal on its own. No such luck. A day or two later, I developed a fever and earache, so I drove to the local hospital's outpatient clinic. I lied to the doctor about what had happened. I made up a story—my nephew had accidentally hit me in the side of the head with his basketball. He seemed to buy it.

He gave me a prescription for an antibiotic and sent me on my way. But over the next few days, I realized the medicine wasn't working. I grew sicker by the hour, lying in bed with a high fever and earache. My husband suggested it might take time for the antibiotic to work. I waited another couple of days. I couldn't eat. Still in bed, I came to a point where it felt as if I were falling down a deep dark hole into nothingness. I practically welcomed it. Anything to escape the pain.

But I mustered strength from somewhere and asked Philip to drive me to the hospital. I couldn't remember ever feeling that sick and weak and abnormal in my whole life, almost as if I were outside my own body. When the receptionist called my name to see the doctor, he took one look at me, checked my vitals, and grabbed the telephone receiver on his desk.

Your blood pressure is extremely low, he said. I'm admitting you to the hospital at once, and we'll put you on IV fluids immediately.

The doctor informed me I had experienced a severe allergic reaction to the type of antibiotic I'd been prescribed, and I would have died if I hadn't sought medical help when I did. They kept me in for several days. My mother came to visit me in the hospital and gave me the prettiest brooch she owned and knew I admired. I remember it was a golden filigreed butterfly, because she said, wouldn't it be nice if we could flit away any time we wished, as if we were butterflies? I guess she meant to comfort me, to let me know she suspected what I was going through. I suppose a mother senses these things.

I left Philip the next winter, the morning after he'd gone on a malicious rampage and destroyed three of my newest paintings. I'd set him off when I said no to sex—a part of our marriage that had become more and more difficult for me to endure. When I saw my studio in shambles that night, I told him in no uncertain terms our marriage was over. I'd finally had enough of his insanity and had reached my breaking point. I ran downstairs and headed toward the phone.

His response was to run past me and rip the phone from the kitchen wall. Next, he took a bread knife out of the drawer and walked toward me. The terror that filled me in that moment I will never forget. I pictured my body lying in a pool of blood on the tiled floor. I had no idea what he intended to do with the knife until he reached out for me to take it. He told me to drive it in him, because if I left him, he didn't want to live anymore.

I begged him to put the knife away. I guess he finally did. The next thing I remember I was lying on the couch, exhausted, wishing I could sleep. Too defeated to push him away, I didn't fight him when he laid down next to me. He pleaded for me to forgive him. Again.

Why hadn't I left him before this? Because I'd believed him when he'd said things would be different. I gave our marriage chance after chance because I thought he would change, we would change, and learn how to get along. I thought his abuse would end. I felt sorry for him when he seemed genuinely remorseful. I guess I still loved him too. All of this rolled up together made me keep trying.

But I couldn't, not anymore. Along with my art, he'd destroyed my soul and the last shred of love and loyalty I'd ever felt towards him. When promise after promise has been broken, love and respect become harder to hold onto. Thankfully, we hadn't had any children to complicate divorce proceedings. I moved back in with my mom, and I tried to put my life back together.

But my emotional recovery was fraught with hardship and setbacks. I fluctuated from days filled with crying jags to weeks of isolation and apathy, to months of hypervigilance and years of deep anxiety. When I thought back on it years later, I realized it was post-traumatic stress. Many nights I cried in Mom's ancient pink bathtub, the same Pepto-Bismol meets dusty-rose tub I once made fun of because it made me think of floating in a giant womb. Now, I needed it. The house and the parent I'd longed to escape as a rebellious rock-and-roll teenager had become my refuge and my agent of healing.

I picked up my paintbrushes again and spent a lot of time enjoying peace and quiet. I was learning how to live without a difficult man and I discovered other things about myself in the process. I was grateful to my mother for the gift of time, to reflect and recover. It gave me a renewed faith in myself and the decisions I had made.

But even after all this time, I've never told anyone the truth of how my eardrum got busted. And every day I have to live with the insufferable knowledge that my ex-husband's abusive rage, however indirectly, came close to ending my life.

CHAPTER ELEVEN

Kat rose from her bed in a foul mood. She should have found a way to collect Marcus from the root cellar yesterday instead of leaving him there overnight to wonder what had happened to her. She'd tried to go, but after lunch Ms. Eleanor had shown up without warning to review and monitor infant and child-care procedures and had stayed for the entire afternoon. When her shift ended, she'd stopped by the wharf on her way to him, only to see a flock of villagers board their crafts and gear up for an evening of black bass fishing. They often took advantage of nights when the sea was tranquil, and after dark when the waters were cooler and the fish bolder and more active. They'd taken the punt out too, she noticed.

Before she could run and give Marcus the scoop, Shyla had sent word for her to come to her dorm room. She'd taken sick with intense menstrual cramps, and as usual the responsibility for her welfare fell to her mentor. Kat had brewed medicinal tea for her from valerian root extract and provided a hot water bottle for her belly, and on Shyla's insistence, brought *Black Beauty* to her from the school library for a reread. Under Ms. Eleanor's orders, she'd stayed with her until morning.

She *had* to put Marcus in the punt today. She rolled together the pile of quilts she'd slept on alongside her ward's bed.

"Good morning." A sleepy Shyla sat up and smiled at her through the milky light of dawn, barely enough to illuminate the bedroom.

"Feel any better?"

The girl stretched and yawned. "Number one now. Thanks for staying with me."

"You should stay in bed until you hear the breakfast bell," Kat said. "I'll check on the rabbit slips by myself."

"OK." Shyla lay back down and closed her eyes.

But her plan was thwarted again. When she tried to escape the dorm, Harper nabbed her in the hallway.

"Schedule change. Ms. Eleanor says all nursery apprentices have to report for duty at once to cover for Yvonne and Nola."

"Well, that blows! What the hell for?" When Harper's face dropped, she instantly regretted her snarky attitude. "I'm sorry. I've been a bit of a crab lately, eh?"

"No worries. The practitioners and senior domestics are to report to the community room in a half-hour. They're overdue for a self-defence refresher course, apparently, and we're already down a girl because Ruby's gone in water taxi to dispatch a baby to Exploits Bay."

"Terrific. Let's get our asses over there then."

When the practitioners came back from their course two hours later, Kat decided to skip her late breakfast and get Marcus instead. But Ms. Jaleena intercepted her in the doorway.

"Headed to the mess hall? When you're done there, could you and Miss Shyla please fill in for an hour at the aviary and hen house? Grace's assistant is helping with the orchard harvest."

Kat knew a polite request from Ms. Jaleena couldn't be ignored any more than a direct order from Ms. Bee. After a quick bite, she fetched Baby Red and put her in her carrier-basket. She tramped off with her ward to the walk-in aviary behind the village outbuildings. A light rain fell, offering cool relief from the blistering late-summer heat.

"The aviary beats nursery chores any day, don't you think?" Shyla asked her on the way. "Anything for a breather from that! So why do you seem so glum?"

Kat grunted. "I have a lot on my plate, kiddo! Can you quit bugging me for once?" Too late, she realized she'd been unnecessarily rude.

"Well, jeepers—pardon me for living. Who pissed in your porridge today?" The girl huffed and ran ahead without so much as a backward glance.

* * *

"Kat, or you, Shyla, hand me the net over there, would you please?"

While Red cooed on her back, Kat urged her ward to help. Shyla glared at her, but she retrieved the long-handled butterfly net from the corner of the aviary and passed it up to Grace. Surrounded by young trees, saplings and shrubs, the nineteen-year-old stood balanced on a limb of the largest tree. She grasped the net blindly, her attention fixed on a red crossbill perched on the branch above her head.

Grace extended her reach and brought the net down in one fluid motion to capture the finch. The small bird cheeped in protest. It flapped and fluttered its wings as it tried to escape the confines of the netted fabric. Gently, she held the bird in a loop of the net and climbed down from the tree using her free hand.

As she had done many times with other endangered species, she brought the crossbill to the long metal table that spanned the rear wall of the aviary and let it go inside one of its eight cages. She told Shyla she would give the bird time to relax before she introduced the yellow female that hopped around in the cage next to his.

The girl knelt down and peered in at the crossbills. "This is a super place to work. I adore horses, but I'm into birds too." She glanced over her shoulder and gave Kat a reproachful look. "Hey— don't you have a sister-ward, Grace? Any girl would be lucky to work here with *you*."

Kat snatched up the feed pail by the door, stung by the remark. Her ward's implied insult did not escape her.

"My hands are full, between caring for the preschoolers *and* working in the aviary."

"Oh my, yes, I forgot. That makes sense." Shyla grinned up at her.

Grace crouched down to admire the birds with her. "Now if it were this easy to capture the rogue, we'd be laughing." She gave a nervous giggle. "Thanks for lending me a hand, by the way. A couple more chores left, and I'll head back to the children with you guys."

Kat opened the screen door of the enormous wood-framed cage and walked out to the adjoining open-air yard and chicken run, where a flock of white leghorns preened and cackled. They scratched in the dark soil for worms, their hackle feathers flared to discourage their yard mates, the ducks, from moving too close. The stout rooster of the flock strutted toward her with a loud squawk, tilted a watchful eye, then headed back to renew his busy pecking near the hen house.

From a 55-gallon steel drum near the wire fence, she filled the pail with grain feed and spread it over the ground for the chickens and ducks. Bright-red comb and wattles aquiver, the rooster charged back for his share of the fresh offering. Kat re-entered the aviary with a basket for Shyla to gather the eggs laid in the chicken coop since the day's early collection. The teen snatched it from her hand and stomped outside without a word.

"I wouldn't worry about the stranger, Grace," she said, gauging her words. "I'm sure if our peons find him, they'll take him down in a jiffy."

"Yeah, you're probably right. Providing he's a lone maverick and not an outrider, scouting ahead for a whole mess of them." The soft-spoken girl gave a shudder while she cleaned out an empty cage with a soapy cloth.

Kat nodded, admitting such a scenario as a valid concern. However slim, the possibility had nagged at her since she first laid eyes on him.

When Shyla and the other wards left for afternoon classes, Kat settled down to rock an unusually fussy Red. She brooded about getting away to the cellar. "Why is she so cranky?" She fumed at the tearful little girl.

Yvonne observed the child from her rocker. "She's drooling a lot. I bet she's cutting her teeth. If you tried—"

A riotous commotion erupted outside the nursery. Yvonne and Falon sprang from their chairs and hurried to the door. Others ran to the nearest window and squealed in alarm at the scene.

"Oh, my stars!" Yvonne clapped her hands. "Come and see, girls. They've arrested the dirty rogue already!"

Kat's heart plummeted. She elbowed her way to the window to see Caleb and two more of their burliest peons restraining a shirtless Marcus with ropes. Why on earth hadn't he listened to her and stayed hidden?

"What will they do with him?" Falon shrilled, her cheeks drained of colour.

Kat realized this was the only outsider most of them had seen alive, a wholly different experience from finding a rotten corpse in the wreck of a long liner.

"Come on," their supervisor said. "Let's go see."

Falon and the other apprentices followed suit. Two of them hugged babies to their chests. Amid the uproar, Red had stopped her fussing and had somehow drifted off in Kat's arms. She plunked the child down in her crib and dashed outside.

She prayed they didn't hurt him.

The scene was a unique one for all of them: the trapping of a rogue. They'd heard mythical tales of such events time and time again, legendary variations shared at Sundown Circle where the stories ended on a positive note for the sistership. In some of the legends, the interloper became either successfully indoctrinated into a peon or refined as a consort. In others, he was deemed beyond redemption and put to death to prevent harm to anyone. With either outcome, it was a method of teaching the pitfalls of any confrontation with a rogue male.

But this was no rehashed, campfire folk tale, nor a journal reading from the archives. This was cold reality, and Kat couldn't picture a positive outcome for their prisoner. Hard to watch, yet she couldn't tear her eyes from the spectacle.

A throng of women and teenagers swiftly gathered. From the schoolhouse down the road, Ms. Naomi and her class of older wards came running. Directly behind them streamed the primary schoolgirls, racing ahead of their teacher, Ms. Lynn. The teachers must have gotten wind of the arrest and dismissed their students from class to witness the hoopla. Even Grace and the preschoolers had run from the playroom to the yard to see the man. They lined up, pressed against the fence, the little ones peeking through the pickets.

The three captors, dressed in rain-soaked, standard-grey peon issue, held fast to lengths of rope to detain their prisoner. The two ropes they had used to lasso the stranger were cinched around his bare torso. His wrists were tightly bound behind his back with the third. Drenched and filthy with rain and mud, he struggled against the restraints, his bitter protests filling the air.

Kat willed him to stop. Couldn't he see his struggle was pointless? The rough fibres of the rope cut into the tender flesh of his naked chest and waist the more he twisted and thrashed. Blood ran in thin, dark rivulets to his hips. It mixed with sweat and rain and seeped down through his wet pants.

It was all her fault. Suddenly lightheaded, her mouth turned dry as dust.

The well-muscled peons remained impassive as they held him. They appeared to derive no enjoyment from the seizure of this man. Nor did they show any trace of distaste, the incident implicit with their purpose in life: to uphold the laws of the island by whatever approach the elders deemed necessary.

The rain had dissipated, and in its place hung a ghostly mist. Wards ran to their mentors for comfort. Kat scanned the semicircle of small groups for Shyla. The girl clung to Falon, Harper, and their wards instead of her.

The youngest of the girls hid their faces behind their hands. A cluster of older women arrived, out of breath. They'd abandoned their chores at the fishing wharf, the greenhouses, and the textile mill to size up the captive for themselves.

The four elders observed from the sidelines, expressionless and silent. Kat found their show of decorum perverse. They didn't act any more bothered than if Marcus were a trapped bear, or a wild horse or bull in need of tethering for public safety.

None of them knew what she knew about the stranger. They had no need to mistreat him. The real danger was for him if he didn't submit. The situation could veer off into a horror show at any moment.

At last he looked in her direction, his eyes wide in recognition. She gave a near-imperceptible shake of her head, clinging to the odds no one else had noticed her or gauged his reaction. She hoped he read the message her face tried to convey: *Resistance is futile! They will beat you and they'll kill you if you don't give in. For your own survival, you must admit defeat and surrender!*

As if he understood, the fight left him and he stopped struggling. Ms. Bianca took note of this behavioral change and stepped forward to stand close to him and the peons. Though Kat tried, she couldn't make out her words. When the elder finished speaking, the peons led their captive away.

The questions erupted at once as the crowd flocked around the elders.

"What will they do with him?"

"What does he want? Did he mean to hurt us?"

"Does anyone know where he came from?"

"Will you naturalize him or execute him, Ms. Bee?"

The chief elder held up her hand. The voices gradually fell silent.

"The show is over, my sisters. The rogue will be presented for viewing to the schoolboys and then confined for the time being. Run along please, back to your duties and your classes."

Her reply didn't sit well with the girls. Their tense questions bombarded the elder, sharper and more defiant.

"They're curious to know your plans for him," Naomi said evenly, above the queries and complaints. "And frankly, so am I. An attempt at integration, I presume?"

"Definitely," Ms. Bee answered. "A perfect opportunity has presented itself to learn how effective our integration process works on an outsider, and a mature one at that. A game-changer, if we are successful." Before she left the gathering, she told them they'd discuss it further at their meeting that night.

Kat shuffled back to regular activities with the others. She held onto the fervent hope Marcus would obey the peons, not provoke them. With this arrest, the trajectory of her plans had been jettisoned. She couldn't envision how to help him now. Tonight's meeting of the Harvest Moon, Shyla's hostility toward her, and now this.

Remembering Naomi's worried face yesterday, she knew much more lay in store at the meeting besides a discussion of Marcus's fate. The weight of foreboding in the pit of her stomach stayed with her the rest of the day.

CHAPTER TWELVE

Marcus spent the early hours of his captivity berating himself for getting nabbed so easily.

He hadn't realized the root cellar and woodland river were so close to Kat's village. Within minutes, the men the two boys alerted had overtaken and lassoed him, seized his knapsack, and strong-armed him back to the hub of their community. Marcus realized at once these muscle bound men were the so-called peons the girl had told him about.

His abductors led him from the mob of curious females and paraded him along a dirt road that curved around the bowl of the cove. They passed a string of tidy cottages and a scattering of boxy, two-storey homes, all with solar panels mounted on their rooftops. They paused at another bungalow, also with solar panels and a fenced playground attached to its side. When the peon named Caleb whistled a signal, startled faces popped up in the windows that faced the road. Seconds later, two dozen boys of various sizes and ages flooded out of the front door.

"A living, breathing rogue!" one goggle-eyed lad cried out. A few of the older ones mocked and jeered at his state of undress, his patchy beard, and his long hair. Most gaped in awe and fascination.

From that display, the peons tugged him to the end of the road and through the gate of an immense outdoor enclosure with a high wooden fence. Caleb relinquished him to a larger, barrel-chested male.

"Thank you, Caleb. And please bring me the collar right away." The goliath of a man loomed over Marcus and detached the sliding loops of wet, bloodstained rope from his waist. He held fast to the rope that bound his wrists. "Now, let's get those wounds taken care of. Come with me."

Marcus scowled with open defiance at the brown-skinned hulk. But he had no choices here. His flimsy attempt at bravado vanished. Shoulders drooped, he limped along in silence.

The man led him halfway through the community to a two-storey structure set back from the road. A short flight of steps led up to its entrance. The whitewashed building reminded him of the deserted cottage hospital in the Quebec township he'd lived in years ago.

When they entered, the peon nudged him into an empty reception area and down a long, claustrophobic corridor. He rapped on an open door marked Examination Room 4. Inside the brightly lit room, he untied Marcus's wrists and handed him over to yet another man. This one was much slighter, younger, and dressed in skin-tight pants and an immaculate white, short-sleeved shirt. He leapt from a chair behind his square of a desk to greet him. Marcus guessed him to be about twenty.

He'd have no trouble handling this guy, given the opportunity. But how would he get by the Hercules?

"His shot, first and foremost. Check his leg too. He might have a broken ankle."

"Thank you, Bryce."

"I'm right outside if you need me." His captor left them alone and closed the door.

Marcus assumed the comment had not been directed at him, and this Bryce dude served as necessary muscle if he, the "rogue," caused any trouble.

The frail fellow gestured to a chair, his head lowered. "Have a seat. I'll clean you up and examine your ankle, but before that I must give you an injection."

Marcus watched closely as he opened one of the four metal counter cabinets behind him. When he swung back to his patient, he held a glass syringe and a sealed bottle of clear liquid.

"What's that for?"

"To prevent and fight disease and infection. Hold still, please." He prepped Marcus's upper arm with a damp swab that smelled of alcohol and plunged the needle in.

Was this the drug—the extract from the plant? A clear possibility! He memorized the room number for later.

The young attendant filled the steel basin at the counter with water from a hand pump that sprouted waist-high from the floor. He washed Marcus's bleeding wounds with a soft, beige sea sponge. He then applied cream-coloured gauze with deft fingers, winding it around his waist and wrists where the coarse ropes had broken and torn the skin.

"What do you people want from me?" Marcus winced at how his voice cracked at the end of his question, but he pushed on. "Am I a permanent prisoner here now?"

The man lowered his head and squinted at the stone tile floor. "Buddy, I'm not the one to ask. We are rarely privy to the elders' plans. Your fate is as much a mystery to us as it is to you." He bent to scrub his slender hands at the sink. "This is all so bizarre—you're a rare entity around here. Outsiders haven't set foot on our island in a long spell. At least not since the poor bastard who washed up in a wreck a few years back."

Marcus thought of the women who'd swarmed around him earlier, particularly the old woman in the long skirt. "Are you people Mennonites or in a religious cult or something?"

The attendant seemed amused. "Is that what you think?"

"What gives any of you the right to hold me?"

No answer. Instead, he handed him a pair of dark green trousers and a matching shirt. "Take off your pants and put these on." He leaned against the counter and crossed his lanky arms.

"And if I don't?"

"Would you prefer our friend Bryce dress you instead?"

Marcus swore, but bent and untied his laces, stiff with mud. He retrieved the rabbit's foot and concealed it under his thigh. *Fat lot of good it's done me up to now.* When he'd removed his boots and stepped out of his filthy cargos, he slipped on the new clothes. The trousers were thin and loose with a drawstring. He cinched the waistband and slid the lucky foot into his pocket before sitting down again.

The attendant brought the chair over from behind his desk, sat in front of Marcus and rolled up his pant leg.

"You a doctor?"

"I'm an intern and lab technician here. The name's Zealand. And yours?"

"Marcus."

Zealand examined and manipulated his ankle and questioned him about his injury. He said it didn't appear to be broken. He sponged the bruised area with a generous amount of solution he called a pokeweed root wash, telling Marcus it should help heal the sprain. He wrapped it in a compress from the arch of his foot to the top of his calf muscle and instructed his patient to stay off it as much as possible until it healed.

"Wear these until we take off the compress." He held out a pair of odd sandals with wide, woven straps. "We'll get your boots cleaned in the meantime. I don't think I wrapped it too tightly. Stand up and see how it feels."

Marcus complied and though it still hurt a bit, he said it felt fine.

"Good stuff. Are you hungry?" He looked directly at his patient at last.

For the first time since he landed on the island, Marcus's wolfish appetite had disappeared. "No. Could use a drink, though."

"As expected." He swung the door open and gave a signal. The gargantuan man stepped back into the room, ducking his head as he entered. In his hand, he held a short rawhide belt attached to a length of heavy link chain.

"He's ready," Zealand told him. "Please get him a drink too."

"Of course." Bryce threw Marcus a half-grimace. "You must wear this," he said in a deep voice as he looped the belt around his captive's neck and buckled it so tightly it pressed on his Adam's apple.

"This is not necessary." He tried to swallow against the collar. "I couldn't outrun you on this leg, and I'm not an animal, goddamn it!"

"Come." The brute gave a firm tug on the crude leash, jerking Marcus through the doorway and out through the hall. "The elders are eager to talk to you."

He drained the mug of water in three deep gulps. Thirst marginally quenched, he shoved the mug back to Bryce.

"Let's go." The big man tugged on the leash and led him briskly out of the clinic. They crossed the gravel road to a long and winding footpath.

Marcus hobbled along as best he could. The sky had cleared during his treatment and he squinted into the slant of late after-noon sun. The sinuous path took them westward and away from the cove, village houses, outbuildings, and sheds. He saw a small flock of sheep, lazily chewing their cud. They passed by a trio of horses in a paddock, munching on grass and clover. Their tails occasionally twitched to flick flies away. Two of them were majestic beauties with flowing manes and lustrous coats of brown and chestnut. The third horse with its dusky coat of spotted grey looked older, judging by the sway in its back and its bony withers.

They turned onto a narrow alley that led toward the shadowy backdrop of mountains. The alley brought them to an elegant, white garden gate with tall granite pillars for gateposts. When the peon lifted its latch and swung it open, a brass bell on the gatepost jangled.

The gate opened onto a meadow of sunflowers, buzzing with furry bumblebees. Clumps of cow vetch and yarrow sprouted in front of them, among a mass of dandelions that had dwindled to silvery puffs of seed. The peon jerked harder on Marcus's leash to pick up his pace.

They passed an acre of tranquil green pasture, dotted with grazing cattle and late-summer oxeye daisies. Marcus stared at the cows with longing as they passed. A dozen head of cattle there, at least. How they would have rejoiced back home to have such easy access to beef and milk, and to have the wherewithal to breed them! He couldn't stop staring until the peon yanked on his leash to hurry him up again.

He almost tripped and fell but caught himself. "Come on, man! What's going on here? What are your plans for me?"

"Don't fret, almost there. We mean you no further ill treatment —unless you make it necessary."

Directly ahead, on a hillside that sloped gently onto the pasture's edge, stood a yellow saltbox house with creamy-white trim, a sheltered front veranda and a manicured lawn. Two giant weeping willows grew on either side of the well-tended property. Rounded flowerbeds and shrubbery in a profusion of layered colours and textures wrapped the corners of the house and bordered the wide front steps.

Four women sat together on the wide veranda, two in a porch swing and two in wicker chairs. Bathed in the last golden light of the dying day before the sun dipped behind the mountains, their static arrangement put Marcus in mind of the faded portraits of his great-grandparents, mounted in oval frames on the walls of his childhood home. The women watched, quiet and expectant, as they approached.

The imposing senior woman with the white hair acknowledged the peon. "Thank you, Bryce," she said in a rich, resonant voice which belied her advanced age.

"You're welcome, ma'am."

She studied Marcus, her expression unruffled. "Young man, allow me to introduce ourselves. We are the elders of Wild Cove. This is Naomi, and here on my left are Jaleena and Eleanor. My name is Bianca. What is yours?"

He told her, then skimmed his eyes over the women: Naomi, who he guessed to be somewhere in her thirties, Jaleena, dark-skinned and mid-seventyish, and Eleanor, a short, rotund woman of about sixty with a florid complexion. She waved a pleated fan at her face and neck. If she were slimmer, she'd be a dead ringer for his departed grandmother. Three wore shorts and tank tops, whereas the woman named Bianca wore a high-necked blouse with sleeves to her wrists and a long plain skirt.

"I presume you've been treated decently since your capture?"

He pulled at the tight collar and glared at her. "I'm not a dog or wild animal, so no."

Bianca's calm demeanor evaporated. She rose from the porch swing and stepped close to the rail, the tail of her skirt swirling around her ankles. Her tanned countenance, toughened to leather by a life spent outside, drew into focus as she leaned against the rail. She met his glare, her intent scrutiny as cold and hard as flint.

"Oh, but you are a wild animal to us, Mr. Marcus the Rogue. We can't possibly trust you with any sort of freedom yet. If ever, in fact. We must protect the others from any threat you might pose."

"I abhor violence and I'm not a threat to anyone, so this extreme use of force by your goons is a waste of everyone's time!" His voice broke at the end of his outburst. He wished he had more water.

"You came to our island with a specific intention, correct? You don't expect us to believe you were on a sightseeing excursion, do you?"

He lowered his head. "No, not exactly, but—"

Bianca cut him off. "I didn't think so." She folded her spindly arms across her chest. "You see, life here goes much smoother for those who cooperate."

"You mean to keep me here? What if I need to go back to where I came from?"

The wizened old woman tut-tutted. "You can't go back, I'm afraid. You see, the need to keep you here is twofold. First of all, if we let you go, you might bring more outsiders back here with you, now that you've seen how special our island is. And what, pray tell, will happen then? We can't gamble on the hope that your kind won't muck it up for the rest of us. Second, your arrival has presented us with a tantalizing opportunity. How successful is our system of governance? Is it possible to assimilate you, to integrate you to our way of life? Or will it prove to be an exercise in futility? Either way, you'll never leave this island again, young man. The sooner you accept this immutable fact, the better your situation will be."

"So, there is no free will here for me or any of my gender. You hate men, keep them as slaves, and believe yourselves superior."

"Free will? Please. Not for you or for any outsider. And precious little is granted to any of our male population." She walked back to the swing and sat down. "Why should you feel enti-tled to such license after the havoc your gender has wreaked on the planet? Entire countries have met their end because of your care-less stewardship, your greed for money and power and your propensity for violence and aggression. The division and strife you've created, the effects of global warming—worldwide floods, famine, disease—caused by man's heedless practices, have brought us to the absolute brink of extinction. And let's not forget other life forms, Mr. Marcus." She regarded him with a wistful air. "Count-less species of animals and plants have met their end, vanished forever. Some were endangered right here on the island, and without our involvement would have died off too. We've rescued several species from extinction through our judicious hunting prac-tices, wildlife conservation, farming, and our burgeoning livestock ranch."

A murmur of agreement rippled from the other elders.

"All of this should illustrate to you why we hold you in contempt for what you have done. But we don't hate men. Rather, we love the earth!" The elder sighed. "Can't you fathom the need to heal the natural world and its remaining life forms, without men like you standing in the way?"

"Of course I can," Marcus said, "but the world was in trouble long before I was born. I had zero to do with it."

"And you'll have zero to do with it here as well." Bianca shook her head. "The irony is we need your seed for survival. Despite the advances of science there is still no way to reproduce without you, we admit. You may already know attempts at reproductive cloning in the Old World met with limited success. Consequently, we employ the basics of egg and sperm the old-fashioned way, at least for now."

"So the plan is to use me for procreation?"

"Your intended use will be revealed when necessary. Let's stick to the present. The time has come for you to tell us your story." Bianca motioned to the Naomi woman. "Please fetch a drink from the house for our new recruit, and a chair so he can get off his wounded leg. This could take a spell."

The woman reappeared with a Windsor chair and a beverage. She passed them down to Bryce. Marcus took a long swig from the tin flask and seated himself, still tethered to the peon. The position of his chair on the lawn below the elders made him feel small and inferior. He knew this intimidation tactic was no accident. Under their close inspection, he noticed his legs twitch and tremble as if they had a will of their own.

The senior recrossed her arms. "Please tell us what life has been like for you. Has it been as harsh as we imagine? Where exactly are you from?"

He tipped the flask to his lips and drained the rest of the pleasant, fruity drink, making her wait. He could share plenty with the old woman to satisfy her, without revealing his covert plan. He told her about the family farm in Quebec he'd left behind.

"The summer I turned ten, we were forced to relocate to a township near the Labrador border."

"Forced? How?"

A spiderweb stretched from the bottom rail of the veranda to the trimmed shrubbery underneath. Marcus fixed his gaze on a brown garden spider as it crept across the delicate web. "In an instant, our entire world was torn apart. My parents and grandparents were already struggling to support us, but we were making it, living on whatever we could grow or hunt. But then..." His voice faltered. His chest ached with emptiness, the way it always did when he thought of the murders, and of the chasm of grief that had plagued him for years. Retelling the horrors of that nightmarish chapter of his childhood felt almost as raw as reliving it, but he didn't want his interrogators to suspect he had anything to hide.

Naomi spoke up. "What happened?"

The spider reached a captured housefly, tightly wound in silk near the center of the web. Marcus was seated close enough to watch the creature's fangs dip into its victim, to liquefy its insides with venom. "We'd thought the worst was over. That the influx of immigrants, the wars, the chaos, and the mob rule we'd heard about had finally come to an end. The wildfires of Western and Central Canada and the U.S. which sent people fleeing to the north had burned out ages ago. Most of this had happened long before my lifetime. So we weren't prepared for the new band of migrants that tore through our region that summer."

"Let me guess," Bianca put in. "They weren't a friendly sort, were they?"

He choked back a bitter laugh. "Are you kidding? For starters, they took over my uncle's farm south of us, but he and my aunt managed to escape harm." He paused to swallow down a renewed twist of rage that threatened to strangle his words. "Two nights later, ten or twelve of the low-lifes invaded our farm. Two of them came at my grandfather with axes and beheaded him. And it didn't end there—they hacked my father to death, while another son of a bitch stabbed my mother in the chest while I watched. That brutal enough for you?"

Naomi's hand flew to cover her mouth. "Mother Almighty," she whispered.

"When they took possession of our property, my aunt and uncle took my grandmother and me and fled east to escape death ourselves. My grandma passed away days later—from a broken heart, no doubt." He purposely excluded his brother from his narrative. To do so would raise more questions and concerns. "We eventually found a place to resettle in Labrador near Minipi Lake."

Bianca left the swing again and paced the veranda as he spoke. When he finished, she stopped and faced him, her sparse brows knitted together. "That is quite the horrendous tale. We had heard bits and pieces of this post-war terrorism and anarchy you speak of," she admitted. "But we had no way of knowing how many had survived the continental wars. We only knew the majority of our citizens who joined the fight didn't come home. We took in many of the displaced flood victims from the Maritimes, but most invaders to our shores came right before war broke out. And since it ended, rarely any. Wasn't life better for you in Labrador?"

"For a long while it was. The climate was cooler there than in Quebec. A scattered herd of caribou and a few moose still roamed, and we had fish to catch, such as char and northern pike."

"Have there been other attacks from vagrants since you moved east?" asked the grandmotherly Eleanor woman.

"Not as bad. We see a few now and then, but the dust has settled for the most part."

"Well, that's good," Bianca said.

"No, not good. There's simply nothing left to fight over. The inland climate is growing hotter by the day. It's harder to find anything to forage or hunt, and the lake fish have nearly disappeared." The spider had polished off its meal. On long, striped legs, it nimbly danced away from the empty black husk. Marcus glowered up at his abductors. "But at least I was my own man and not forced to live like a trapped animal."

His admonishment triggered the end of the old woman's patience. She stepped toward him. "The burning question is this, Mr. Marcus: what did you hope to gain by coming to our island?"

Alone in his rathole of a room, he tried in vain to decompress and clear his mind, but the pain in his bandaged leg had intensified. All the muscles below his knee were stiff and tender to the touch. The spruce boughs he'd used on his previous nights on the island rivaled the comfort of the thin mattress that lay between him and the floor. Adding to his discomfort, the makeshift bed felt damp, smelled of dust and mould, and straw poked through the fabric into his back.

The peons had barred him in here at sunset with a tray of food, a jug of water, and a sharp admonishment not to knock or cry out because both would go unanswered. On the opposite end of his rude accommodations stood a chair with a chipped chamber pot placed upon it. He highly doubted if Bryce and the rest of the peons lived in such squalor.

He ruminated over the day, sifting through the emotion-charged events that brought him here. The adrenaline rush when the pair of teenagers spotted him on the forest trail. His racing heart and his pointless struggle to break free when the peons surrounded and arrested him. Kat witnessing it as they dragged him, a curiosity and an aberration, into the midst of the village children and the rank and file. And the oppressive anxiety of facing their leaders, his mysterious fate in their hands.

The girl had given the impression she hadn't disclosed his arrival to a soul, nor their brief acquaintance. To protect her own ass at this point, he guessed. If her leaders discovered how she'd tried to hide him and planned to help him escape back to the mainland, he imagined she would suffer harsh discipline. It hadn't seemed a big deal to her, the dangers she might have placed her people in if his motives proved suspect. Hadn't they taught her to watch out for trespassers and potential marauders? Or had his earlier assessment of her been confirmed correct? Did she possess a stubborn independence and an iron will of her own?

He still had no appetite for the meal of fried fish, greens, and cherry pie on the tray. Feeling dehydrated, he drank more water from the jug. His head ached from the barrage of probing questions. Bianca and the other female elders had interrogated him for two hours, wresting from him every detail they could about his life and his experiences as he sat fettered before them.

Marcus had shared with them everything he could think of, without revealing the existence of his ailing son, his quest for drugs, or his brother's impending arrival if he failed to come back. When the youngest elder named Naomi showed sympathy for his plight, he almost threw himself at their mercy. He almost told them about his child. But why would they give up any medicine for him or for the people he lived with? Kat had warned him, as an outsider, he shouldn't expect any help from her leaders. Instead, he told them of his search for a better place to settle, his implied purpose for coming here.

Once satisfied with his answers, Bianca had repeated her words of caution.

"Remember this," she'd reiterated before Bryce took him away. "Life will go much better if you yield to our bidding. I do appreciate you've had a hellish childhood and a hard go of it ever since. But because of your past, I predict you'll eventually come to view your capture as a lifeline, even a blessing. We take no pleasure in treating you harshly but mark my words: we will not tolerate any resistance from you. And if you pose even the slightest hint of a threat to our citizens, you won't live long enough to regret it."

He had no doubt of her sincerity, solidifying his distrust of her administration. In the black, deathlike silence of his stuffy room, he struggled to contain his mounting despair. He grasped at his uncertain friendship with Kat. In his mind, she remained his sole possible ally.

Overnight, his mission had become a whole lot tougher than he'd ever imagined.

CHAPTER THIRTEEN

"Welcome, sisters. Latecomers, please take your seats. This meeting of the Harvest Moon is called to order."

The rumble of conversation subsided and a hush fell over the packed assembly. From her seat in the third last row next to Harper and Falon, Kat looked to the stage podium where Ms. Bianca stood tall and proud.

For a woman who would mark her eighty-eighth birthday in a few months, she was a stunner. She wore her hair loose this evening, long silver waves swirling in elegance over thin but perfectly postured shoulders. In spite of her years, her eyes still flashed with the vitality of youth. Even the deep lines carved in her face didn't detract from her regal bearing; if anything, Kat thought they gave the chief elder a more dynamic presence. For the occasion, she had donned her finest traditional costume, a floor-length sheath dress of a metallic hue made from the softest and finest of harbour sealskin, embellished with intricately adorned patterns of white shell beading on the neckline, wrists, and hem. Her preferred attire for special events, the dress accentuated her silver tresses and handsome figure. New leather-braided sandals completed her outfit.

Behind the matriarch stood her fellow elders. They wore their usual meeting apparel of long hemp skirts and tailored blouses.

Ms. Bee beamed over the sea of female faces. "Sisters, we have cause for much celebration this fall. We have had our most successful growing season to date, thanks to the skillful supervision and planning by our food production manager, Ms. Jaleena, and I'm proud to see how hard our citizens are working to harvest the bounty. Once we have picked, reaped, gleaned, gathered and stored the yield from our fields, orchards, and greenhouses, the elders of our island will set a date for this year's Harvest Festival at Grand Lake. I'm sure you look forward to it as keenly as we do.

"We have two items on our agenda tonight," she continued. "They are of equal importance, but let's commence with what I'm confident is on everyone's mind since the excitement of this afternoon." She paused for effect. "What are our next steps, now that we've apprehended a rogue?"

"Holy shit!" In her seat behind Kat's, Ruby clapped a hand over her mouth. Some tittered at her outburst, while a smattering of cheers gave way to vigorous applause. Those who'd been engaged elsewhere this afternoon, Kat realized, had only now learned of the arrest.

Ms. Bee took a sip of water from a cup on the podium. "To know the right direction to take, let's review how far we have come. Yes, we are simply a small island country in a vast and distressed world, but we've proven that a lifestyle under our network of protective matriarchal leadership is the way to peace. The successful management of our peons and consorts and their roles in our society of villages speak for themselves. Since the inception of the Assimilation and Refinement Solution, we haven't had one relapse. Not one.

"And now with a live rogue in our custody, we have a golden opportunity to test the Solution on the adult male. Will we succeed? I cannot say. But if we do, any male newcomers to our island will also undergo a naturalization process. And the future as we forge ahead will be ours and ours alone, only stronger."

A more enthusiastic round of applause swelled from her attentive audience. When the clapping tapered off, the senior elder grew sombre.

"We will now proceed to our second item of significant import."

Kat sat up straight and held her breath.

"As many of you have already learned or may suspect, in the recent handful of years we've incurred a disturbing increase in the number of miscarriages, stillbirths, and premature infants who perish shortly after delivery. We have contacted the other villages of the island and they report similar issues. Why this is happening, we have yet to ascertain. It might be related to the sperm quality from our consorts. Our system of integrating these young men as compliant and suitable breeders, particularly with regard to the pharmacological component, will be reviewed for possible modifications.

"Whatever the cause, our population growth has stagnated. We have fewer offspring to take over when we pass on and, needless to say, this is counter to our ambition. To tackle the stagnation of births and the uptick of newborn deaths while we probe for answers, we will launch a major amendment. As you know, our breeding program, under the direction of our community health elder, Ms. Eleanor, opens for women at age twenty. This has been the suitable age since its inception and it has served all our villages well. We have yet to determine why, but this age is no longer deemed appropriate. Therefore we are lowering the age of enrollment into the program to eighteen, effective immediately. In addition, participation will become one step short of mandatory."

A heated clamour of protests burst from the assemblage.

Kat felt blood rush to her face. One step short of mandatory—what did Ms. Bee mean? Kat was eighteen. And they expected her to make a baby *now*? What in the actual prancing, dancing, flying fuck?

The chief elder paused until the roar of objections decreased. "As you older girls know, reproduction has been voluntary but with many enticements to make it more attractive. These incentives will remain. Full discretion in choosing your sexual partner from our pool of consorts, and to change partners if no conception takes place within six months. Prime and pampered residence at the Origin Suites, our elegant, private chalets for impregnation, gestation and delivery, for as long as it takes or up to two years. Distinct rights, privileges and freedoms throughout pregnancy. Except for first-year breast milk production, the exemption from nursery duties and child care afterwards, if desired. Two healthy births, as dictated by the previous program. And as ever with It Takes a Village, anonymity from the children birthed and immunity from the myriad of challenges which go along with it.

"The cherry on the cake? Your reward: the liberty to choose a vocation as you wish and for as long as you wish from our index of occupations after two deliveries. And as always, if your vocation is to birth more than two offspring, that choice will also be sanctioned."

Kat gasped in disbelief. Two births? Surely, this new order didn't include her. No way. She was going to Western Path! Her blood pounded in her ears.

Ms. Bee's voice crackled on, echoing throughout the room. "Along with this restructuring and hand in hand with the benefits, we must implement a new series of deterrents to make your induction into the program more attractive. If you decline enrolment, your exclusion from participation in free days and celebration day activities will come into effect. You will receive no special privileges or indulgences of any kind. And most importantly, the vocations you have chosen for yourselves will be revoked. For the rest of your life, your work detail will be chosen as we see fit."

Kat sat rooted to her chair. The elders couldn't impose pregnancy on them at such a tender age, but the alternative was so offensive, it bordered on enforcement. Having her ranch plans revoked if she didn't comply, her cherished dreams smashed if she didn't reproduce? She seethed with rage. It was blackmail.

"Please tell me I'm hallucinating!" Harper leaned toward her, fists white-knuckled to her chest. Next to Harper with a face as pale as milk, Falon appeared on the verge of a panic attack. Around the crowded room, other faces mirrored Kat's anger and confusion. Several girls raised their hands. Kat was about to raise hers, but Ms. Bee wasn't finished.

"I realize this is stressful news for many of you, and you have questions. But because of the added business and the preparations for our festival, we will dispense with journal reading and the question and answer segment. We will meet with each of you and address your specific concerns in the days to come."

Renewed cries erupted. Obscenities blasted from a few daring souls in the back of the room. Kat felt like joining them.

Ms. Naomi stepped forward to stand abreast of the chief elder. In unison, the two women held their hands up and waited for silence. When the complaints dwindled to a murmur, Ms. Bee stepped back and Ms. Naomi walked to the podium.

"Over the next few days," she announced, "all girls who have reached our new coming of age will take instruction from Ms. Eleanor and submit to preparations. As for the rogue and his status, expect a progress report at the next Sundown Circle. This concludes our meeting of the Harvest Moon. In honour of the occasion, a special banquet of refreshments will be served in the community room. Thank you, dear sisters!"

The elders struck up the traditional chant:

"Mother of Nature, come what may
we are strong and here to stay
each of us is but a spark
together we outshine the dark..."

Where the entire assembly ordinarily joined in the chant, most of the voices remained silent. The response fell flat and lacklustre, even among the elders. After two rounds, the senior women filed in silence from the stage and out of the assembly hall.

Falon grabbed her wrist. "This can't be happening!" she blurted in her ear. "We're girls, not women. Dear Mother Almighty!"

Harper stood up slowly, her face a tight mask of shock.

Kat leaned toward her. "You alright?"

Her friend came out of her daze. "I thought we had two more years. Now I don't know if I'll ever be ready. Are you scared?"

"Scared isn't the word I'd use," she said as they streamed out of the hall. "Royally, savagely pissed is more accurate."

Yvonne slithered up from behind. "Dissention in the ranks?"

Kat threw her a dirty look. "This has nothing to do with you."

"But aren't you curious to find out what sex is all about? This way, you get to do it a whole two years earlier, and with the elders' blessing!"

Falon blanched.

"Preauthorized sex with a cute consort is hardly the end of the world, little bitches." Yvonne said. She threw in the annoying snicker that always got under Kat's skin.

"I don't know," Falon said. "Intimate relations with one of those groomed bucks? My worst nightmare come true, is what it is."

"And the way they've engineered this new directive makes it damn near impossible not to submit," Kat said. "Who's up for having their work choices taken away forever? It's unethical and backward." She had to talk to the elders. Perhaps she was getting worked up over nothing. Either way, she would not give in without a fight.

"Plus," Falon added, "we would lose our free days and celebration days."

"So, you comply," Yvonne said. "Then you'll have the rest of your life to do whatever your heart desires. Sounds heavenly to me."

Harper stabbed a finger at Yvonne. "Kat's right, this doesn't affect you. You've already had your attempts at pregnancy, and let's not forget your plum practitioner post."

Yvonne stuck her chin out. "I wish for nothing better than to devote my life to our wee ones. That, and sex with no strings, expectations or consequences." She drew away and caught up with Ruby.

In the softly lit community room, a delectable blend of sweet and savoury aromas greeted them. Buffet tables covered in creamy-white tablecloths skirted the perimeter of the room, each laden with various delicacies often synonymous with their monthly meetings.

This time, however, the elders had provided a greater than usual array of treats to placate them, and the change of venue from the usual mess hall added a celebratory air. Shrimp tacos, steamed mussels, sliced meats, cheese, and sushi; crab canapes and spinach-potato bites; crudités and fruit kabobs; frosted corn-flour cupcakes and jam pastries; and punch bowls filled with jewel-coloured potables—every treat that appealed to their appetites beckoned. Dining tables filled the middle of the room, draped in red cloth, glowing with candlelight, and a new addition: each table, save for the sister-wards' table, had been furnished with bottles of the elders' coveted berry wines. Though a few teens had snuck wine in the past, Kat included, to have it served to them was a first.

She seized the opportunity to speak to Ms. Naomi alone at the elders' table while the others filled their plates.

"Please tell me this change doesn't involve me."

Naomi's eyes were downcast as she poured herself a glass of wine. "I'm sorry, dear. I can appreciate how it feels unfair to you, but no one is exempt from these amendments. And I assure you, your ranch career awaits you, if and only if you fulfill your obligations."

Her throat tightened. "But I was hand-picked for that job!"

"It isn't being taken from you, merely postponed for perhaps as briefly as two or three years. You're young. You'll still have your whole life ahead of you."

"Might as well be a hundred years," Kat said through clenched teeth. "Promises don't mean diddly-squat around here!" Sweet fuck-all, in other words. Without waiting for a reply, she pivoted on her heel and stomped back to the others.

Her eyes swept over the cornucopia of food and drink at their disposal. But her appetite had vanished. She felt sick. Correction: she had an acute desire to grab a bottle of wine and down it on the spot. Falon and Harper weren't eating either. They sat at a table together and stared into their laps.

The room buzzed with conversation. They had been given gobs to discuss, but she was in no mood for talk. She pulled out the chair next to Falon and Harper, seized a bottle of cranberry wine, and poured a glass. She offered the bottle to Falon. "Here. You could use this too."

"I don't know. Wine will make me queasier, if that's possible."

Harper snatched the bottle and poured her own goblet full. "Remember the awful journal reading a few months back? The one Grace read?"

"The Rape? You bet I do." It had been the creepiest story from this past year, and Kat wasn't easily frightened. The cautionary tale had stayed with her longer than any of the others. What had chilled her the most? The rapist had been known to his victim and had escaped punishment. He'd also threatened the woman with a repeat occurrence. The revelation of every horrid detail, graphic and unvarnished, had overwhelmed the teens at that meeting. Falon and Harper had stayed up all night, wide-awake and restless. Others like Kat had suffered alarmingly vivid dreams.

Harper hunched over her wine. "Well, that's how I see it, as if they're handing me over to be raped."

Kat gave her hand a quick squeeze. "I hear you, but as nasty as it sounds, I'm sure it won't be violent. We women run this show, don't forget." She wanted to believe her words, but in truth, the lack of choice sickened her more than the thought of sex with consorts. The "Queen Bee" and the other elders were the only ones truly in charge.

Harper sipped her wine and said nothing.

"But what if I don't get pregnant right away?" Falon whined. "What if I must do it over and over for months on end?" Her voice broke as tears brimmed on her eyelids. "Or for years, the way Yvonne did? I don't know if I can take it!"

Ruby joined them, nibbling on a bacon-wrapped scallop. Yvonne reappeared behind her with a goblet of wine and a plate piled high with sushi and mussels.

"Aw, what's the matter?" She pouted at Falon, plopped herself beside Ruby, and laid her banquet in front of her. "Still belly-aching over the new directive? A necessary evil, girls. Think of it as a minor sacrifice for the best interest of the island. And for your sacrifice, you shall be rewarded."

"Are you *trying* to make us puke?"

Yvonne's eyes darted to Kat. "As expected, you've a problem with it too. No great surprise there."

"You know damn well I do. And your holier-than-thou attitude stinks. You make yourself out as virtuous when it's an open secret how you can't wait to spread your legs. And not for procreation either."

Yvonne snorted and gave an exaggerated shrug. "But attitude

makes all the difference, tough girl. That's pretty much what it boils down to." She lifted a fat wedge of sushi to her lips and bit into it as she glanced at a mournful Falon. "Listen, I know exactly what it's like with the consorts, bless their hearts. I could write a book. They're under oath to the elders to present the sexual act as a pleasant and generous experience, if you catch my drift. If they break the oath, they'll face serious consequences."

"Don't knock it 'til you rock it," Ruby put in as she bit the head off a spear of broccoli smeared in yogurt dip.

"Ruby's right," Yvonne said. "Come on, gals. Have we ever enjoyed such a scrumptious banquet? And with wine!" She raised her glass. "Cheers."

Kat tossed back her own wine, jumped from her chair, and stormed out.

Later, when she and the others had gone to bed, she lay staring at the ceiling. Shyla had rebuffed her again, coldly ignoring her when she'd gone to her room to say goodnight.

Her headache pulsed and her guts churned. She wished the girl was her only worry. She couldn't remember Ms. Naomi or any of the elders letting her down like this—at least not since they sent Wren to Labrador. In the darkness, she smoothed her hands over her flat belly and sighed. Pregnancy had not been something she'd ever thought about much, but now she had no choice.

In the bunk next to hers, Falon tussled with her bedclothes and whimpered into her pillow. Kat knew tonight's bombshell weighed heavily on her. The girl had always given her the impression of a child who hadn't quite grown up. For a buttercup such as her, the expectation to mate against her will must have disturbed her deeply. Tortured by her own timidity, Falon was often reduced to a quivering bag of nerves whenever she crossed paths with the peons and consorts. Heck, she was even tight-lipped and anxious around Ms. Bee.

Having her ranch position put on hold galled Kat the most. Her life's goal had been snatched from her and held out of reach. How could she fix this without sacrificing herself to produce two island offspring?

She had to find a way.

CHAPTER FOURTEEN

With the rumble of dissent and speculation since the pivotal announcement, Kat didn't have much time to stress over Marcus, or Shyla's continued avoidance of her whenever possible. Two days later, she still hadn't absorbed the entire scope of the updated directive, let alone resigned herself to it. How could they rob her of the life's work she'd set her heart on six years ago? Whatever happened to self-determination and achieving one's full potential?

She'd taken a stand against the injustice, locking horns next with the breeding coordinator, Ms. Eleanor. Shouldn't they allow her the wisest use of her talents for the collective good? They should not simply allow it but applaud it. Wasn't this what they'd been taught? But Ms. Eleanor flatly dismissed her objections and reiterated the necessity for the adjustments. Sweeping reform was essential if they expected their population to survive, let alone flourish.

Getting nowhere with the elders, she tried to see the new directive from their viewpoint and frame it in the most philosophical way possible. But the lack of say in the matter repulsed her. Ambitions crushed, she forced it from her mind until she'd have no choice but to confront it head on.

Her thoughts flitted back to Marcus and his future. She knew the peons held him prisoner, but where exactly? And how were they treating him? As much as she still questioned his intentions, she hated to think of him roughed up for their own amusement.

The image of his haggard face from two days ago tormented her. Once more, it prompted the childhood memory of the rogue who had tried to run off with her. And something else. Was that rogue the same one she had seen the peons hang from a tree? Though the savage memory lingered, she couldn't say for sure. The rest of the incident stayed buried, repressed in the murky recesses of her subconscious.

The rain, drizzle and fog had lifted overnight, giving way to gentle winds and a cloudless sky. Instead of checking snares, she decided to take the *Serendipity* out early for the forty-five-minute row to deeper water, to haul her gillnets for redfish. If there was enough breeze when they finished, she would put up the sail on the way back.

Shyla was all for it, instantly bubbly when Kat entered her bedroom at dawn and shook her awake. She breathed easier at the change, grateful her ward hadn't held her grudge too long and had welcomed her back into her good graces. Shyla sang their campfire song, "Already Strong" when she had a go with the oars. As they worked side by side hauling nets, she chatted about her school friends and their fall semester course load. She shared, too, how they couldn't wait for the Harvest Festival with its contests, races, and the enormous celebratory feast at its finale. Maple candy apples and baked pumpkin fries served with sour cream were her absolute favourites, she told Kat.

The light wind freshened as they pulled and emptied the last net. The yield had been ample enough in each of the nets to drop them back down instead of moving them elsewhere. Their arms and shoulders ached and sweat drenched their backs from the strain of hauling in the trapped redfish, along with a decent bycatch of halibut. Kat welcomed the draft. With the favourable wind direction, they wouldn't have to row their way ashore.

"I'm sorry you can't start your apprenticeship as expected," Shyla said. She leaned into the curve of the gunwale while her sister-guide unfurled the sail. "You must be awfully disappointed. I'd be rotted if I were you."

Kat scanned the ocean horizon. "You don't know the half of it."

"I can't picture it. You, of all people, making babies."

Kat didn't answer. Had Shyla's pity for her dissolved her former resentment?

The sun gleamed on the billowing sailcloth as Kat maneuvered the punt back to port. As they entered the harbour, a pair of saddleback gulls and a flock of arctic terns wheeled and swooped overhead. The terns squealed like excited children, their scalloped wings luminous white upon the brilliant blue sky.

She took in the sail as they glided inland and leisurely rowed the short distance to the wharf. As soon as they moored the boat, the wharf workers approached with baskets to collect the fish. Comprised equally of women and peons, they took possession of the bountiful catch to be gutted and cleaned on the fishing stage platform. The workers started splitting and salting the redfish to dry upon flakes later. The halibut would be prepared for the table at once, to reappear as golden-fried steaks on little beds of lettuce for their supper that evening. Chef Vicky would see to that.

Kat told Shyla to grab breakfast for them both, and she'd meet her at the nursery.

When the girl left, she acted on impulse. Under the pretext of checking slips if questioned later, she stole through Wild Cove to the peon quarters, hoping to catch a glimpse of Marcus. It was ludicrous but because she'd failed to hide him and bungled his escape, she held herself oddly accountable for his welfare.

Since she'd overheard the latest gossip last night, she felt doubly sorry for the man. Yvonne's current peon paramour told her what Bryce had disclosed: Marcus had confessed to the elders that he'd fled from his homeland years ago when most of his family had been murdered. It sounded as if he'd been through the throes of hell and back again.

The consort and peon quarters lay on the southern border of the village near Poplar Forest, in full view of the lofty elders' residence. Kat hoped none of them were watching her.

The consorts' rectangular dorm, the annexed boys' wing, and the male schoolhouse were sheltered from wind by the mountain range to the west and a dense growth of balsam poplars and trembling aspen to the south. A robust, emerald-green arborvitae hedge offered privacy from the peon quarters. The peon compound's four one-storey structures, closer to the cove and exposed to the elements, were built of cinder block, unpainted and austere. From the main building in the forefront jutted the connected peons' exercise yard.

With zero space between its high, planked walls, the yard looked more like a stockade or pen. Kat was in unfamiliar territory; she had little cause before to explore the grounds at close range. She heard male voices laugh and holler from behind the high fence. Two wide gates stood open on the side of the yard that faced her. She lurked closer and ducked behind a thin copse of dwarfed damson trees. Craning her neck from behind the trees, she peeked through the gates and caught a glimpse of activity.

A senior peon supervised archery practice with a handful of preteen boys. By a wide margin, one boy's arrows had missed the bullseye painted on the opposite fence. The other male children taunted him until the peon reprimanded them into silence.

But no sign of Marcus. She left the shelter of the damson trees to investigate the rest of the compound.

"Hello, Miss Katrena. Can I help you with something?" Caleb

lumbered toward her. He led a subdued man by a chain, hitched to a rawhide collar around his neck.

At first glance, she didn't recognize him. Since she'd last seen Marcus, he'd received a major makeover. His hair had been clipped short, his scruffy beard shaved off, and he wore sandals, an ankle bandage, and the standard, dark green garb of the peon recruits. The sun gleamed and bounced off his freshly-washed haircut.

He seemed much younger to her—and distinctly more vulnerable.

"No, I..." Her mind raced to come up with an excuse. "I wanted to check the ripeness of the damsons, is all." She stole another glance at the rogue.

Caleb raised his bushy brows at her and winked.

He didn't swallow her story for a second. She felt her cheeks burn. "I better go." She gave him a nonchalant wave.

"See ya later, Miss." Caleb tugged on the chain, jerking Marcus toward the exercise yard.

Unwilling to give up, she made moves to leave but skirted around the enclosure. When she hid behind a large trash bin against its exterior wall, she heard Caleb's booming voice.

"I'll come back with your food soon," he said. Then he shouted, "Breakfast is ready, boys! We'll wrap up target practice when you're done."

She heard the youngsters run from the yard. Finally, the metallic creak of gate hinges.

When Caleb left, she came out of her hiding place. The gates had been barred horizontally with a long wooden beam. She slunk around the rear and hunted for a gap along the high fence. A crevice, a knothole, anything. Her search came up empty and she circled back to where she started.

Whistling a tune, Caleb reappeared with a tray. Kat scrabbled away to conceal herself behind the trash bin again. From her crouched position, she overheard him somehow speak to Marcus through the fence.

"Breakfast for ya, bud." The quick screech of a latch. "Eat up. You're gonna need it to build up your strength. Your basic training kicks off at dawn tomorrow."

She peeked around the corner. Caleb's hairy arm pushed the tray through a horizontal hatch she hadn't noticed, about one-and-a-half feet wide and six inches high near the gates. As the peon closed the shutter to the hatch, she ducked lower and waited until he strolled back to the mess hall.

Before she lost her nerve, she flew to the hatch and opened it a few inches. Marcus stood in her line of vision, holding a tray of food. The chain and collar around his neck had been removed.

"How are you?" she whispered with urgency.

He flinched and almost dropped the tray. "Cripes! Take a goddamn guess." He sidled closer. "For starters, your cabal of elders treated me to a flashback from the Spanish Inquisition, your band of thugs had a blast last night making me a laughing-stock, and to top it off they locked me in a miserable hole in the wall with a stinky straw mattress as thin as an onion skin." He sneered at her. "Other than that, I'm jim-dandy."

Kat had no qualms about standing close to him with the fence between them, and yet when her eyes met his through the slot, an odd flutter filled her chest. She noticed his bandaged wrists. "How bad—"

"Superficial wounds," he cut in, "and my ankle isn't broken, only sprained."

"How did they manage to catch you?"

He put the tray on the ground and stuck his hands in his pockets. "I took a swim in the river that runs through the woods. They saw me when I headed back to the root cellar."

"The peons?"

"A couple of their scouts, I presume. When I tried to escape on this bum leg, I didn't know I was running right into your posse. Two of those jeezly big titans roped and tackled me on the barrens."

"Did they mention their plans for you?"

"Something about basic training or boot camp, but I still have no clue what they intend to do with me. Should I be freaking out, right about now?"

"They'll try to integrate you."

"But how? Not with torture, I hope."

She wrinkled her nose, aghast at the thought. "I hope torture isn't part of it either. I've heard bits and pieces of the process used on the boys, but not in any detail. What I do know is if you fail to come through it successfully, they'll eliminate you like a rabid fox."

"Precisely what that old battle-axe Bianca told me. What gives them the right?"

"Marcus, whatever the rest of the world is like and whatever form of government you're used to, it isn't here. As a man on this island, you have few rights."

"So I've heard." He stared down at his food tray with longing. Ignoring the fork, he knelt in the dirt and ripped into his meal of boiled eggs, bread, and fried potatoes with his bare hands.

Kat couldn't contain her curiosity as he devoured the food and drank from his tin flask. "How *is* life out there in the rest of the world?"

"Don't ask me. I only know what I've lived. Violence, hunger, and misery, most of it. No order, no government. Just ghost towns and a scattered hamlet. Clusters of people here, a family or two there, doing whatever they can not to starve or get sick."

"Any clue how many are alive on the mainland now?"

His face shone under the unforgiving sun. "There's no way I can answer that."

"I heard about what happened to your family in Quebec. I'm really sorry."

"Forget about that now. How do I get out of here? You'll still help me, won't you?"

Obviously, he had no desire to bring up the horror of his slain family members with her. She couldn't blame him. "I did say I'd help you but that was before you went and got yourself captured."

"I realize your predicament if you were found out, but please, come up with a scheme to spring me from this pen and get me in your boat." He wiped his mouth with the back of his hand. "You can't desert me now!"

Guilt jabbed at her. She avoided his pleading gaze. She hated to abandon him, but what choice did she have? Her eyes fell on the flask. She gave a quick thumbs up and said she'd think about it.

They'd added a critical ingredient to his drink this morning. They'd given him his first dose of the mysterious elixir last night, Harper had overheard and relayed. She'd asked Ms. Eleanor at supper how hard it would be to integrate a grown man, and the elder admitted Dr. Olivia had prescribed the same elixir they used on the other males, though at a higher dosage.

Marcus didn't know it yet, but his assimilation had already begun.

* * *

When she joined her ward for their own hasty breakfast, they learned it was their shift to mop the floors of the Gathering House. Kat collected the cleaning supplies from the building's utility closet, and they swabbed the assembly hall and community room first. When they finished those rooms, they refilled their pails with clean water and soap and tackled the mess hall and kitchen.

"Can we go for a horseback ride when I get out of school or after supper?" Shyla brushed damp hair out of her eyes. "The perfect reward after this dreary work!" Little pearls of perspiration stood out on her top lip as she plunged the yarn mop into the soapy water. With vigor, she wrung it out and swished it back and forth over the mess hall's time-worn hardwood floor.

"No argument here," Kat said, impressed by her energy and diligence. Since their rift and subsequent reconciliation, she realized she'd lucked out with Shyla as a ward instead of one of the younger, more rambunctious children of the cove. Not that she'd ever admit it to anyone. Her mixed emotions about the whole mentorship deal had not gone away. The memory of Quinn's hatred toward her and Wren's transfer still rankled. "We'll check to see if the horses will be available. They'll probably work in the fields today gathering the livestock hay and feed, so they might be too tired later. The peons have borrowed strong horses from Exploits Bay too, to get the job done faster. We might have to wait for another evening to ride."

"Oh! I heard about that village having two new draft horses from crossbreeding at the ranch. Can we go see if it's them on our lunch break?"

But when they returned to the nursery to check on their charges, Kat found out their breeding coordinator had made other plans for the rest of her day.

"It's time to begin your enrollment," a businesslike Ms. Eleanor announced from inside the doorway. "Same goes for Harper and you three, Falon, Grace, and Ruby. The practitioners will train older women to take over child care and domestic duties going forward, and you will each be assigned to your choice of a less strenuous, afternoon internship. Tomorrow you will continue with your usual morning and evening mentor duties. Come with me, please."

The five teens left with Ms. Eleanor. Ruby walked alongside the elder, with Kat and Grace behind them. In silence, Falon and Harper brought up the rear. Falon's pale, pinched face was the incarnation of anxiety.

Grace, on the other hand, hummed a cheery tune. A moment

later, she stopped short. "How do we manage this, along with our mentoring?" she stage-whispered. "Are we expected to mate with children around?"

Ms. Eleanor eyed Grace and laughed. "I heard that. You're not expected to engage in sexual intercourse around the clock. That isn't how it works."

Grace gave Kat an exaggerated wink. "Yes, of course. What was I thinking? Gotta come up for air at some point, I suppose."

Surprise, surprise. Grace usually came across as quiet and introverted, so Kat had thought her shy like Falon. Now she saw her in a new light. Perhaps she'd grown bored with her aviary and toddler duties and wished to try something new.

"Where are we going?" Harper asked, echoing her thoughts. "To the Suites?"

"No, it isn't time to go there yet," Ms. Eleanor said.

The tract of luxury log chalets which comprised the Origin Suites were pleasantly situated along the rolling foothills of the Long Range Mountains. They spanned the outskirts of Wild Cove behind Poplar Forest and overlooked Timber Pond. Kat and the others had passed through the vicinity countless times, though children—and teenagers, up until now—were not permitted inside the handsomely appointed suites. Word of mouth from previous breeders had furnished scant details of what lay inside those walls. The groups of twenty comfortable chalets built in every island village were relics from yesteryear, once used as part of the island's tourism industry long before the world economy began to flounder. They had been diligently maintained ever since for their beauty and for their current fundamental purpose.

"To begin," their elder said, "each of you will require a thorough examination at the clinic. We'll meet up with the other new breeders there."

By reflex, Kat glanced down at her bare legs in brief buckskin shorts and at the scar snaked around her lower right leg. When she was five years old, a four-hundred-pound black bear had blindsided her in the woods while she and Ms. Naomi were collecting mushrooms. When the animal roared and gave chase, she'd scaled a spruce tree to escape harm. But it reached up and clawed her with its enormous paw, tearing into her leg with one swipe.

It would have killed and eaten her if Bryce and Caleb hadn't been nearby chopping wood. Alerted by her elder's shrieks, they'd come running to help the younger Kat. When Caleb had thrown an axe into the bear's flank to distract it, Bryce had shot and felled him with poison arrows. The attack prompted the use of traps near their villages for black and brown bears, and even for the possibility of polar bears, from thereon. As the clinic loomed up to meet her, memories of that painful day surged back.

During her early childhood, people had seen the odd polar bear. Starving and emaciated in their migration from the arctic, they'd had no choice but to swim south in search of sustenance. The bounteous north and polar ice cap where once they'd thrived was no more. Since then, the endangered animals had disappeared, gone the way of the great auk, the eastern wolf, the northern cod, and so many more. It had been at least ten years since the last reported sighting by islanders and northerners alike. She'd survived a bear attack, but she harboured no animosity toward any animal. And to think of the extinction of those magnificent white mammals of the north discouraged her to no end.

The clinic which serviced Wild Cove and four nearby villages had been reproduced in four strategic locations for the other twenty communities around the island. Eagle Inlet, Battle Cove and Muddy Tickle in coastal Labrador shared their own health facility.

Aside from treatment for the bear attack, Kat seldom had occasion to visit the two-storey clinic, since illness was rare. All citizens had received the necessary shots for disease prevention, so unless someone needed their tonsils or appendix out, broke an arm, or sustained some other serious injury, they had little need for medical attention.

Under Dr. Olivia, Surgeon and Chief of Medicine, the staff included two female physicians, a male consort as lab technician and intern, Ms. Eleanor as health coordinator, and two all-purpose assistants. When not engaged with day-to-day health care, the staff kept active with research projects and the study of natural pharmaceuticals, to advance new ideas and develop better medications, anesthetics and treatments. At a meeting two months ago, Ms. Eleanor relayed that Dr. Olivia and her team were working hard to synthesize the island's depleted stockpile of Immunity-2.

The new recruits to the breeding program trooped single file into the health facility. Their elder led them past reception, down a long corridor, and into an airy office with a picture window, an administrative station, and a row of chairs. Five teen girls Kat and the others knew were already seated. Three closed doors lined the opposite wall.

"The staff are expecting you and will call each of your names when they're ready. Afterwards, meet me in the break room." With a wink at them as they sat down, Ms. Eleanor left.

She hadn't even opened the book she selected from the browsing material on the table when a thin woman in a white coat emerged from one of the rooms, calling out her name. Ruby and Grace gave her encouraging looks while Falon and Harper stuck their noses back into their books.

She followed the medical officer into her examination room. A neatly folded patient's gown had been placed on the exam table, but her gaze flew to the stirrups.

"Hello, Katrena," she said in a voice as smooth as warm maple syrup. "I'm Dr. Prudence, and I'll be your physician for procreation prep and enrollment. How are you today?"

"Honestly? If it's the truth you're after, I'm rotted. This is the last place in the world I care to be." She glared brazenly at the doctor.

"Aahhh!" Instantly, the physician's sunny stance adjusted to a much cooler setting. "A malcontent, I see. How fortunate to begin my residency with a bitchy teenager! You better be careful what you say from now on. We don't need you spreading your malignant negativity to the others. Now please get undressed and put on the gown." She picked up the slim folder on her desk. Kat spied her name on the tab as she strode past. "See you in a few minutes."

As soon as the door closed, she kicked off her hikers as hard as she could. They flew across the room and banged against the wall.

But she did as she was told.

Journal Reading #3

Old World Anthology – Adult Memories Archives of Physical & Sexual Abuse
Volume 2: Sexual Harassment & Sexual Assault in the Workplace
Entry recorded: January 11, 2017

MY ACCOUNT OF SEXUAL VIOLENCE AT WORK

My name is Althea, I am twenty-nine years old, and I come from the city of Manila in the Philippines. Because my English is not great, I have help recording this from a friend who writes English better than I can.

In the summer of 2012, when my babies were toddlers (my daughter Trisha Mae was three and my son Jasper, one and a half) we need more income to make ends meet. I move in with my mother, alone since my father passed, and she survives on a meager pension. My husband, the children's father, deserted us last year. I don't know where he lives and he not help to support us in any way.

I found a job in a nearby food market, and my mother took care of the kids. I enjoyed the work I had to do there, but the pay was awful. I worked for a few weeks and have no luck finding a better job, but I hear about a program in Canada where they hire temporary foreign workers for much better pay.

I hated to leave my family, but I long to make a better life for my mother and my babies. I didn't know what else I can do. If I get accepted to the program and my employment goes well, I consider immigrating to Canada permanently and my family join me. I dream of taking night classes to further my education and get more skilled work.

Along with a few of my coworkers at the market, I apply for a work visa and a passport and my application is sent. Next thing I know, I'm kissing my little ones good-bye and flying to Newfoundland, Canada with four other Filipino women, same as me. We share a tiny basement apartment there in the city of St. John's and start our jobs with a commercial cleaning company.

I work hard at my new job from day one. During orientation, I work days. But once trained, I have to accept the permanent night shifts I'm offered. The job has no union, and yet the status quo is that those who have seniority, who for most part are Canadian citizens, work permanent dayshifts.

For three months straight and with no complaint, I work nights cleaning offices, banks, and other places of business. It is hard because trying to sleep in the day is next to impossible for me. The advice for working nights recommends you stay on the same sleep schedule on your days off too. This way, you will not be disoriented by the change in schedules. I hoped after a while I get used to it.

I need the job to send money home to support my family, and to qualify for permanent status. Another hire on nights came from the Philippines a year before with her entire family of six. She is dog-tired most of the time. When she supposed to be sleeping, her husband work days. And with school out for summer, her children are left on their own. They are older kids who do not need a sitter, but the apartment is never quiet enough for her to get quality sleep. She not get much domestic support from her husband, either. He works full-time and believe his duty to the family ends when he passes over his paycheque.

At the end of the fourth month, I find out other new hires received a bump up in their wages. Not on the last paycheque, but weeks ago. Why not me? The more I ask around, the more I learned. The Canadian men get wage increases, but not us, the foreign workers, or Canadian women. I call to my recruiter and left a message to contact me. When I don't hear back three days later, I decide to ask for a short meeting with the boss of the cleaning company. He put me off for a couple of days, but in the end I got my meeting.

I get ready for work early to give me time to go to his office and have a few words. I plead my case for a raise, and ask if I might be able to work days and nights alternately like some others of the cleaning staff.

His answer to both of my requests is an unequivocal 'no, not at this time'. I ask why the men get paid more, when we do the same job.

"Because they are men," he says, putting out a cigarette in the ashtray on his desk. "They are the main breadwinners in their households, therefore they need more money than you do. You have husband? I imagine his wages are higher than yours, therefore you don't need a raise."

"No, I have no husband, but I have children back home," I argue. "I'm the main breadwinner. And I know there are men who got raises who don't have children, and some aren't even married!"

"No, but they might have a family someday."

This makes no sense to me, but I not getting anywhere. "Well, is there a way you let me rotate shifts? It's hard for me to work nights all the time."

"We need men on the dayshift because that's when the vans need to be loaded and unloaded with cleaning equipment and supplies. Surely, you not say you are capable of loading vans like they do, are you, miss? As for your kids, well, this is not my problem. I didn't make you get pregnant. And I certainly didn't make you find a job in another country so you can wash your hands of them."

I sat there, speechless and in shock. How dare he insult me this way! Shaking and disappointed, I go to leave his office.

He stood up too and walk over to me when I reach for the doorknob.

"Maybe, miss," he says in a different voice, "we can come up with a solution which works for both of us." He touches himself down there and moves closer. His bulging belly shoves against me.

My heart pounded and I froze. His tobacco breath hit me in the face as he unzips my jacket and rub his groin on my hip. His hand touched my breast through my uniform.

"What you are doing?" I shrieked. I shoved him away with all the force I had.

"We can arrange for you to earn bonuses here and there," he said, ignoring my cries, "to make up for your salary." He brushed past me, tore my hand off the doorknob and locked the door. "You want to make extra money, don't you?" He holds my wrists in an iron grip with one hand and unbutton the blouse of my uniform with the other.

The strong smell of his cheap aftershave fills my nostrils, making me urge. My throat hurt and my voice cracks as I cry for help.

"No one can hear you, miss. When there's a shift change, no one's around this part of the building." He became impatient with the buttons and rips my blouse open, exposing my bra. I try to twist out of his hold, but he hauled up my bra, exposed my breasts, and grabs one, squeezing hard.

I not see through my tears, but I stop crying for help.

"There's a nice girl. I will make you feel a lot better. No husband, hey? Wait until I give you what you really came for." He rubs his bristled face into my chest and bites. I cry out. "Or would you rather...go down?" He groaned in my ear. "A job's a job, right?"

I struggled to free myself. I hear my uniform rip. But he is big and strong compared to me. I can't fight him off. When he clutches my throat, I afraid he will kill me. This is why when he propelled me to the couch behind his desk, I gave in and let him to do what he wants. When he flips me over, I certain he will tear me apart. I cried into the smoky couch the whole way through.

At last, he was done with me. Trembling, I dress as fast as I could. He wouldn't look at me afterwards. He sat down at his desk to shuffle papers as if he is all business. But before I escape his office, he told me to wait.

"At least you don't have to worry I knock you up with another bastard. Run along to your shift, and next time, don't put up such a fight. I know you're hungry for it."

I try not to cry and run to the door.

"Oh, and if your plan is to report this little romp? I say you asked for a raise and you offer sex to get it. Your word against mine. Now go to work."

I manage to find my way out of there without losing it completely. I can't bear to see that swine ever again. I rather die first.

I think, what I am going to do? More than anything, I long to go back home to Manila to hug my babies and not ever leave them again. My mother be crushed if she knew what happened. I can't tell her or anyone. I am filled with shame. But I have no other job. I have my family to think of. They depend on me. We need the money.

Racked with pain, I run to the bus stop on quivering legs. I miss the eight o'clock bus for my shift at the suite of offices downtown and wait twenty minutes for next one. When I arrive, my supervisor tapped her watch in irritation. She berated me for my tardiness and said she will report me to my recruiter if it happens again, adding migrant workers didn't get special favours over other employees. I don't know how, but I made it through the shift and only break down once in bathroom. I keep my mouth shut and do my work.

The next day is my day off. I decide to contact my work liaison officer again to see if I can work somewhere else. A fast food restaurant or a seafood plant—any job, as long as I do not ever be near the lowlife piece of scum who raped me.

This happened five years ago now. I have better job in a nice restaurant where my bosses are a decent man and woman. They are kind to us workers. My babies and my mama came to live in Canada and are with me now and they are content.

My friends ask why I don't have boyfriend. One said she fix me up with a guy she knows but I say I too busy, and anyway, I rather spend my free time with Trisha Mae, Jasper and my mom.

A man is the last thing I need.

CHAPTER FIFTEEN

·

While they awaited their test results, Kat and the other breeding novices attended Ms. Eleanor's information session on all aspects of the new directive.

The elder briefed the young women on the importance of a nutritious prenatal diet and safe, regular exercise to ensure healthy babies. Once they achieved pregnancy, they were not to indulge in wine, cannabis, hallucinogenic mushrooms, sexual intercourse, overly strenuous activities, or any negligent behaviours which could harm the developing fetus.

She emphasized that labour and delivery didn't involve the clinic. Births took place in a special room at the Origin Suites where the village birth doula and assisting baby catcher oversaw labour and delivery. The ideology of the elders, teachers, doctors, and these assistants asserted pregnancy and childbirth were not illnesses, therefore they shouldn't be treated as such. If complications did arise which required medical intervention, a clinic physician remained on standby to assist.

They revisited the philosophy of It Takes A Village. Each newborn would be transferred to a distant village to eliminate the parental link between breeder and biological offspring. At the same time, Wild Cove would continue to love and raise the children transferred in. This practice ensured the nurture and development of each child within a network of attachment figures as opposed to one primary mother figure. The philosophy was in keeping with the conviction of the elders that a child's self-esteem and well-being is highest when no one exhibits favoritism of one child over another.

"Affectionate guidance in equal measure for all," Ms. Eleanor explained. "How was it ever accepted in the past to only care about the children *you* bring into the world, to put their needs ahead of anyone else's child? Where is the justice, the altruism, the honour in that?"

Grace held up her hand. "I have a question."

Yes, dear, go ahead."

"It concerns favoritism—not toward children, but toward the consorts. What if more than one of us desires the same sexual partner?"

Ruby giggled.

"In the event you can't settle on one consort each, then you will share the consort in question on alternate days or nights. This method has worked out on several occasions, and hopefully that will be the case this time around. But they are all suitable young men. Now, let's get back to birthing."

To avoid any initial emotional attachment, the elder also told them they would not hold, feed, or even see the infants they delivered. Following the release of the newborns, they were expected to provide breast milk for one year, expressed manually via the Marmet technique and fed to the incoming exchanges by nursery staff. Former breeders would provide them instruction on the technique.

The girls returned to the waiting room for their results. Kat's tests came back normal. The one issue Dr. Prudence uncovered was the questionable size of her pelvis, likely too narrow to push out a full-term newborn. She might require a C-section instead of going the natural childbirth route.

"Surgery? What a bonus!" Kat ignored the doctor's withering look as she tore out of the examination room.

Having no apparent issues, Harper and Ruby were cleared for reproducing. Like Kat, Falon received the same diagnosis. To their disappointment, the pelvic condition was not deemed serious enough to exclude them from the program.

Of their group, Grace fared the worst. The one teen who welcomed the new directive would not participate because of an overgrowth of uterine tissue and irregular periods. Kat bristled at the irony.

Ruby hovered over her and squeezed her hand. "Perhaps they can fix you up with surgery."

Grace's lower lip quivered. "They tell me it's too severe for that."

"Does this mean you'll go back to aviary and toddler duty?" Falon asked. "You could try an apprenticeship for another job."

"It isn't my fault I can't conceive. Where's my opportunity to earn free will?"

"Grace, I'd get clarification if I were you," Harper said.

"No, it isn't your fault," Ruby agreed, "so it shouldn't deprive you of your right to choose a vocation that appeals to you." She dropped a freckled arm around Grace's shoulders and whispered in her ear.

Kat would bet her next meal Ruby was recommending a sex romp with a buff and willing young peon as consolation.

The next step in their enrollment was the selection of breeding partners. Along with the five other Wild Cove females from the ages of eighteen to twenty who had yet to breed, Kat, Harper, Falon and Ruby were instructed to attend a meet-and-greet that night at the Origin Suites Lounge. Other females of age and young consorts from the three neighbouring northwest villages would also attend. Drinks, conversation, music and dancing would facilitate the mingle-fest, Ms. Eleanor hinted, and help smooth the awkward edges off the selection of partners. The same scenario, they learned, would play out in groupings of the twenty-eight island and allied Labrador villages, with varying numbers of participants.

The fledgling women and the crop of consort participants had never met, at least not in a formal way. They may have caught glimpses of one another now and then—Wild Cove and the other villages were indeed small communities—but because of their gender segregation, particularly from the consorts, these men were virtual strangers to them.

Kat rubbed her temples to ease the beginning of a tension headache. She wished it was her with infertility issues instead of Grace. She would have switched places in a blink with her or Yvonne to escape this ordeal.

Or would she? At least once the two pregnancies and milk production were over, her body and her life would belong to her again. She could choose whatever she desired after this hateful period had passed. And she already knew what she desired most of all.

When the rest of the sistership left for Sundown Circle at the beach that evening, the fresh batch of potential procreators traipsed off to the Suites Lounge. Upon their arrival, a senior supervisory consort at the welcome desk gave the attendees nametags. Kat quickly scrawled her name on hers with the offered charcoal pencil and pinned it to her tank top.

"I hear most of them are new to sex like us," Ruby told her while she pinned her nametag to her generous bosom. "According to Dr. Prudence, this will give us the best chance of producing strong and healthy children."

"Virgins all around?" Kat snorted. "Who you trying to kid?"

"I mean...like *most* of us." Ruby's cheeks glowed pink under a swarm of bright freckles. With a sheepish grin, she pulled away. "Good luck!"

The introductory segment of the meet-and-greet presented a speed-date format to encourage matchmaking in a timely manner. Kat noticed the consorts outnumbered them, presumably so every female would more easily find a suitable match. As per instructions, each teen would remain seated at her table while the consorts rotated from table to table to chat. According to Ms. Eleanor, the young men had been well briefed on the new directive and carefully selected for their health, fertility, intelligence, temperament, and attractiveness.

Kat parked herself at the nearest table, crossed her arms, and stifled a yawn.

At the end of the four-minute time slots, a whistle sounded, signaling the consorts to switch to the next participant's table. Halfway through the candidates, she hadn't met anyone who appealed to her, let alone bowl her over with charm or witty conversation. The handpicked consorts, immature and bland to her, left her cold. She seethed at the thought of enduring another half-hour of this silliness, and she flirted with the idea of hiding until the farce of an evening ended. The one element that made the event halfway tolerable was the bar, where berry wines poured on demand.

While the youth who sat opposite her waxed lyrical about his much-loved tome on organic chemistry, her eyes wandered to the next table where Falon actively avoided eye contact with her current speed date. Poor girl. She even felt a twinge of pity for the unfortunate victim Falon evaded, a pasty-faced guy who—dare she think it—was prettier than most of the girls. What was with these dudes? What had happened to their masculinity? Along with aggression, had too much testosterone been bred out of them as well?

Not one of them bore the slightest resemblance to Marcus.

Down to her last two dates, she hit upon a possible prospect. Reed, a pleasant chap with a slim, sturdy build and impossibly long lashes, met with her tentative approval well before the four minutes ended. As weird as it felt to spend such a chunk of time among consorts, he was the first candidate to disarm her and chase away her sour mood. His dark sense of humour and cynical attitude to these bizarre goings-on piqued her interest the most. At least they shared that mindset.

"This set-up is wack, hey?" He grabbed the chair across from her, swinging it around before he sat, using the back as an armrest. He glanced at her nametag. "So, Kat, how does it feel?"

She tilted her head to one side. "How does what feel?"

"Ah, you know. To be inducted into the new teenage order of doe-eyed, sacrificial virgins, ripe for the picking. Awkward!"

She chewed on her thumbnail. "I imagine the same way it feels for you—just another smart-ass in a stable of pedigreed stallions, stamping your hooves and chomping at the bit."

"Touché. But I'm yet to see anyone fall over themselves to ride me. You up for it?"

Despite her intentions to remain indifferent, she found herself smiling at him. When their time was up, she decided he would suffice.

But as it happened, Harper also chose him. "Reed is the only guy here I can stand," she said emphatically as soon as the last whistle blared.

"Me too," Kat replied, puzzled. "Huh...does this mean we have to share him? Or should we fight each other for him?"

Harper arched her eyebrows. "Fight with you? I don't want him that bad."

Kat punched her in the arm and grinned. Harper's soft feminine type wouldn't stand a chance going one on one with a badass like her.

To her annoyance, she didn't win Reed, but neither did Harper.

Once he caught a glimpse of statuesque Ruby in all her ripe, curvaceous beauty, he was smitten and she in kind. Ruby's choice had been made.

Kat must have been foolish to think he'd go for her. She knew she appeared somewhat androgynous with her super-short cut and her wiry build with a mere rumour of a bosom. Her face may have been agreeable enough but compared to the other girls, she suspected her appearance and her no-nonsense attitude put most guys off.

She and Harper consoled each other, dreading the next part of the evening. The Dance. The band, comprised of two female singers, a guitarist, a violinist and a drummer, set themselves up at the front of the lounge next to the bar.

The bar staff lowered the lights and lit candles on each table, bathing the dance floor in an amber luminance. The band opened with a tender, sentimental song, the soft harmony and strains of the violin setting the mood. From the sidelines, Kat checked to see how many had lucked out and how many had struck out. Along with four of the twenty-year-old women who sat at the bar, she and Harper were in the clear minority.

"I can't believe this." Harper pointed to the middle of the dance floor. "Even Falon found a guy!"

"What? No!" Kat spotted her, slow dancing with the pasty pretty-boy. Ah, no wonder. She had matched herself up with the mildest, most unthreatening male in the room. And though Falon acted pleased with her choice, the lad seemed vaguely uncomfortable to be in her arms to begin with.

A group of other young men, at least a dozen or more, stood to the side of the dance floor. Kat ventured a glimpse at those closest to her and Harper. One leaned against the wall as if fed up, hands jammed deep in his pockets. The stocky fellow next to him guffawed repeatedly at his own remarks. Another fidgeted with an empty wine glass, twirling it around and around like a globe. All rejects, same as her.

"Let's get drunk."

Harper grabbed her wrist. "Come on."

As they quaffed down goblets of wine at the bar and brooded over their exclusion, the next song exploded with the singers performing a Capella at a much faster tempo. Two of the rejected youths promptly came forward. Kat remembered their faces and nametags from the speed rounds but not much else.

The shorter fellow pitched her a cautious smile. "Hey, no point wasting this excellent song," he murmured. He put his empty glass on the bar and held out his hand. "Care to dance? Kat, is it?"

She sized him up more closely, thinking she might've seen him somewhere before. She almost declined, but when his smile evaporated and he dropped the proffered hand to his side, she forced a nod.

She squinted at his nametag. "Hell, why not?" she breathed, squaring her shoulders. "I'll dance with you, Colt."

"Great! Let's do it." He tucked her arm under his, as if afraid she might reconsider and run away.

Harper agreed to dance with the other consort, and the four joined the crowd frolicking on the dance floor. They bopped and swayed to the catchy beat. Kat didn't know if it was the wine, the song, Colt himself, or a combination of all three that slowly warmed her to him.

I suppose he'll serve the purpose. She mirrored his capricious grin when the song ended. When she rejoined her friend at their table, the consorts headed to the bar for another round of drinks.

Harper panted from exertion as she straightened her ponytail. "What's your guy's name?"

"My guy? Sheesh, I don't know if I'll ever call him that. But he is a little stallion."

"How do you mean?"

"His name is Colt. Ha! What's yours?"

"It's either Leif or Reef. I couldn't hear over the music and the handwriting on his tag is atrocious."

Kat laughed. "Alright, I'll claim Colt as mine if you settle for Leif or Reef or whatever his name is. Agreed?"

"Yeah...whatever." Harper stared at the candle flame between them. "This is really hard for me, you know."

"Not exactly easy street for me either, sister."

"I don't think you get it," Harper said. "This goes against my nature. Let me put it this way: you know how fond I am of carving and whittling."

"Uh huh."

"I can spend hours at it to perfect the tiny details, sanding smooth my new creation until I get it exactly right and it pleases my eye. But what if, suddenly, the elders forbade it? Say they took away my pocketknife and sandstone and my blocks of wood, and gave me a big, ugly anvil and a forge instead? What if they forced me to become a blacksmith or something else I'm not made for?"

"Ah. Say no more—I understand."

Harper's eyes shot up to meet hers. "You already knew?"

"I had an inkling."

"I...I'm quite fond of you, Kat. Always have been."

On impulse, Kat patted her hand. A warm tingle rippled through her. She wasn't entirely surprised by the declaration, but it pleased her to no end to finally hear it put into words. She remembered how Harper tried to cheer her up when she returned from her ranch stint years ago. When she'd gifted Kat with the tiny horse she'd carved, she'd had a hunch about the depth of Harper's feelings. "You've always meant a lot to me too. It's weird to be around so many males at once, isn't it? Don't worry—we'll talk more about it later. This part of the deal will be over soon anyway."

The smiling men rejoined them with more wine.

"What will be over soon?" Colt handed Kat her glass as he pulled a chair closer.

"This meet-and-greet deal."

He leaned toward her and dropped his voice to a murmur. "Any chance you'd like me to be, um... more than your dance partner?"

"Actually, I was about to ask you."

He moved closer and kissed her on the mouth. "Wanna get outta here and get better acquainted?"

Kat touched her lips in surprise at the impetuous kiss—firm, yet as warm and soft as a baby's cheek. "Are we allowed already? I mean, tonight?" She couldn't remember the proper protocol from Ms. Eleanor's info session.

"Can't see why not. Come on, let's go back to my dorm. Or yours?"

Though he looked slightly familiar, she hadn't been sure if he lived in Wild Cove or one of the other villages. This would make the situation easier. "Aren't we supposed to use the Origin Suites?"

She swung around to Harper for input, but she'd already headed back to the dance floor with Leif. Or Reef.

"Right-o!" Colt said. "One of the chalets next door. Why did that slip my mind?"

You're as skittish as I am, that's why. She drained her glass and jumped to her feet. "Okay. Let's get out of here." If she became pregnant quickly, this portion of her martyrdom would be mercifully over. She tried to frame it as the first hurdle to her true destiny.

She waved goodbye to Harper and followed Colt out of the lounge. Two senior consorts stationed at the exit with clipboards blocked their way.

One of them addressed her. "Have you selected your consort for the Origin Suites, Miss Kat?" he asked after he read the tag on her chest.

"Evidently." She gestured to Colt at her side.

Charcoal pencil poised, he squinted at the paper on his clipboard. "Here you are—a Wild Cove citizen." He checked her name off.

The other man came forward and checked off Colt's name.

The first senior consort dropped a red-painted key in Kat's palm. "In your suite, you'll find a letter on the bed you both must read. It will give you assistance and final instructions. Your suite number is engraved on the key."

"Thank you," they said in unison.

Colt glanced at her shyly as they walked next door to the sprawling vista of log chalets, nestled in the foothills against a background of dark evergreen trees and spectacular soaring cliffs. Each of the luxury units boasted a cherry-red door, twin picture windows, and a wraparound deck under a sloped roof with wide, supported eaves. The grounds of the chalets had been landscaped with privacy in mind, each separated by chokecherry shrubs, copses of white birch, and mature willows.

By the time they'd crossed the threshold to Suite 12 and locked the door behind them, Kat's stomach was performing backflips and somersaults and her hands trembled. She took a deep cleansing breath to overcome her trepidation.

It didn't work.

Her introduction to sex was one thing. She liked Colt well enough, and on a rational level she understood why they were here. That understanding did not, however, erase her aversion to getting pregnant. She hated to relinquish control of her body and her future to the elders, but how could she not? She couldn't bear the thought of a future without choices.

"Whoa." Colt's mouth dropped open as he scanned the interior. "Quite the digs."

They stood together, speechless as they took in the loveliness of the suite. The entryway led them into a tastefully decorated sitting room with a cream-coloured sofa and loveseat. On the oval coffee table, a mixed bouquet of yellow snapdragons, sunflowers, and orange tiger lilies had been arranged in a pewter vase. Kat recognized the vibrant perennials from the elders' garden. She leaned over them and inhaled the blend of sweet floral scents.

At the back of the room, an airy flight of stairs led to an overhead railed loft. A wood-carved media console faced the sofa. It displayed a turntable stereo and an impressive vinyl record collection which filled the open shelf underneath, a notable detail she remembered hearing about from Yvonne. What caught her eye, though, was the gorgeous Tiffany lamp on the console. She ran over to admire it.

"I read about these lamps in a book from our library!" she exclaimed. "*Clara and Mr. Tiffany*. A true story apparently." She frowned. Yet another account of talented work done by women, for a man who had received all the credit.

She entered the adjacent room and stepped into a fantasy. "Now isn't this the finest kind!" Never had she seen such a charming and elegant bedroom. She pictured the stark monotony of her dorm and her narrow bed. Even the comfortable rooms in the elders' house didn't compare to these.

The walls of delicate seafoam-blue showcased a collection of paintings, rendered in watercolour. Subtle images of birds, butterflies and botanicals of assorted species surrounded them. A braided ivory area rug under the queen-sized four poster bed covered most of the polished pine floor. Antique oil lamps with pale-pink glass chimneys sat on floating shelves on either side of the bed. A trifle overkill on the feminine décor, but the bed did look tempting to her —for a marvelous night's sleep.

She crossed the room to the window with its multicoloured border of stained-glass panels. The window presented a picturesque view of Timber Pond, especially tonight. She took in the sky and the galaxy of stars over the water, pinpoints of white light sprinkled around the full orange hunter's moon. Someone had left the side window open a few inches to cool the room. A waft of fresh air fluttered in on her bare legs while the gentle rhythm of waves lapped the shore. She heard the lonely cry of a loon on the distant side of the pond. Her throat felt suddenly full.

What the hell? *Smarten up, you chickenshit. You've got this.* "Hey," Colt called from the adjoining bathroom. "Come here and get an eyeful!"

Kat swallowed down her quaking nerves and left the window to see what he had found.

An iron clawfoot tub stood in the center of a shiny, tiled floor. Next to it, an assortment of fragrant soaps, bath salts, sea sponges and towels were stacked on a white ladder-back chair.

She ran to the tub and turned on the twin faucets. "Hot and cold running water. Geez Louise—where the heck are we?"

"And here too! The modern plumbing folks used to have." In the corner of the room, Colt pulled back a white lace curtain to reveal a stone-tiled stall with its own faucets and a showerhead. "Could get used to this pretty quick, huh?"

She stared with yearning at the tub but decided it might take too long. She needed to get this night over with. She strode to the bedroom window and drew the drapes closed.

"Think I'll grab a quick shower."

"Go on," Colt said. "I'll get one after you."

Her consort sat on the edge of the bed, utterly out of place on the pastel, patchwork quilt with its bank of pillows and lace dust ruffle. Kat plucked up her courage and asked him if this was his first time too.

"Shows, does it?" He rubbed the back of his neck. "To tell you the truth, I'm kind of curious to see what all the fuss is about."

She re-entered the bathroom and closed the door. Before starting her shower, she pulled up her brief wrap skirt to pee in the commode.

"Whaa?" Those belly backflips had morphed into menstrual cramps. Splotches of dark blood stained her underwear. "Well, fuck me!"

"Uh, yeah..." Colt called out, "but can't we use the bed?"

She laughed. "Hang on." She jammed a thick wad of disposable bathroom cloth in her crotch and cleaned up as best she could.

Back in the bedroom, she shook her head at the young consort. "Murphy's Law. I started my period."

"Eww." Colt jumped off the bed as if she had popped and deflated his nervous excitement like an enormous soap bubble. "We aren't expected to go through with it now, are we?" He held up the envelope he'd found on the bed.

"Hell, no—I don't care what the rules are, that ain't gonna happen." She snatched the envelope from him, ripped it open, and skimmed over the letter inside. "It says I'm supposed to live here, and you are to visit daily or nightly for sexual intercourse. The upper loft is for you if you stay overnight. But what's the point if we have to wait? I need to go home and change, so I might as well hit the sack while I'm at it." Along with the cramps, dizziness from the wine she'd imbibed made her long to lie down.

Colt made a hesitant step toward her and squeezed her hand. "So, I'll see you in about—"

"Five or six days," she finished for him. "I'll let you know."

He couldn't get away from her fast enough, she noticed.

She cursed her dumb luck and scurried home. How silly of her, expecting to put this behind her tonight.

A separate part of her, though, rejoiced in the reprieve.

Back at the dorm, she went to Shyla's wing to make sure she'd done her homework. She found the girl crying on her bed, inconsolable. She asked the other girls in her room to give them some privacy.

Kat sat on the bed and rubbed her shoulder. "What's the matter?"

The girl sobbed, trying to catch her breath. "It's our Thunder. He's dead!" She fell into her mentor's open arms.

Kat caught the contagion of her ward's grief. Her eyes misted over as they hugged, but she blinked it away. "Let's go out to the common room and talk about it." She wrapped her arm around the weeping girl and guided her out of the bedroom.

In the common room, Shyla told her she'd gone to the stable after Circle to treat the horses to a carrot apiece. Grace had accompanied her. When they got there, they'd found Thunder lying in his stall. Shyla had tried to coax him up, but he hadn't budged. Grace then opened his stall and confirmed the worst. She'd told Shyla he'd probably died in his sleep.

Kat knew the old horse's appetite had flagged in the past year and he'd lost weight. His death might have resulted from cancer or a gastrointestinal condition. Caleb had mentioned in August they would need to euthanize him soon, as a horse of twenty-seven years old could not be treated successfully. She tried to relay this to the girl as gently as she could.

"At least he's not in pain anymore," Shyla said, sounding mature beyond her years as she dried her tears in her nightshirt sleeve and walked back to her room with Kat. "And we still have Joy and Pippa."

"That's right. We'll have new horses too, one day soon. Try to think about that."

Shyla's chin trembled as she forced a brittle laugh. "I don't know why I'm so upset—I didn't even know Thunder that long."

Back in her own wing, Kat held it in until she made it to a shower stall. She stood under the stream of water until she'd cried herself empty. She'd known the dapple-grey horse all her life and couldn't picture Wild Cove without him.

CHAPTER SIXTEEN

As the lone student in the nondescript classroom, he sat at a student desk in the front row, his right ankle—his good one—chained and fastened to the desk leg. Light-grey shiplap walls surrounded him, with a wide blackboard at the front, three half-open windows to the left that nearly reached the ceiling, and a rear wall covered with a faded world map and a poster of the solar system. Five rows of simple wooden desks filled the room, facing a teacher's desk laden with a stack of heavy textbooks, most with cracked spines, a three-ring binder, a pot of ink, and an assortment of writing instruments in a widemouthed mug. An ancient brass bell stood next to the binder.

The consort teacher, slim, handsome and about his own age, introduced himself as Reggie. He told Marcus his education and intelligence level needed to be assessed in comparison with the other peons.

He leaned on the edge of the desk, selected a book, and opened it with a professional air of detachment. "We're fortunate to have the classroom to ourselves today. The younger boys are on a field trip. Have you ever taken an I.Q. test?"

"Nope."

"You have learned mathematics?"

Marcus nodded. "My mother taught me the basics when I was a kid." Oddly, the memory of his murdered mother didn't hurt quite as much as before.

"Ah. Homeschooled, eh? What other subjects were you taught?"

He yawned, his eyelids heavy. He'd slept well the last couple of nights. Still, he found himself drowsy at times throughout the day. The drowsiness was not unpleasant. Soothed, dreamy and more relaxed, he also noticed he felt healthier since living among the peons. He attributed the improvement to the sudden abundance of wholesome, delicious food he now scarfed down three times a day. He speculated on what would be served for lunch later, then promptly berated himself for his selfishness.

"We covered the basics: reading, writing, geography, world history and social studies. And a smidgen of basic French. Some of the sciences too."

"Excellent. We'll get you underway with a series of multiple-choice questions. Each question has four possible answers. I can provide paper and pencil to help you if necessary, but you are to answer orally. Are you ready?"

"Ready as I'll ever be," Marcus said. "I'll give it a go without paper and pencil."

"Very well. We'll lead off with math. I'll read a sequence of numbers. It is your job to determine the pattern they follow and tell me what number is next in each sequence."

He had little trouble answering correctly for each sequence. Growing up, he'd passed all the math tests his mother had given him, before she was taken from them. Their aunt had taught the rest of his and Trent's schooling.

With the series of questions and answers completed, Reggie selected another book from his desk.

"Well done, Marcus. You're obviously a bright guy. Next, let's see how you do with logical reasoning. I have ten problems to read to you, and you are to answer with the most favorable solution. Number one..."

* * *

With the I.Q. test, an E.Q. test, and science and geography quizzes completed by noon, they broke for lunch. Reggie rang the teacher's bell to summon the peon outside, who escorted Marcus back to their mess hall. Bryce had told him at breakfast that starting today, he'd no longer eat or sleep alone but would share the peon quarters with the rest of them. His integration also extended to physical skills exercises as well as afternoon lecture and study sessions with the other recruits. If all went as planned over the coming days, Bryce added, they'd take off his ankle restraint permanently, but the recruitment exercises would progress under constant supervision.

He accepted the steaming bowl from the elderly peon ladling out the food. The old man grinned at Marcus. "Here, stuff dat in yer gob. You need to put some meat on dem bones."

Under close guard, he ate his meal of chicken and vegetable stew at a picnic table with the teenaged recruits. They all wore the dark-green, peon-in-training issue. He devoured the savory stew with three wedges of cornbread and asked for another bowl. As with each meal they had served him so far, a flask of the tasty, fruit-flavoured beverage topped it off.

Right away, he noticed the non-recruits and older peons at the other tables. They drank from mugs instead of flasks. He arrived at the conclusion that the fruity drinks were served to recruits because they needed more calorie intake for their strenuous physical training and workouts.

Or had a more potent ingredient been added to the drink? He

finished his second bowl of the tasty stew and stared at his flask with a dubious eye.

After lunch, the peon guard brought him and the other students to a cramped, rudimentary library attached to the back of the boys' schoolhouse. Two walls of shelves were jammed with books from floor to ceiling. Three upholstered armchairs and a cracked leather couch occupied half the room. When they sat around the table near the window, the guard once again fastened Marcus's ankle chain to the furniture. The other recruits studied him with open curiosity. Several whispered.

A different consort, fortyish with a scarlet brush cut and a wildly prominent overbite, swept into the library and introduced himself as Jeremy.

"Greetings, young men." On the end of the table he placed an earthenware mug with his name painted on it, next to a world globe that had seen better days. He beamed a toothy welcome in Marcus's direction. "Your classroom is being used today for the younger boys to write exams, so we've taken the library this afternoon. Normally we'd pick up with our lecture from the World Cultures curriculum, but because we have a new student joining us, we'll put it on hold for now. Instead, we will review the Great Collapse to bring our new student up to speed. We will also summarize our local origins: a look back on the Old-World Newfoundland and Labrador history. For tomorrow's class, we'll take a comprehensive overview of our more recent New World history and how we arrived where we are today."

A collective groan filled the room.

"But sir, we were getting to the best part." A heavy-set youth with beefy arms and bad acne glared at Marcus, clearly blaming him for the change in lesson plan. "Last time you told us we'd learn more about cannibalism. No fair!"

Marcus recognized the youth at once as one of the peons who'd captured him.

THE WOMEN OF WILD COVE

"Mind your monstrous appetite, Rory!" put in the boy next to Marcus. "Hmm...should we be forewarned?"

The other students erupted in peals of laughter.

"Alright, boys, that's enough," Jeremy said. He gave Marcus a couple of sheets of paper and a charcoal pencil. "These are condensed lectures only. We'll get back to the cannibals the class after next, Rory, I promise. Feel free to take notes, Marcus."

He grunted to show his indifference, but soon grew absorbed in the consort's lecture.

"Decisions made by the majority of world governments— chiefly and historically led by male leaders since time immemorial —have resulted in widespread and relentless aggression, destruction and disaster. Because of inadequate policies and mismanagement of key issues, because of divisiveness, warmongering and greed, and due to the gross negligence of ignoring world-wide environmental crises which confronted us all, these leaders have brought the world close to complete annihilation."

Growing more animated, Jeremy paced the floor in front of his pupils. "Global warming came first. Some experts believed we could have done little to prevent it and its effects, while others blamed its rapid acceleration on over-industrialization and ignorance. The rainforests had been nearly destroyed. The oceans became highly acidic, choking shorelines with seagrass and kelp and affecting numerous species of marine life. Floods devastated many areas while drought and wildfires destroyed others, driving entire populations to northern regions.

"The cautionary signs were there for decades. Mother Earth was in peril. If those signs had been acted upon at the outset, the fallout may have been reversed and avoided. But the warnings were dismissed because of money and the unquenchable thirst for power and control. The downward spiral persisted."

"We were in plenty of trouble here earlier than that," another boy interjected. Jeremy gave a thumbs up. "You're correct, Howard.

Prior to the global floods, fires and famine, our island along with Labrador had already lost much of its valuable natural resources to climate change. The northern cod, lobster and snow crab stocks had all but vanished due to ocean acidification, but with the economic crumbling of foreign markets, the commercial fishery was doomed anyway. The long-lived industry ended. Next, the oil industry foundered when prices plummeted due to worldwide overproduction and surplus. So yes, your point is well taken.

"Scientists back in the 2010's asserted Canada was warming up twice as fast as the rest of the world, and they've been proven correct. Although this spelled disaster for most of the country, one study prediction proved true: certain areas of the globe would benefit from climate change. As it turned out, that prediction included us here on our little rock in the North Atlantic, doubtlessly due to the melting of the Greenland ice sheet which keeps our waters relatively cool. Since then, the island has experienced a drastic evolution from when we were known as the easternmost province of Canada." He walked to the window and threw up the sash. A light breeze wafted in, cooling the stuffy library.

"Our new temperate climate was ideal back in 2059 when we won our independence from Canada and established ourselves as a sovereign state. Our government came up with the brilliant business proposition to convert the island into a year-round vacation resort. Fogo Island, our largest offshore island since lost to sea level rise, made it happen in the 2020's. Using their success as a model, those in power forged ahead.

"For years, Newfoundland enjoyed unprecedented prosperity as a renowned and lucrative cruise-ship and escape destination with its picturesque resort villages, state-of-the-art vacation chalets, new marinas, and of course its rare, idyllic weather compared to the rest of the continent. Sadly, the government in power barely paid lip service to conservation stewardship. Protection of plant and animal life did not take priority as it should have. Who can tell me what did?"

"Making gobs of money," Rory said, "off the scores of wealthy clientele flying in from every corner of the earth. Greed took over."

Jeremy nodded. "Exactly. They commercialized the bucolic model of our culture and sold us out for the almighty dollar. Tourism became a gold mine, catering to the world's rich and elite. Vacation homes, inns and travel packages were booked up months in advance and the government coffers overflowed with profits. With the revenues, they replaced existing infrastructure with new, geared toward making the island even more attractive to tourists.

"As money poured in, multiple greenhouse construction became the next major project. Along with new farms and orchards, the greenhouses guaranteed we would have food aplenty year-round."

He sauntered back to the table and spun the faded globe absentmindedly. "Unfortunately, nothing can live for long in a bubble. The rest of the world's economy had tanked. Cruise lines and airlines went out of business. Tourism revenue diminished as, one by one, the niches of rich customers with their private jets declared bankruptcy, found other refuge, died, or were murdered by the have-nots. Outsiders began to invade our shores, trying to stay here for nothing. This initiated fortification of the entire perimeter of the island. More lighthouses and lookouts were built with heavily-armed security."

Marcus held up his hand. "That security is no longer the case, though, is it?"

Jeremy's bristled hair glowed, burnished a deeper red by the afternoon sun streaming through the library window. "We haven't felt the need to keep our lookouts strictly occupied like we used to. It's been a long time since we've had invaders or outsiders—until you showed up, that is."

"Doesn't mean others aren't out there," Rory put in. "Am I right, Mr. Rogue?"

"We'll call Marcus by his real name from now on, boys." Jeremy hurled Rory a stern look. "Now, let's revisit the world scene during pre-collapse. Ahead of the economic downturn, the blatant call came from major government players to divide and conquer. With it—and despite the strides made in the promotion of peace, unity, and equality—a horrifying reverse trend took hold. Xenophobia, homophobia and misogyny experienced a revival. Racism thrived, and extremism and terrorism took a dramatic upswing. This unrest became the front and centre issue for years in virtually every country.

"Division between nations escalated. Vital ecological concerns were ignored and our physical world suffered. Heavy reliance on fossil fuels amplified the greenhouse effect. The consequences? Vast regions of the southern hemisphere became uninhabitable. Many perished from heat stress or from drinking contaminated water. Uncontrollable fires destroyed entire forests while sea rise permanently flooded countless coastlines." He strode back to the table and took a long drink from his mug.

"Thus, the chronic mass influx of illegal immigrants to the north. This overcrowding into the northern hemisphere gave rise to the Eurasian and North American wars, which led to total economic, industrial and technological breakdown, and extensive loss of life across those continents.

"Malnutrition and poverty abounded. Deadly pandemics broke out. Any human and animal who'd managed to survive the wars, the disease, the ravages of the collapse and the aftershock migrated even farther north to stay alive." He gestured to Marcus. "It appears this included your predecessors."

"The result is the life we know today: a more primeval culture with an inability to rebuild to its former status. For valid reasons—

with the need for population growth aside—our elders prefer it this way." Jeremy paused. "Any questions?"

"I have one."

All attention swung to Marcus.

"The floor is yours," Jeremy said.

"From what you've said and what I've witnessed up to now, I get how the governing system is successful here. What puzzles me, though, is why the men don't revolt. Has there ever been any push-back? Why is it that the peons and consorts don't simply take over and demand to lead, or at the very least, demand to share in the leadership?"

Jeremy paused, looking thoughtful. "Before I respond to your question, I have one for you. Did you know matriarchal societies are nothing new? Granted, there were few, but female supremacy was not uncommon in the past. In ancient times, women ruled much of Northern Europe and the Mediterranean. Crete had been ruled by women for much of the Bronze Age. China has had a history of matrilineal systems, where ancestral descent is traced through maternal instead of paternal lines. Pre-Incan Peru was matriarchal."

"I didn't know there were that many," Marcus admitted.

"Many Native American tribes, too, had been matrilineal, some matriarchal. My point is these types of governments can work. In times of great change, upheaval and disaster, the world particularly needs more female leadership—sustainable and peace-loving societies that work cooperatively with nature. It's a necessity of our times, in my opinion."

"But does it make your male population feel powerless, even unworthy?"

"Marcus, I have confidence in our administration and great respect for the elders. And we as consorts and peons are given care and respect in return." The consort halted his pacing by Marcus's desk. "Are you aware of the corresponding mentorship that exists for the boys on this side of Wild Cove? Their dormitory and schoolhouse are behind the peon and consort quarters, albeit with more rigid supervision, the same as they are in our other villages. So as you can appreciate, the elders do care about the upbringing of all the island's children, not only the girls." He crossed his arms in front of Marcus as if to challenge him. "I trust these leaders to make the right decisions. Decisions and policies to afford both genders satisfying and fulfilling futures. Why would we or anyone revolt against that?"

* * *

When Jeremy concluded his lecture, a stooped, elderly man escorted Marcus to his new dorm sleeping quarters inside the peon compound. The modest room was void of any furniture besides the row of four wood-frame bunks with a crate footlocker at each. It smelled of pine, oiled leather and lye soap. Two screened and shuttered windows overlooked the bunks. Utilitarian accommodations, but far superior to the hovel of a room he'd slept in up until now.

His bed, identical to the others, had a firm but comfortable mattress, a feather pillow, and a blue and grey patchwork quilt. Inside the footlocker he found two more shifts of peon-recruit clothing and underwear, soap, two towels, and other toiletry items.

"This way," the senior peon said in a gravelly voice. He shuffled out of the bedroom, leading Marcus across the hall to the communal lavatory, complete with a pair each of urinals, commodes, shower stalls, and wash basins with hand pumps and ancient, smudged mirrors.

"The common area is down past the mess hall." The old man squinted up at him with watery blue eyes. "I can show it to you now if you like, before we go eat."

He asked if he could shave first. The peon agreed and called for backup. A man his own age quickly joined them. He held the chain to the ankle restraint and watched over Marcus as he shaved at a wash basin.

At supper, he lined up with the others, holding his plate. A senior peon had removed his restraint and stood guard at the door. The peon named Caleb dished out everyone's share of mutton from a roaster and an assortment of steaming vegetables from a blackened tureen. Sourdough bread waited in straw baskets on their tables.

He sat down to eat and slathered two of the fragrant slabs of bread with thick layers of butter. As he bit into one, another flask of the mystery drink materialized. He ignored it.

He saw Caleb study him as he chewed his meat and stabbed at his carrots. The peon came forward and picked up his flask.

"You haven't drunk your Assimil-Lixir." He held it under Marcus's nose. "Down the hatch. Now."

Assimil-Lixir. That's what they called it? Because of the gradual adjustment in his general attitude since his capture, he'd wondered if they drugged him by some means, and now he knew for sure. Was this how the elders kept every single man in line? He stared at the peons as he swallowed another morsel of mutton. They were like sheep too, as were the consorts, apparently, never complaining or thinking twice about their governance. He beheld the flask in Caleb's hand with new contempt.

But he could not draw suspicion or create a scene. He accepted it and took a swig.

Whenever Caleb glanced in his direction, he lifted the drink to his mouth and faked a few sips. At one point when the teen alongside him turned to chat with his friend, he made a bold move. With the peon also distracted for a moment, he switched his flask with the youth's near-empty one.

After three days in custody, he had devised a strategy. He swapped his flask for empty ones or dumped it on the sly. He noticed the older peons drinking the elixir at breakfast only. If he managed to trick his captors and keep his dosage down to one a day instead of the prescribed three, he could control this so-called assimilation. Easier said than done. Unexpectedly, curbing use of the elixir took enormous willpower because he found its effects pleasant and addictive.

It was a struggle not to succumb to the beauty of his new habitat, the daily indoctrination, and to the effects of the mystery concoction, but not impossible. Submission to the wishes of the peons, the elders, and the spell the island had cast over him could be likened to the ease of slipping into a warm, protective cocoon, or yielding to the intoxicating comfort of a lover's embrace.

He understood how their methods might succeed on someone with no other agenda beyond integration and island citizenry, but he could never lose sight of his crucial purpose. He would not let them brainwash him. He had to get his hands on the medicine. He had to enlist Kat to help him carry it out.

First, he must convince her of his successful integration. But how long could he afford to wait? If he acted now and appealed to her sense of humanity and compassion, might she agree to help anyway? Wouldn't she want to save his sick little boy too?

CHAPTER SEVENTEEN

With the nursery stint behind her, Kat had three new internships to choose from: textile and outfitter apprentice, clinic assistant, or food management trainee.

She accepted the clinic assistant internship. She chose it partly because the biology aspect of it appealed to her, but mostly it allowed her to work alone more than the other selections would. Depending on how long it took her to conceive, the new half-day assignment might last anywhere from six to eight weeks to two years. Ms. Eleanor informed her she would begin her orientation on Monday afternoon.

Apart from the new job, her duties outside of sexual intercourse—her initiation on hold for a few more days due to her own biology—still included mentoring Shyla.

At dawn the next day, she took her ward to Black Spruce Forest to check snares, gather chanterelle mushrooms, and to pick medicinal teaberries and evening primrose. The girl was subdued. Dear old Thunder was still on her mind, Kat guessed.

As soon as they arrived, she brought up the changes in schedule with her ward, including the end of nursery duty which opened up entire mornings to themselves. She saw at once how the news brightened Shyla's world, relieved she'd no longer assist with babies, toddlers and domestic work. On their way back from the forest, she was rife with suggestions on how to spend the remainder of their free half-day.

"Why don't we go for a swim at the pond, or better yet, in the beach tidal pool? June and Ruby swam there last week and they—"

Kat fought against the swell of irritation in her gut. "Forget swimming, will you?"

Shyla's face dropped. "Why are you mad at me? It's not my fault you have to be a breeder! And why do you hate swimming so much?"

"I'm sorry for shouting at you, Shyla, I really am. And I hope you aren't upset with me again." Kat sighed. "I don't hate swimming—we'll go another time."

The teen recovered quickly from the outburst. "Let's go out on the water, then. Ms. Jaleena says the skipjack tuna are back this week. We might even spot a cat-shark or two. Think they're dangerous? Have you ever seen one?"

"No, not yet. The sharks our fishers have seen were scarcely a foot long, so you needn't worry too much about them. Maybe we can go later when the wind dies out. Too choppy out there now." She fell silent at the mess hall where they dropped off the rabbits and their baskets of mushrooms. "I have another suggestion. After we take these berries and primroses to the clinic, why don't we see how the rogue is managing?"

"Sure," Shyla answered as she clasped her mentor's hand.

Kat pulled it from her with a jerk. "Don't you remember what I told you about handholding?"

"Yeah." The girl's lips tugged into a defiant pout. "We shouldn't become too attached to each other. No one is more important than anyone else. For the good of the village. For the welfare of our people. Blah, blah, blah. But why the heck not? I've noticed how you've attached yourself to the rogue!"

Why the heck not indeed. The memorized precepts sprung from her lips anyway. "Listen up. I'm not attached to a rogue, a peon, *or* a consort. Nor any man. Remember that. And I'm sure I already told you this. We're free to like each other, but no playing favourites, no displays of affection that single one another out and create jealousy and rivalry. We are sisters and equals."

Little Quinn had acted as if the precept meant her sister-guide didn't like her, but Kat considered Shyla mature enough to know the difference. She didn't speak of how too much fondness between them could carry a heavy price. She winced from the familiar stab, the persistent thorn in her heart.

After they dropped off their woodland pickings, they headed to the peon compound. "Come on, I'll race you!" Kat sprinted down the dirt road while Shyla trailed close behind.

Catching their breath as they neared the exercise yard, they both saw the rogue at the same time. Again, his new groomed appearance confused and flustered Kat. His clean shave not only made him look youthful, but more appealing.

Outside the yard, Marcus, two teen peons-in-training and a senior peon with a tanned bald head and faded arm tattoos stood on the sidelines as a third teenager climbed a rope that hung over the high fence. The youth made it to the top with ease, clambered over, and rejoined the group through the open gates.

The peon instructor waved Marcus over next. Kat noticed his chain restraint was gone. With no hesitation and ankle still wrapped, he grabbed onto the rope. He pulled himself up, planting his feet on the fence planks.

As he scaled the fence wall, a warmth flowed over her skin. With his long hair gone, the defined curve of his jaw and the flexed muscles in his neck and shoulders were more visible. The way he propelled his lean body to complete his ascent, then rested atop the fence to dry sweat from his hands on his trousers before descending on the other side...

This reaction to a member of the opposite sex was foreign to her—an odd and alarming excitement she had no name for. Just when she thought she knew her sexuality inside out. She squelched the bewildering sensation and turned her back to Marcus as he rejoined the trainees. Maybe Shyla had been right after all.

Screw this. Why hadn't any of the consorts from the meet-and-greet stirred her that way?

A scrawnier youth stepped forward to take the rope next, but had trouble pulling himself up. The instructor strode over to help him.

Kat edged closer to Marcus while Shyla watched the youth struggle. "How are they treating you?" she whispered. "Your leg is much better, I see."

"Could be worse, I guess. And yes, the ankle is coming along well. But listen—we need to talk."

"I know. How long will your integration take?"

"Nobody's telling me. I'm the first adult to ever go through it under your elders, so it's a learning process for your people too."

They observed as the youth climbed halfway up the wall and slid to the ground with a yelp, his hands bloodied from the friction on the rope. His instructor tugged strips of cloth from his waist pocket, wound them around the teenager's hands, and ordered him to give it another go.

Still wearing a grimace from his wounds, the lad pulled himself up again.

"I better get out of here."

"Wait." Marcus stepped closer and out of earshot from her ward, who watched with amused interest as the lad slid down the rough rope the second time. "I'm due at your clinic for a follow-up round of immunization after this exercise. Any way you can meet me there under some pretext?"

After a moment of indecision, she told him she'd try. She could show up there under a guise of curiosity about Monday's orientation. She waved to Shyla and signalled her to follow.

"I don't see that poor squirt as peon material," her ward said on their way to see the horses.

"Neither do I, but this is how they weed them out. If he fails basic training, the elders will find a use for his talents in another capacity."

In lieu of lunch, Kat snatched a plum and a hunk of cheese from the central kitchen and hurried to the clinic. She met a familiar consort at the front desk, dipping his pen in an inkwell and scratching numbers on the chart in front of him. Darned if it wasn't the sweet-looking boy who paired off with Falon at the meet-and-greet. She checked his official nametag.

"Hello, Robby."

He squinted up at her. "May I help you, miss...?"

"The name's Kat. I start orientation here on—"

"Monday," he interjected, his voice crisp. "Not today. Or did I not get the update?"

"I'd like permission to take a gander around. Get my bearings for next week."

The consort drummed his fingers on his desk. "I don't believe it's permitted without an escort. I'm the new assistant, and this is my first week since I finished my own orientation. Please have a seat. I'll check with the doctor."

When he left, the door opened and Bryce walked in with Marcus. The rogue was no longer collared, tethered or restrained by the ankle or otherwise, which calmed her. Bryce's eyebrows lifted when he saw her but he remained tight-lipped as the two of them walked down the corridor.

She seized her chance before Robby reappeared. Creeping

down the corridor at a safe distance, she saw Bryce lead Marcus through a door marked Examination Room 2 on the right side of the corridor. She crouched behind a laundry trolley and waited.

Another consort in a white lab coat walked with purpose up the long corridor, entering the same room. Kat peeked out and held her breath as Bryce left the room, lumbered past her, and exited the clinic.

Now what? Afraid Robby would come back and catch her, she pulled a lightly-soiled peon housekeeping tunic from the trolley and slipped it on. She stole down the hall with her head low and entered the empty examination room marked with a 3, next to the one where Marcus waited. She left the door open an inch to spy through.

Robby scurried past on his way back to the front desk. No doubt he was trying to figure out what had happened to her, but she couldn't concern herself with him. Her heart thrummed in her chest at the prospect of being discovered. Behind the closed door of Room 2, voices murmured. The consort exited and left, but she still heard Marcus talking to someone. Must be the doctor, she thought. *What the hell am I doing here?*

She froze at the sound of voices.

"...give you a quick physical exam in the next room, get you weighed, and give you your shot. Go in there and undress, and I'll come back in a few minutes."

"Whatever you say, doc."

Kat dropped to the floor and slid under the desk across from the examination table and the physician's weigh scales. She listened as the door creaked open and closed.

When she peeked out from under the desk, she saw Marcus remove his green shirt and pants. When he'd stripped naked, his body instantly aroused her. Her own body reacted, flooding her with an exquisite warmth from her groin all the way up to her neck.

She stuck her head out. "It's me," she whispered.

"Good lord!" Red-faced, he covered his genitals with his hands.

"You did want to talk to me." She averted her eyes while he lunged for a sheet to cover himself.

"Yes, about that. I have a confession to make, Kat. As much as I hate to admit it—being captured and all—you and your people have made such great strides here. Your elders deserve a lot of credit for their organization and its philosophy. I've come to respect their point of view and to appreciate your way of life. I find it all so intriguing."

"For real?"

"With no outside help *or* interference, you've realized a means of not merely subsistence, but peace and productivity. It's fantastic what you've achieved, and I'd like to be a part of it."

"You sound as if you no longer care to leave." She gave a little chortle.

"But here's the deal. I don't think I do!"

"Are you shitting me?"

"What do I have to go back to? A desolate land with nothing to live for, the grim memories of losing my fam...my parents, my grandparents, and my home? Would you wish to go back to such a life?"

"Well, no. But are you prepared to sacrifice your independence to become a peon? Or a consort?"

"There are far worse stations in life. I mean, what's wrong with the pursuit of good, old-fashioned honest work, and to be needed to help grow such a resourceful society?"

"So, you see yourself content in the role of either one?"

"When I consider the alternative of going back to that hard, lonely life, I'd be nuts not to cooperate with your people. I'd have a new purpose and I'd get to share in the countless comforts you take for granted. The wholesome food you grow and catch here, the healthy and lush environment, the camaraderie—it's a no-brainer."

She nodded slowly. "When you put it that way, it *is* a no-brainer."

"Besides that, you have medicine here. Do you realize how rare meds are where I come from?"

She paused. Should she be discussing this with him? "Yes, we have Immunity-2, but we'll run out if a new source of the extract isn't identified soon. Wait—do you mean you no longer need my help? What about the relatives you've left behind?"

He seemed to deliberate on his reply before answering. She thought it odd how relaxed he was today and not apprehensive about his plight. How had he accepted his fate this quickly? Were the effects of undergoing assimilation already obvious?

"I'll mention a rescue of what's left of them once I'm integrated as a reliable citizen and in a better position to make it happen. But there's something I need to ask you—"

They both heard a door close in the corridor.

"I have to get out of here." She crawled out from under the desk and bolted to the door.

"Can we talk again soon?"

"Sure." She withdrew from the room, pulled off the house-keeping tunic, and flicked it back in the trolley as she fled. She rounded the corner without anyone seeing her.

Robby sat at the front desk. He shot to his feet and glared at her. "Where did you go? You were told to wait!"

"Relax, Robby," she threw over her shoulder as she left. "It's all good. See ya on Monday."

* * *

"I hate you," the little girl cried. Water dripped down her forehead from her soaked blond curls, joining the tears that coursed down her cheeks. "You're a bad person and a horrible sister-guide!"

"Don't be such a sook and quit the snotting and bawling. You're melodramatic about everything."

The girl vanished.

"Kat...Katrena..."

"Please, Wren, don't leave me here. I'll be better, I promise. Please come back!"

"Why would I, Katrena? You don't listen to a word I say lately. You disobey me and you're always taking off by yourself. Something awful could happen to you in the woods and you'll be gone forever. And I would get the blame."

"No, Wren, come back. I promise I won't let you down anymore. Please don't hate me. I'm not a bad girl!"

"Kat..."

"Where are you...don't hide from me, please..."

"Kat. Wake up."

Someone was shaking her by the shoulders. She woke up to Falon hovering over her.

"Must've been one ghastly nightmare." She sat on the edge of the bed. "Care to share?"

She quickly turned away. "Nothing but a dumb dream. You know how they are. No rhyme or reason to them. Go back to sleep."

CHAPTER EIGHTEEN

The week marched past for Marcus, his waking hours filled with a bustle of activity: strenuous physical conditioning, chore duty training with the younger recruits, and classroom information sessions on everything he needed to know about island life. He learned all inhabited villages were coastally located, as it was too hot in the interior to thrive, or even survive, comfortably. Because of this, the water taxi system had been adopted as the main source of transportation from village to village.

He listened to lectures on the local customs, mores and taboos. He was further briefed on the philosophy of the matriarchal administration and the finer principles of It Takes a Village. He learned of the new age of enrolment for breeding and particularly wondered what Kat thought of it.

Time was flying much too fast. As each day ended, he worried over what was happening at Minipi Lake. He had to get back there with medicine before Trent came searching for him. They had agreed he would wait three weeks, and though half of that remained, he hated to think what might happen if his brother ever stepped foot on the island.

They gave him back his boots. His ankle had healed, he felt strong in his arms and his back, and he'd gained much-needed weight. At breakfast, Bryce announced the time had come to harvest all remaining crops as quickly as possible. They needed every able body to pick, gather and store the essential food to get them through the dormant months of winter. He assigned Marcus and the other recruits to work in the cornfields after their morning workout.

He had already helped harvest the orchards of its apples, pears, plums, nectarines and wild black cherries. Most berries had been picked and were already jammed or pickled, and the women tended to the greenhouses year-round for their yield of tomatoes, lettuce, spinach, onions, sweet peppers, and a variety of culinary herbs.

Grains such as oats and wheat were grown on other village farms, Marcus had learned, and as part of the Harvest Festival held annually at Grand Lake, growers from around the island traded with each other, bartering with their surplus of grains and produce so each village had ample shares of what was needed. They also traded meat. Farms that raised pigs and turkeys came to trade their surplus for salt fish of various species and quarters of beef.

The peons left him and the others to their weight-training routine in the exercise yard. Kat came to see him again, announcing herself with a low whistle through the hatch in the fence. Her inexplicable interest in him was apparent, though he noticed she tried not to let it show too much to the others. That interest was already working to his advantage. He dropped his dumbbells and walked over to her. He could see only her forehead and eyes through the aperture.

She commented on his healthier appearance and asked again if he'd truly accepted his new life. Her question told him she still clung to doubts over his sincerity. Going forward, he needed to work harder to gain her confidence. Time was of the essence.

"I understand it isn't your goal to restore your world to the way it once was," he told her. "What you already know and I've come to realize is the answer to the survival of the natural world and humanity is not to attempt a renewal of industrialization and superfluous technology. This appears impossible anyway. Many of those advances helped to land the planet in the shocking mess it found itself in."

"By golly, I think he's got it." Her eyes crinkled at the corners. "Pure common sense if you ask me. Then you'll become a peon?"

"They are grooming me as one." He flexed and unflexed his hands, his fingers stiff from lifting weights. "I'm up to speed already on most of their responsibilities."

"In that case, you must be helping with the harvest today."

"I'm headed to the cornfields shortly. It feels great to contribute, to have a purpose. And no more shackles! I suppose they realize I'm no longer a flight risk." Privately, he congratulated himself. His scheme to fool the peons into believing he'd been naturalized, and so rapidly, was working. "But I am curious about something I didn't get a chance to ask you at the clinic."

"Fire away."

"I have an adequate sense of all peon duties, but they haven't told me what I assume the consorts are for."

"I guess they'll cover the subject soon as a part of your integration," she said. "What is your assumption?"

"They're used for one essential purpose. Their fertility."

The girl didn't answer.

"That's it, isn't it? It must be."

"It's a key part of their purpose, yes. But they're also employed for their intelligence and abilities in skilled areas that don't require physical fortitude. For instance, medical research studies as well as ecological and agricultural studies. They carry out practical research too, for the betterment of our way of life, such as construction of larger generators, solar panels and better plumbing."

"How much autonomy are they given?"

"None. The elders approve, direct and supervise each activity every step of the way."

Marcus chuckled. "You sound highly well-versed about the goings-on here. Are you the exception, or is every girl your age a Miss Know-it-all?"

She dipped her head. "Some of us pick up details sooner than others... more or less."

He thought about her imminent role as a breeder. "Here's another question for you. How do you feel about being expected to procreate at your age?"

Through the hatch in the fence, a blank stare. "I'm not exactly doing cartwheels about it."

"I get that. By the way, am I correct to assume peons don't do any of the procreating?"

"To father offspring? I don't believe so. The question hadn't occurred to me."

Now it seemed to weigh on both their minds.

"Strikes me as unfair to deprive those guys of female, uh, companionship, for lack of a better word."

"I agree. But let me put that particular worry to rest." She dropped her voice to a whisper. "The peons play another role."

"Which is?"

"They fulfill the needs of other women in our society."

"You mean...your elders and teachers?"

"I don't know who specifically." She picked at a loose splinter in the aperture and peeled it off. "Some women take peons to their beds after hours, I hear, but they're discreet about it and they don't cohabitate. We will always remain segregated. Women who have fulfilled their breeding contracts or who've moved beyond child-bearing age use them too. Still, others have no interest in men for that purpose whatsoever. To put it simply, the consorts are for procreation whereas the peons are, for lack of a better word, for recreation."

"Oh, really? Simply another job for us peons, eh? Apart from your elders, do all the women of the island live in dorms like the men?"

"No, our dorms are for sister-guides, wards, and primary school-girls, plus two live-in dorm nannies who take care of the littlest ones. Nola and Yvonne live at the nursery, and the rest of the women live in the homes you see scattered around the cove. Every village is set up this way, more or less."

Marcus tried to wrap his mind around this new information. He puzzled briefly about a peon having the right to refuse a woman he didn't find attractive. Most likely not, if they had so few rights to start with. All academic, anyway—he wouldn't be sticking around to find out. "Then, the chosen peons are invited to these homes when needed?"

"So I understand."

He grinned. "And here I was, under the impression the older women lived like nuns."

"What are nuns?"

"Kat, you're so knowledgeable, I'm amazed you're not familiar with the term!"

She let out an uneasy laugh. "Gonna tell me or not?"

"They're women of a religious order or church who take vows of chastity and poverty, and obedience to their spiritual beliefs."

"Ah. That's why I didn't know. We haven't been taught much about traditional faiths."

"Oh? Do none of you believe in a supreme being?"

Her voice took on a patient, pragmatic tone. "We've been taught to believe in a Mother of Nature and the Golden Rule. We care for and respect the environment and each other. But traditional religion as you know it, no. Our elders say many of these ancient belief systems can be dangerous because they promote intolerance and fanaticism. There have been more wars, bloodshed and death because of religious groups than from any other cause. Not to mention how many of their beliefs contradict hard science."

"Hmmm. Good point." Marcus heard the peons coming to get him. "Time to hit the fields. You better go. Is it tomorrow you start your job at the medical clinic?"

"Yes," she whispered. She shut the little hatch in his face and vanished from his life once again.

* * *

"Marc?"

"Yes, Ava?"

"When will you come back? Why have you left us? Do you still love us?"

"You know I do. How can you ask such a question? My life is dedicated to you and our son!"

"Then why don't you come home?"

"How can you call that godforsaken hell-hole a home? We need medicine for our boy and I can't come back until I find it."

"But he's getting sicker by the day. He can't recover if he doesn't get relief from the fever and cough soon."

"I realize that, dammit!"

"Do I have to spell it out? Don't forget you couldn't—"

"How could I forget? I'm doing whatever is in my power to prevent it from happening to Hudson. And I've found a lovely new home for us, away from that wretched place."

"Where? Isn't the whole world like this?"

"No, it isn't. I've discovered a wonderful island with trees and animals, and flowers and fruits and vegetables, with clean air and fresh water and plenty of other food. And lots more people are here too, who are healthy and thriving and living peaceful, productive lives."

"How can this be? Where is this marvelous place?"

"Not far, darling. It's the island of Newfoundland. And guess what? They have a cure for our son!"

"They do? Oh my God, we can save him?"

"Yes, we can save him. But I need a bit more time to get my hands on it."

A ray of hope crossed her face, but then her eyes misted over. "Hurry, Marc. If you're not back soon, I'll have to take him with me."

"Please, angel, not yet. Let him stay alive for me. I swear I can do this—then this misery ends."

She sighed. "I'm afraid, Marc. He won't eat and he's barely drinking. He's wasting away before our eyes. We're lucky if he lasts through the week."

Marcus cried out in anguish, as if his heart were clamped in a steel vise. "No! Please don't take him, Ava. I know how much you miss him, but he must stay with me. I need him. The world needs him..."

He woke up with a start. Oh, how he missed her! He missed the raw, pure energy of their union, the way they fed off each other, even during the long, hungry nights—especially during the long, hungry nights when they'd clung together for mutual comfort. He choked back a sob, realizing all over again his beautiful Ava, his soul mate and the jewel of his life, had died. Gone forever, only to visit him when he slept.

He jumped from his dormitory bed, aching with the emptiness that followed these powerful visions from his nightly dreams. The dreaded sickness had stolen his wife from him months ago, and it threatened to steal his boy next. He knew why she haunted him.

Though he needed no reminders, her visits were for their child's sake.

Today, Kat had been more receptive to him than ever. Time was running out, but before it did, he needed to tell her about his son.

CHAPTER NINETEEN

Her period was finished. The elders were done with postponements and ordered her back to her Origin Suite as soon as possible, for the duration of the program. They expected her to have intercourse with Colt repeatedly until she conceived. With this pervading her thoughts, Kat decided to broach the subject of Marcus to Ms. Naomi after tonight's Sundown Circle. If she waited any longer, it might be too late.

The sister-wards had practised a new campfire song at school this week. They were keen to perform it, particularly since they'd learned to sing it in three-part harmony.

Their rendition of "Harvest Bounty," as close to flawless as a glee club of little girls could attain, drew enthusiastic applause. Eleanor and Jaleena dabbed at their eyes while Ms. Bee praised the singers and their teacher for the delightful performance.

Ms. Naomi beamed with pride at the children, and her smile warmed Kat too. It bolstered her courage to broach her proposal later. And she mustn't make it sound like she favoured Marcus over any of the other males. The junior elder often listened when she made helpful suggestions about other matters. She would see her viewpoint and help make it happen.

Her recent chat with the newest peon recruit convinced her of his readiness to convert to their society. Mulling it over, she also thought of him as a possible friend. She hadn't had a close relationship with a male before, growing up and living separately from them. Unless you counted Bryce and Caleb. She'd known them her whole life.

What could be the harm in nurturing their friendship, especially if it resulted in a fruitful union?

When campfire ended and the others retired to their dorm, she sought out Ms. Naomi and asked for a word in private.

"By all means, dear. Why don't we go for a walk in the apple orchard? The night air will do us good before we turn in. I'll meet you out front in a bit."

Kat nabbed Yvonne as she left for the nursery, enlisting her to ensure Shyla went to bed on time in her absence.

"No problem," she said easily. "You can do a favour for me later on."

And I'm sure you won't take too long collecting, Kat nearly answered in reflex.

Hmm. Perhaps the time had come to cut the woman some slack. *We all have our needs and wants, now, don't we?*

The apple orchard was silent and bewitching at night with the rising moon. Around them, trees stretched in silhouettes of charcoal against a starlit sky. The muted radiance of blackberry solar lights bordered the winding path and the sweet scent of fermenting windfall apples lingered in the air. A short stroll to the heart of the orchard brought them to a glade with a garden bench. Ms. Naomi suggested they sit for a while.

The elder got straight to the point. "What is on your mind, dear?"

Hunched over, Kat took a deep breath. "This is simply a

suggestion, but would it be possible to..." She imagined how ludicrous her idea would sound out loud. She paused. "Now that I'm actually saying it, I'm almost sure you won't agree. But I hope you will."

"Agree to what? What's this about?" She laid her hand on Kat's forearm.

"This matter of getting pregnant. It's about Marcus. I realize he's being groomed as a peon, but if I pick him to become my—"

"Your consort?" Ms. Naomi pulled back her hand as if burned.

"Well, I thought we could—"

"You can't have an outsider as a consort, my dear. I shouldn't need to tell you this."

"But if he becomes integrated with us, why ever not? Why couldn't he become the exception to the rule? Or, with his unique history and set of circumstances, why not have him work as a peon *and* use him as my consort?"

The elder shook her head firmly. "Such an arrangement is impossible at this juncture."

"Please hear me out. There's another reason I propose this. I've studied biology. We're passing up a golden opportunity here to introduce new genes into our population. Why can't we approve it for the betterment of our people?"

"Because we can't take that chance yet. Kat, you're an intelligent young woman, and you raise an excellent point about gene flow. But what we are attempting with him is experimental, and it's far too premature to mate him with one of you girls. What is wrong with the consorts we have? Why do you prefer Marcus? What attracts you to him?"

"It isn't one quality in particular. Rather, more of everything in general." Her own candor surprised her. In the subdued light, a warmth spread from her neck and face up to the roots of her cropped hair. "He makes me feel alive in a way that's new to me. Colt from the meet-and-greet is satisfactory, but he doesn't compare to what..." A faint sigh escaped her lips. "I can't explain it properly. I don't know what else to say."

"It's called infatuation," Ms. Naomi said, "and not the least bit unusual. But you can't act on it. Not with Marcus or with any rogue you may ever encounter."

Kat hung her head again and fell silent.

"I need to tell you something. You remember the journal reading, The Rape."

"Well, yeah! Possibly the creepiest story we've ever heard."

"Years ago, an infiltrator sexually assaulted and murdered one of our women."

She gasped. "Oh no!" A thread of memory emerged, the one that resurrected at any mention of the rogue from before. Running through the woods with little Kat over his shoulder. The reek of his sweat and body odor, his greasy hair, the filthy rags he wore. Biting him. Scratching him. Screaming for help. "Which woman? Do I know her?"

"You were too young to be told about it. We kept it a secret from all of you children. He brutally raped her, strangled the life out of her, and left her body on our beach under a mound of kelp. The crows and gulls found her first."

"How hideous!"

The elder drew a heavy breath. "She'd disappeared while we had that other stranger from the mainland among us. He'd convinced us he'd come to the island in peace and promised his cooperation. But Bryce told Ms. Bee he'd seen the bastard talk to her a few times and had suspected him as soon as we discovered her body."

"I don't remember. Who was she? Did the man confess?"

"Yes, he made a complete confession. We'd considered an attempt at integration before the murder, but none of us could stand the sight of him after what he'd done. So we authorized Bryce and Caleb to execute him by hanging. We learned a hard lesson that year, Kat. We realized we'd been foolhardy to take in an outsider at face value. Never again will we trust a newcomer without using the Assimilation Solution. We can't risk putting your tender lives in such peril. And the mixed martial arts classes you attend? That tragedy prompted them. We initiated self-defence instruction to give each of you a fighting chance against any new rogue or, perish the thought, if one of our own men turned rogue."

"I remember the hanging."

"What?" Naomi gaped at her, eyes wide. "You saw it?"

"Bryce and Caleb didn't know, but I watched from the bushes in the woods. They put his neck in a noose and strung him up from a tree. Revolting, to watch someone die that way, and the only time our peons ever frightened me. I didn't know why at the time, but..."

Another fragment of memory bubbled up from that painful period of her life when she'd felt discarded and unloved. Her gut connected the dots.

"No." Cold disbelief washed over her. "Not Wren," she whispered in the deep hush of the night. "Please don't tell me it was my Wren this happened to!" She already knew the answer. She squeezed the young elder's arm, her fingernails digging into her flesh.

Ms. Naomi's sad face told Kat her worst fear was true.

"You lied? She didn't get a transfer? My sister-guide was raped and...*murdered?*"

Illuminated by moonlight, the elder's eyes shone with tears. "You were out in the woods on your own, collecting healing herbs. Wren went to look for you. When you came back alone, you told Ms. Eleanor and me how you bit the rogue to get away from him. Wren told you to run and hide, but you didn't see what he did to her. No one knew until much later." She reached for Kat's hand and held it in hers. "We couldn't tell you the truth or tell any of the minors about such a heinous crime. We wanted to protect you from the pain. We could only learn from the tragedy and move on. Wren saved your life the day she died. Knowing her the way I did, she would have sacrificed herself for the rogue to let you go." Ms. Naomi sighed. "That's the kind of sister-guide she was."

Kat stared at her, unblinking. Her body shivered and her teeth chattered. She clamped her jaws together to stop it. "Why didn't you tell me?" Renewed grief for her childhood mentor coursed through her. "If I hadn't let that monster catch me—"

"Another reason why we didn't reveal it. You might have blamed yourself, and that would've been too much guilt for any girl to carry."

She sat mute, sucker-punched into silence. The horrifying knowledge of Wren's violent, premature death plunged into her like the blade of a knife.

The last scrap of hope for a reunion, gone forever. She gulped for air, the shock too huge to handle.

When Ms. Naomi opened her arms, she collapsed into them and wept. All the tears for Wren she'd bottled up for far too long fell at last, soaking the elder's chest. Part of her felt betrayed by the lies she'd been fed, but she was too broken to pull away.

Her cries diminished to sobs. After a time, they too subsided.

The elder walked her back to her dorm. "Please don't tell anyone about this yet. With the issues the new outsider's presence has raised, it might be a good idea to introduce what you've learned as a cautionary tale to our journal readings."

Kat dragged herself to her bedroom, a cold, hollow ache in her chest. She hid her grief from the other girls as they readied for bed and fell asleep. She lay awake, curled into a fetal ball, tortured by Ms. Naomi's words.

Crying into her pillow, she mourned afresh for Wren, dead at the hands of that evil piece of human garbage. She'd been wrong about her sister-guide. Wren hadn't stopped loving her. She hadn't rejected her. All the reasons why she'd blamed herself had been products of her imagination. And it wasn't her fault the rogue had tried to take her. She'd only been a child, gathering herbs in the forest.

In all likelihood, that loathsome man had used her as a lure to capture Wren. He bore one hundred percent of the blame.

Still, however disturbing Naomi's disclosure, however horrendous Wren's demise must have been, she didn't see Marcus as a man they should have doubts about. She couldn't imagine him carrying out any of those atrocities.

But had she been gullible, taken in by his approachability? Could no outsider ever be trusted?

Drained, she tried to fall asleep. But when she closed her eyes, she saw poor, frightened Wren, fighting for her life until she couldn't fight anymore.

* * *

The next day she crawled out of bed, lethargic. The previous night's revelation came flooding back, leaving her woozy.

As she dressed, she resigned herself to her plight. She would pluck up her courage once more to fulfill her obligation. She'd tell Colt she'd meet him at her suite tomorrow night after martial arts class.

She met her ward for breakfast when the bell rang. The smell of toast and the usual babble of voices filled the mess hall. With no room left at the table to join Harper, Falon, and their wards, they slid into an opening across from Yvonne, Ruby, and little June. While Kat picked at her meal of sea trout and hash browns, she overheard their conversation. Ruby was regaling the nursery supervisor about her consort Reed and his insatiable sex drive, which kept her busy at her suite every night.

Yvonne bit into a forkful of trout. "You'll be knocked up in no time," she said, drawing a giggle from June. "I'd love to know how

Harper is making out with her consort. Let's go ask her if she's turned over a new Leif yet!"

Ruby let out a loud guffaw, spitting out her tea.

Kat slammed down her fork. "Really, Yvonne? Around the children? And Ruby, do you think your sex reports are appropriate for little girls' ears?" She pushed back her unfinished plate of food.

"Why don't you mind your own damn business, tough girl?" Ruby snorted. "Kat isn't getting any yet. Betcha that's why she's acting all crooked."

"Falon says she isn't faring much better," Yvonne said. "Robby couldn't get it up, apparently. Three tries and counting!" They fell against each other in gales of laughter.

"Go to hell, the both of you. Are you done, Shyla?"

"No, not yet. Jeepers, what's got you steamed now?" She buttered another slice of toast and topped it with a thick swirl of partridgeberry jam. "Are you worried over Marcus again?"

Yvonne leaned across the table. "Is that what's eating you? Oh, relax. He's not one of your rescue animals from Western Path, you know."

Ruby tossed Kat a saucy grin. "I don't believe it's worry. I'd say she has the hots for him. He *is* handsome, and we wrote the book about crushing on peons, didn't we, Yvonne?"

Kat jumped to her feet. "I'll meet you at the stable, Shyla."

When the girl caught up with her later, Kat had finished grooming Pippa with the curry-comb and brush. She instructed Shyla to groom Joy while she changed their water and put down fresh hay from the loft.

Her ward's face creased with concern. "Something new is clearly bothering you."

"I can't talk about it. Forget it, alright?" She dumped the buckets, scrubbed them out, and refilled them at the well. A pair of orange tabby cats took a break from their mouse hunting to play around her. They meowed and bunted their heads against her legs while she worked.

Shyla grabbed the first refill to take back to them. "I hate to see you down," she said. "Feel like a ride after we feed them?"

"I'm not great company, but ok." She pasted on a smile for her ward's sake. "And it'll have to be a light ride. They'll need their strength to help wind up the harvest later."

"Oh, right. I almost forgot. Ms. Naomi said afternoon classes for the older students are cancelled today. We're helping with the harvest too."

* * *

After a gentle horse ride together and a midday meal of tomato soup and grilled cheese sandwiches, Shyla hurried off to go to the farm fields with her classmates.

Kat prepared for her initial session of clinic orientation. On her way, she met Yvonne on the road, carrying a covered woven basket. Her eyes were red and swollen from crying.

"What's with the sour puss?"

Yvonne slowed her pace. "On my way back from Puffin Bight."

Kat came to a standstill. "Not another newborn!"

She dashed away a stray tear. "Twins this time."

"Mother Almighty—what's happening to the babies?"

"No one knows for sure, but in the case of these latest two, they were conjoined and not viable once they left the womb. Oh, your peon wishes to have a word with you."

Kat bit back a cutting retort, taking Yvonne's frame of mind into account. "Listen, he's not *my* peon. Did he say what it's about?"

"Nope, but it sounded important. He's at the exercise yard."

She headed east to the peon quarters. The last time she'd

spoken with Marcus, she'd secretly wished he could become her consort. Now, she didn't know what to think anymore.

The yard gate stood open when she arrived. She poked her head in, but the yard was empty. Then she saw four peon recruits trundle toward her in single file, wheeling bales of hay in wheelbarrows.

Marcus lagged behind with a fifth load. When he saw her, he told another peon to go on—he needed to grab a drink from the well. The peon nodded and they carried on.

He left his barrow and walked to the well on the side of the exercise yard. With a quick look around, he tipped his chin in a gesture for Kat to join him.

Two senior peons walked past her and murmured hellos. When they disappeared inside the yard gate, she jogged over to him. Marcus grabbed her hand and pulled her along until they were both out of sight behind the yard's rear fence. A vein pulsed at his temple and the hand that clung to hers trembled.

"I have to say this fast. We don't have much time."

"What's up?"

"It's time you knew the truth, Kat. The real reason I'm here. I need medicine for my little boy, Hudson, and I need you to get it for me."

"What!" She pulled her hand from his. "You have a little boy? Where is he?"

"Back in Labrador," he said in a hushed tone. "He's contracted the same disease that killed my wife and wiped out most of the people in our hamlet. We believe it's tuberculosis. That's why I came here—we heard a rumour about drugs on the east coast that might save him. I chose to start my search here. Maybe I should've brought him with me, but I was afraid the trip would be too hard on him."

He'd lost his wife. Kat digested the rest of his words.

"You have access to the drug at your clinic, and once you get it, your plan to put me in that boat is back on. Please. Hudson is all I have left in this world. He's only three. If I don't get medicine to him soon, he won't survive."

"But why didn't you tell me before now?" Was it already too late? Another enormous secret? First Ms. Naomi, now Marcus?

"I didn't know who to confide in. I'd thought about stealing it myself, but it's impossible. They hardly let me out of their sight." His voice cracked and his eyes pleaded with her. "I wouldn't ask you, but I'm desperate. I hoped we were friends by now and you'd understand."

She struggled for the right words. The last thing she needed was to see him cry. It might unleash her own tears, still precariously close to the surface since last night.

"I hoped we were friends too," she said quietly. "But friends shouldn't keep such huge secrets from each other. And I believed you were becoming one of us."

"I was scared. I'm sorry." He glanced over his shoulder. "I...I am being integrated. But there's no elixir or drug, no brainwash or indoctrination or *anything* that will make me forget I'm a father. I can't disown my son."

"Who is he with now? Who is taking care of him?"

"My half-brother Trent and a few other people. The upshot is Trent will come for me soon if I don't return. Can you get enough for me to treat the others too?"

She thought it over carefully. If he didn't get the drug and leave, they'd soon have another outsider to deal with. Marcus was not to be her consort, but she could still help him. "Alright. I'll try to get the drug for you."

"Thank you! The shot they gave me the day they captured me —that guy Zealand took it from a cabinet in Exam Room 4. I don't know if you'll still find it there or not."

"This is my first day of orientation, but I'll do my best...Marc."

He bent down and pulled her into a tight hug. When his cheek grazed hers, she smelled his earthy male scent. His heart thumped against her collarbone through his sweat-streaked shirt.

"I'll be forever in your debt." Chin quivering, he let her go. He pulled the rabbit's foot from his pocket and pressed it in her palm. "Your turn, for whatever it's worth."

She gave him a crooked grin and pocketed the furry paw. "Better catch up with the others before someone sees us together." She peeked around the side of the fence as he ran back to the wheelbarrow and rolled it down the dusty road.

As she continued on to the clinic, concern for the sick boy eclipsed everything else. It shouldn't take much medicine to cure him. If his father got back to him in time, and the boy recovered...

She might never see Marcus again. But how could she not help?

Ms. Eleanor met her in the entrance. "Dr. Prudence is waiting for you in the staff lounge. I hope you have a great first day."

She nearly stopped Ms. Eleanor then and there. Would it be better to tell an elder about this? Wouldn't they try to save a sick child if they had the power to do so? But they wouldn't necessarily believe anything that came out of an outsider's mouth. After what she'd learned last night, she realized they had plenty of reasons not to trust his kind.

Marcus had convinced her of his sincerity and his genuine need for help. But why had he waited until now to ask? Either he'd told the truth, or she'd fallen for a fictitious sob story. Did he really have a sick boy? Or was it an elaborate lie to hide his actual intent, and his friendliness part of a strategy that might threaten their village or the whole island?

Could her ability to read people and her intuition be so unreliable?

Journal Reading #4

New World Anthology – Adult Memories Archives of Physical &
Sexual Abuse
Volume 1: The Early Years
Recorded: October 7, 2116

MY ESCAPE FROM SEX TRAFFICKERS AND STARTING A NEW LIFE

My name is Tori, I'm nineteen years old and I was born in the town of Avalon Shoals, Newfoundland. I do hereby swear my story is entered as truthful and to the best of my ability.

Twelve years ago when I was seven, my mother committed suicide by swallowing a lethal dose of pills she'd bought on the street. We had moved into her boyfriend's run-down hovel of an apartment in Grand Avalon only days before.

I had never met my real father because he left for work in Western Canada before my mom gave birth to me. She told me he'd landed a job in pipeline construction, but after a few weeks of work, the company folded. She said he went from that job to fighting out-of-control forest fires in Alberta. He died two months into the job from smoke inhalation.

The police arrested my mother's boyfriend for pimping and drug-dealing shortly after my mother had passed. Because I had no other family, social services placed me in foster care.

The family that took me in were as destitute as my mother. They lived in downtown Grand Avalon too, but they cared more for the neighbourhood alley cats they fed than they did about me. They nearly starved me and they never bought anything for me. I wore hand-me-downs from their other foster kids and learned from those kids how to shoplift to keep my stomach full.

After one year, I ran away from my foster home because the

oldest boy molested me. When the police caught me stealing bars and chips in a drugstore, I got placed in a new foster home with other girls. Around the time I was eleven, one of the new girls started being nice to me. Charlotte, or Charlie as we called her, was thirteen. She brought me food and snacks when she could because she thought I was too skinny. She told me I had beautiful hair and she'd comb and braid it for me. I came to depend on Charlie because no one else in my life seemed to give a damn about my wellbeing.

That was the same year the government, deep in deficit and with nowhere to borrow from, dropped the rates for foster care-giver allowances and expenses. Our foster parents had no other choice but to cut back on grocery costs. No surprise why I was so thin.

One evening, Charlie took me with her to her friend Willow's house. Sixteen-year-old Willow was nice to me too, though she wore too much makeup and smoked way too many cigarettes and joints. And she drank a lot. But when Charlie and I hung out there, Willow gave me pop, candy and gum. She offered me cigarettes too, but I didn't smoke. Once she bought me a styling new pair of black jeans and a cute, burnt-orange crop top. She told me she bought the clothes, but now I believe she'd shoplifted them too. Another time, Willow pierced my ears with a darning needle and gave me a dangly pair of earrings to wear.

One night, Charlie dressed up in the new clothes she'd "bought" that afternoon. The dress was short and skin-tight, and her shoes had the highest spiked heels I'd ever seen. She told me to put on my new outfit from Willow because we were invited to a New Year's Eve party. Charlie shampooed and straightened my hair, put red lipstick and glittery, gold eyeshadow on me, and told me I looked hot and foxy. When I tried on my new clothes and modeled in the mirror, I didn't recognize myself.

We walked to the party two or three blocks from our foster

home, slinking through the shadows that stank of cat piss to avoid the gangs of punks and delinquents that roamed Water and Duckworth Streets. The city in those days was in a state of decay and diseases were on the rise. Hep C was rampant, and the hospitals were filled to capacity with the sick and dying. Whenever you turned on the TV, it seemed another bad news story was breaking. I remember when the reporter on the six o'clock news announced the resignation of the premier of Newfoundland and Labrador, and no one else was the least bit interested in taking his place. Shortly after, the mayor of Grand Avalon up and quit. The city had become a hotbed of crime and political corruption, a cesspool of illness and addiction, a gutter of poverty and despair.

The downtown was dark and sultry, and the stink of sewage mixed with sea air rolled in from the harbour. When we arrived at the party on Queen's Road, I noticed I was the youngest one there. The row-house upstairs apartment was thick with smoke, throbbed with deafening music, and was filled with men of all ages. Willow and another girl talked and carried on with them, and drugs were all over the place.

This sort of scene was quite normal in those days. A couple of years before the schools shut their doors, my teacher played a video in class about the global crisis, and I remember the woman in the video said the world's youth were in trouble. They had lost confidence in the future and found escape through drugs and crime. She also said overdose reports and the youth suicide rate had skyrocketed to epidemic proportions.

At the time, I didn't realize how true those words were. Drugs, both legal and illegal, were around more often than not and had even taken my mother from me. This was the only lifestyle I'd ever known.

While Charlie got high with a boy on meth or crack, Willow brought me into a bedroom. She said if I behaved like a good girl and didn't give the men any trouble, they would take me in and buy me stuff, and I wouldn't have to live in a foster home ever again. I asked, what men?

Then a big guy with bad teeth and teardrop tattoos on his cheeks came into the bedroom. He gave Willow a wad of cash, patted her on the behind, and closed the door as she left.

That was the last I ever saw of Willow, or Charlie.

The man told me to stay put until he came back with a nice surprise for me. But he looked so scary and mean I didn't believe him. When he left the room, I waited for a bit and snuck out. I saw him near the stairs by the front door, talking to another shady character. Terrified, I ran down the hall to the bathroom and locked myself in.

The teardrop man pounded on the door and yelled for me to open up. I stood on the toilet and peered out the window. I was on the second floor, but a heap of garbage bags and discarded Christmas trees lay on the sidewalk below and would cushion my fall. I'd escape that way! I slid open the glass, squeezed through, and down I jumped. I scrabbled over the stinking trash and took off up the dark street.

But the man came around the corner of the house before I'd run half a block. When he caught up with me, he grabbed my hair, twisted it around his arm, and hustled me into a waiting van. I didn't know what was happening or where I was going, but there were three other frightened girls in the van too. One looked even younger than me. The man in the front passenger seat gave the teardrop man a bunch of money and what I guessed was a bag of drugs, and that was the last we saw of him.

Our ride in the van lasted overnight and into the next morning. Tired, thirsty and famished, I saw the sun come up. When the youngest girl cried, I cried along with her. What would become of us?

The van finally stopped. Through the window, I saw droves of cars and a big rust-bucket of a ferry at a wharf. The older girl who sat next to me told us the driver and his sidekick supplied girls to a sex trafficking ring in Nova Scotia, and we were about to become their newest batch of workers.

The driver parked the van aboard the ferry. Before he let us out, he told us more or less what the girl had said and added if we weren't friendly and compliant with the customers at our destination, he'd have no choice but to mess up our pretty faces and hurt us real bad. His sidekick also informed us they'd kill anyone who gave them trouble during the ferry crossing and throw the body overboard. We had no reason not to believe their threats.

As we got out of the van, I heard a commotion. Four more strange men bounded toward us with rifles and they stuck them into the backs of our kidnappers. They made the two men lie on the deck of the ferry. A crowd of passengers watched.

The oldest man told us not to worry, we were safe. They escorted us off the ferry and piled us into the back of an old pickup truck with Silas, the teenager among them. None of us had a real home to go to, so we put our trust in them. As we drove off from the ferry terminal, Silas filled us in. They'd bring us north to a tiny outport in the Codroy Valley. The women there would give us a decent home and he and the other men would make sure no one harmed or threatened us again.

They were true to their promise and my world changed drastically. I and the other girls were taken to a house with two elderly women who welcomed us as their own. We attended a one-room schoolhouse, learned how to do farm work, and adapted to rural life.

The villagers were not at all like the people I'd known before. No one took antidepressants or meth or heroin and I saw no pimps, prostitutes or criminals of any kind. There were no rat-infested apartments or flooded streets or neighbourhoods filled with rotting garbage and broken-down cars, and no polluted harbour or screaming police sirens that woke you up in the middle of the night.

The village folk didn't have any money like some people had back in the city, but we had healthy food and everything we needed.

As I grew to womanhood, I was blissfully ignorant of what was happening in the rest of the world. Yes, we knew of the global crisis and the war that raged on the mainland, but up to that point it had made only a minor impact on our lives. Our community was tiny and insulated, but so were the other outports due to outmigration and fewer births in the last fifty years.

Silas and I fell in love somewhere along the way, and last summer I became pregnant. Elated, I couldn't wait to have my baby. But in November, Silas left us to join in the war effort. Troops from our communities and from the Grand Avalon region enlisted to fight against the American immigrant uprising and infiltration into Canada. One third of our troops were women. A handful of our soldiers made it home alive, and my Silas wasn't one of them. Our island population took another disastrous hit.

But our elders are unflagging in their crusade to rebuild our numbers. Following the global collapse, a group of women who used to be city social workers and therapists joined our village. They told us the well-to-do townies had long absconded to higher ground elsewhere and had taken with them whatever they could to hide out from the riff-raff. Most of the people still in Grand Avalon were trying to flee the city because of looting and other crimes, extensive flooding, and poverty.

Like them, the women hoped to find a safe place to settle where they could live off the land. They'd brought with them a trunkful of documents and files of client interviews. They told our elders when the government offices and health facilities shut down, they didn't want to see the women's stories destroyed or left behind. The elders have since incorporated the stories as cautionary tales into our monthly meetings. Without them, most of our citizens would have no way of knowing how much times have changed. My entry today will be added to those files.

Along with the city social workers and four other young widows with babies, I and little Bianca made the voyage up the west coast last month to relocate to another community on the Great Northern Peninsula. They needed more women and children there and they intend to train us to teach school and to help run their medical clinic.

My daughter, the same as me, will never know her father, but I will tell her about his kindness and bravery as she grows up. I'm mostly thankful she will not experience the horrid childhood I'd suffered. And I vow to raise little Bee to be a strong, hardworking, fair-minded individual, and a worthy citizen of our new village home of Wild Cove.

CHAPTER TWENTY

Marcus straightened up between the rows of vegetables and caught himself as he swayed backwards. Leaning on his spading fork, he mopped his brow with the back of his work glove. His lower spine cracked with stiffness and his neck and shoulders ached. Unaccustomed to working long hours in high humidity and his endurance still not up to par with the other workers, he took a break and watched his fellow peons go on with their digging.

He couldn't help but agonize over what was transpiring at the clinic.

As the men uprooted potatoes, carrots, parsnips, turnips, onions, and beets, other workers came behind to gather them in hemp bags and woven baskets and stow them on horse-drawn carts. The carts then carried the trade surplus to outbuildings, and the rest of their vegetable yield to storage bins and root cellars before the autumn rains and tempests rolled in. Yesterday, he'd helped finish the corn harvest while others had picked Brussels sprouts, green beans, broccoli, cabbage, and pumpkins. The quantity of fresh, nourishing food the villagers had grown astonished him.

Today marked the culmination of the harvest, and not a day

too soon either. The sun had departed early in the week and the warm but freshening gale smelled of impending rain. Last night, Caleb had announced the advent of hurricane season was imminent. The barometer readings at dawn had confirmed it, forecasting the approach of a powerful and concentrated low-pressure system.

Over the past forty-eight hours, Marcus had toiled nonstop alongside the others to reap the bountiful fields, taking time off only to eat and sleep. Along with the corn, he'd helped harvest and store the hemp crop yesterday, and after breakfast today he'd lent a hand stowing dried hay in the barn for the livestock. He wasn't sorry to see the arduous chores come to an end.

In spite of his break to rest, rivers of sweat poured down his chest and back. His limbs twitched with fatigue. Or was it nerves? Kat had said she'd try to secure the medicine for him today. If she pulled it off, he could be on his way back to Minipi Lake by this time tomorrow. Over and over, he imagined Hudson, healed and happy. He saw himself squeeze the boy in a bear hug, kiss his small face, tousle his wispy hair.

He prayed for a positive end, but his head buzzed with every possible blunder or setback. What if the staff at the clinic busted the girl for pilfering drugs? Or suppose she did give him the drugs, but the peons seized him before he escaped?

Or what if she'd had misgivings about helping him at all?

He hated how the success of his quest rested on the shoulders of an eighteen-year-old girl. Little Kat, doing her utmost to help him. He tried but failed to shake off the torment of guilt and the crushing weight of his doubts.

A group of young girls hurried along as they skirted the farmland. They swung buckets of water, fulfilling their duty in the harvest by bringing refreshment from the nearby brook to the thirsty workers. His throat dry and scratchy, Marcus held up his hand to them, but they kept going.

Kat's ward Shyla trailed behind them. She approached him between the furrows of rich earth.

"Thirsty?" She gave him a friendly smile. "I'll get you a drink. Hang on."

"Thanks." He smiled back, grateful she'd noticed him.

She sprinted off, passing other workers swinging farm machetes in the plot adjacent to his. They were removing the buckwheat cover crop for green manure, and they, too, held up their hands to the girl for drinks. Marcus followed her movements to the brook where other youths had gathered to fetch water.

When he turned back to his spading fork, a distant movement beyond the buckwheat field caught his eye. The dark silhouette of a man lurked between the trees at the edge of the wild cherry orchard. As he stepped from the shadows, he gave a brief, furtive wave in Marcus's direction.

Peering closer, he recognized him instantly. His heart bounced with a sickening thud against his ribcage. Adrenaline flooded through his body.

His brother!

Marcus scanned the fields and the perimeter of the orchard to make sure no one else had spotted him. He signalled to Trent to hide.

He caught the attention of another peon in the field. "Need to take a leak, man." He pointed to the edge of the farmland. "Be right back."

The peon gave a brief thumb up and returned to his work.

He walked to the outer fringe of the cherry orchard. Anxious to hear Trent's news, it took the last ounce of his self-control not to break into a run. He pushed against panic, struggling to act casual in case anyone watched him.

His brother had concealed himself behind a dense stand of trees. He waved Marcus closer. "These inhabitants—I take it they're not a threat?"

"For you they are," Marcus whispered. He stared at the state of his brother in torn, wet clothes. "Don't let them see you! When did you get here—how is Hudson?"

"I made landfall last night. Didn't realize how wide the strait was, and the last half of the crossing was choppy as hell." Trent spat on the ground. "Took on water, the boat capsized, and I lost all of my supplies—knife and all. Thought I was a goner too, but I was close enough to swim to shore." He stared at Marcus with sunken eyes, his broad face ruddy with windburn, his scruffy hair and beard matted with dirt and laced with white brine from sea spray. Berry juice stained his lips and hands. "They're dropping like flies back home, bro. We need that medicine right away, before we all die."

"My son! How is he? Answer me, goddammit!"

"Did you find the drugs or the plant? Do they have it here or not?"

"Yes, they have the extract, but it's in short supply and well-guarded!"

"So why are you wasting valuable time farming, for chrissakes? I knew I should've come instead of you—you gutless wonder. I'd have those drugs by now. I would've saved him and everyone!"

Marcus stepped closer. "Would've saved him? Is it too late?" His chest constricted.

He heard a noise behind him. Shyla headed their way, swinging a bucket of water.

His brother slowly shook his head. "I'm sorry, Marc. We lost Hudson. I buried him myself, right next to Ava and her mother. Less than twenty of us left now. All the women and children are dead."

* * *

He stared at his scrunched fists. He didn't comprehend what he saw. Blood oozed from the raw, pulpy flesh of his torn knuckles. It streamed down his hands and around his wrists in runnels, but he felt no pain. The thick trunk of a tree stood before him, its scaly, grey bark stained bright red with blood.

In a daze, he tottered from the orchard and back toward the vegetable ground. Passing an overturned bucket in the grass, his jumbled thoughts reeled back to Shyla—and Trent. It jolted him out of his shock and he remembered Hudson again.

A strangled cry jerked from his lungs and jammed in his throat. When his feet hit the long footpath skirting the plots of farmland, he broke into a run. Some of the peons paused their work as he fled by. They leaned on their shovels and spade forks, muttering to each other. It didn't occur to him to care.

A heavy hand clamped down on his shoulder. His feet flew out from under him and he fell backward. Someone grasped his arms and spun him around.

"Where do you think you're going?" Bryce barked in his ear. A gasp of alarm replaced his show of anger when he saw Marcus's bleeding fists. "Hey, man! What happened to you?"

Marcus struggled to wrench himself away, but the peon was too strong. His legs buckled and he slumped against him.

"You need to get those wounds seen to, buddy, and whatever the hell else is wrong with ya. Let's go."

He sat in silence on the examination table while an attendant bandaged his hands. When two other members of the clinic staff entered the treatment room, their presence hardly registered.

He didn't answer any of their questions. Instead, he slouched over until his head hit the table. He found it hard to breathe, let alone form words. He covered his face with his hands, shutting them out. A numbing fog filled his brain, but an emptiness dragged his chest down into his gut. The more they talked, the more he shut down. He lay still and wished he could die too.

"We should admit him for observation," a voice said. "Let's get him upstairs."

Two of them assisted Marcus to the second floor and brought him to an inpatient room. When he sat on the edge of the bed, someone shook his arm.

"Here, drink this."

He felt a flask pressed to his lips.

"You'll feel better if you do." The assistant Robby stood over him. Not caring one way or another, Marcus tasted the familiar liquid, the Assimil-Lixir that blunted the sharp edges off every situation. In a half-stupor, he tilted the flask to his mouth in his bandaged hand and drank it down.

"There you go," Robby said. "We'll come back to check on you soon."

Eyes narrowed to slits, he watched as the consort left the room. Through the half-open doorway he spied a wheeled supply cart in the corridor, laden with medical supplies on one side and lined off with eight or more flasks of undiluted Assimil-Lixir on the other. When another staff member pulled Robby aside with curious questions, he saw his opportunity. He rolled off the bed and crept into the corridor. He seized all the flasks he could hold, fled back inside the room, and slammed the door. There was no lock, so he hauled over a nearby chair and jammed it under the doorknob.

The knob rattled violently. "Let me in, Marcus!" Robby shouted from the other side, banging on the door. "Now, this instant!"

As he guzzled down the potent liquid, he ignored the commotion in the corridor. Others had gathered. They pounded at the door and yelled to him, their voices heated and urgent.

A shadow of an intention, a purpose, formed in his brain. A

sense of needing to warn someone. About his brother. And a machete.

A girl? The ghost of an image dissolved before it could solidify. He guzzled down another. And another. The clamour of banging fists and shouts from outside the door faded. As he downed the sixth flask—or was it the seventh? —so did the last vestiges of shock, emptiness, and the burning guilt that had gnawed at him ever since he'd left his doomed son behind.

As he lost consciousness, he dropped the last flask to the floor and fell across the bed.

CHAPTER TWENTY-ONE

The season's first hurricane struck hard and fast in the middle of the afternoon.

At four o'clock, Kat sat in the clinic lab, preparing tinctures from medicinal roots the way Zealand had taught her at the beginning of her shift. She glanced at the medicine cabinet opposite her. She hadn't found the drug in the exam room where Zealand had administered it to Marcus on the day of his capture, so it had to be here in the locked cabinet.

The intern hovered nearby, studying slides under a microscope and making periodic notes in a binder. Kat had hoped she might get into the cabinet when he took his break, but he locked the lab door before he left and told her to take a break too. Since their arrival back, he'd given her no opportunity to access the drug.

At four thirty, Ms. Eleanor tracked her down in the lab.

"Go on home, dear," she told her from the doorway, chest heaving. Her yellow slicker dripped water on the floor and raindrops clung to her cheeks as she caught her breath. "I told Dr. Prudence to excuse you early. I'll run along too, as soon as I collect a few necessities to take back to your dorm. Who knows how long it'll take to wait this one out?"

"Anything I can do to help before I leave?"

"We have it under control. Before the storm ramps up to maximum intensity, the peons are double-checking that every area is secured. They've already brought the livestock back to their barns with enough food and water for the next few days. Oh, and Kat? The Origin Suites are closed temporarily. You don't have to check in for sexual relations until the hurricane is over. Three of the suites' roofs have sprung leaks since the storm picked up, and one of them is yours. They'll need repairs before they open again."

"Sure. No problem." When the elder left the lab, Kat blew out a frustrated moan. She knew how long the hurricane could last. If she didn't swipe the medicine now, Marcus might have to wait for days for her to get another chance. He'll be heartsick! And she couldn't blame him. No, his child's life depended on her now. She couldn't screw this up. She had to come up with another way.

But as the saying went, it's an ill wind that blows nobody any good. She wouldn't have intercourse with Colt quite yet. She thanked the universe for the small miracle.

Zealand sat glued to his microscope. She glared at him, willing him to leave the lab. When he glanced up and urged her to follow her elder's orders, she swallowed her disappointment and took off her lab coat. But she refused to admit defeat. She tried to invent an excuse to come back later.

A gale force gust of wind and rain nearly knocked her off her feet when she left the medical facility. Head bent into the escalating storm, she ran as fast as she could to her dorm. By the time she made it, her clothes were drenched.

She entered the common room of the girls' dorm and cleared the rain from her eyes. A crowd of children milled about. A few were stationed at the window alongside Ms. Jaleena and Ms. Lynn.

"Oh great, Kat," said Jaleena, "I'm glad you're here. You can help me check that the wards are safe and accounted for. Ms. Naomi should be back directly. She went to confirm the boys are rounded up and counted in the male quarters. We'll hold a head count now too, to make sure all women and girls are in for the night."

Minutes later, they realized they were one short. Kat's sister-ward was missing. They checked the bedrooms, the bathrooms, and even the closets, but no Shyla. Kat jogged to the Gathering House next door to find her, despite the fact Chef Vicky and the kitchen staff said they'd left the place empty.

She came back alone. "What about the schoolhouse?"

Ms. Lynn turned from the window. "There shouldn't be anyone there. Only the little ones had classes today because of the harvest, and I made sure they left with me."

"Oh, right, the older girls helped in the field today. Shyla told me this morning. When was the last time anyone saw her?"

"I saw her at the harvest," Grace offered, "bringing water to the peons."

"Me too," Ruby added. "But I don't remember seeing her since then."

Kat gnawed at her thumbnail. "I'll go check the school anyway. Maybe she went to get something. A book from the library, maybe."

"Put this on, then," Ms. Jaleena ordered. She held out her own raincoat.

"I'm already soaked. Back in a jiff." She left the dorm.

This time, the wind at her back helped propel her in the direction of the schoolhouse. She scoured the building, repeatedly calling Shyla's name.

"Where the devil did you go, you stupid kid?" she asked the vacant classroom. Her question bounced off the walls and echoed back to her.

Could she have gone to make sure the horses were alright? Kat wouldn't put it past her, the way she doted on them. But when she arrived at the stable, the horses were alone and everything had been secured. She didn't know where to check next.

Then she had an idea. Shyla may have taken it upon herself to fetch Kat at the clinic. Her ward knew they had to report to their dorm before the hurricane worsened, and she'd wanted to tell her sister-guide! Perhaps they had missed each other earlier. It made sense, didn't it? The clinic was a few yards behind the schoolhouse. She took a deep breath, darted outside again, and sprinted around the school through the driving rain.

Ms. Eleanor met her in the doorway, her shock of grey frizz standing straight up, her mouth reduced to a stern line. Her wide girth blocked the entrance to the clinic. "I told you to go home!" she roared into the gale. "And you're still soaking wet! Put on some dry scrubs and a raincoat before you go out again."

But when she told her of Shyla's disappearance, the elder took it in stride and joined in the search. "If she *is* here, it shouldn't take long to find her. You check the rooms on the first floor, and I'll enlist help to cover the second floor. Dr. Olivia and her intern are staying for the night—I'll get one of them to help me. They're tending to our rogue right now."

"Marcus? What's wrong with him?"

"Not sure. He fell ill during harvest. Bryce brought him in a short while ago."

Kat didn't have time to worry about him now. Probably nothing serious. She told the elder to meet her back at the entrance and they would leave together once they'd combed the premises.

She hunted for Shyla on the main floor. She checked the lab, the operating room, the examination rooms, and the staff lounge. But she couldn't find her charge anywhere. She raced back to the entrance to find Ms. Eleanor.

"No luck for us either," she told Kat. "But Zealand said Marcus asked to see you."

"Where is he?"

"He's been admitted as a patient. They're running tests to see what's wrong. He's in Room 3 upstairs, and I'm going with you."

She did some quick thinking. "Alright. I'll see what he needs, but are you sure we've covered the whole clinic for Shyla? Did anyone check the supply room and the janitor's room?"

"Why would she be in either of those places?"

"I don't know, but we've searched everywhere else. Please, Ms. Eleanor?"

"Very well, but it's getting worse out there. I'll meet you back at reception, alright?"

Kat agreed and took the stairs two at a time to the second floor.

Marcus lay motionless on the bed, eyes closed, face grey against the white pillow. A sheet covered him to his chest. For one breathless instant, Kat mistook him for dead. Zealand stood over him, drawing several blood samples from the inside of his elbow below an elastic tourniquet. When he inserted the samples in the blood tube rack and discarded the needle in a wall receptacle, he saw her in the doorway.

"Marcus wished to speak with me?"

"He's asleep again, but you're welcome to wait." The intern strode past her with the samples, leaving her alone with the patient.

She inched closer to the bed. As soon as the sound of Zealand's footsteps receded down the corridor, Marcus's eyes flew open and bore into hers.

"What's wrong, Marc?" she asked. "What on earth happened to—"

"Trent took Shyla," he whispered.

Her stomach dropped. "What did you say?"

"My brother has her."

"Your brother? He's here?" Her head swarmed with questions. Was this some sort of terrible prank? "Since when?"

He let out a feeble moan. "Since last night...I didn't see him until today. Came across the strait, same as me. I told you he'd come for me, Kat. We're blood, and this is what family does." His eyes filled with raw contempt. "Didn't you read about that in your damn schoolbooks?"

"So you don't need the punt anymore?" she whispered. "You'll go back with him, but you still need me to get the meds? But why did he take Shyla?"

"She's his insurance you'll meet his demands. His guarantee you'll help us."

Like a starburst, the truth dawned on her. "Did you fake your assimilation?"

"Bingo. I faked compliance to get access to the drugs. I dumped most of the dope juice your peons tried to force-feed me and played along, waiting for my chance to get my hands on your medicine. I was trying to save my little boy, don't you get it?" With great effort he sat up in bed, his eyes bloodshot, smouldering with unconcealed rage. "But you don't, do you? The way you were raised, not expected to love a mate or raise a child as your own, how could you? You'll never have to worry about putting someone else's needs ahead of yours or doing whatever is humanly possible to save them!"

Kat shrank back from the bed. This new side of him repelled her. In response, her own temper flared, but she checked herself. She set her jaw in renewed determination. "I know what it is to love. I know how it feels to care." She blinked away an image of Shyla's face. "How could you let your brother take her? You screwed us over, Marcus!"

"Screwed you over? Come on! You haven't the foggiest clue what I've lived through. You and your people in your insulated world are oblivious to the horror going on out there. Ava was an extraordinary woman who brought joy and purpose to my life. Can you imagine how it felt to lose her, and my stillborn daughter before her? And now..." He fell back on the bed. Tears glistened on his pale cheeks. "Hudson is dead. My brother came to tell me my son couldn't hang on any longer. I failed him and I failed my wife. It's over."

Kat's heart went out to him. "I'm so sorry," she said, her voice hoarse. "Is that why you're here in the clinic?"

"I wish I was dead too. My life has no point anymore."

"Listen to me, Marc. I'm miserable about your son, but what does it have to do with your brother and Shyla? Where has he taken her? What does he want?"

"An exchange. The immunity drug for Shyla's release. And don't tell the others. If you do, or if you don't take the drug to him by first light tomorrow, you might have signed the girl's death warrant." He rubbed his gauze-wrapped hands over his arms. "If it isn't too late already. I should've told you sooner."

"Oh, no..."

"You agreed to help me today. Did you find it where I told you to look? Trent needs enough for himself and for what's left of our people back home, before they all fall victim to TB or whatever it is."

She shuddered. "I found out it's kept in the lab. I tried to get it but I'm not here alone, and the meds are under lock and key. I can't simply waltz in and take it! I was waiting for my chance—"

"No, you can't wait! My brother is nothing like me. He can be cruel, and he's only gotten meaner since his pregnant girlfriend died last summer."

"Well, that's enough to harden anyone—but surely he wouldn't hurt a defenseless kid!"

"You must make sure Shyla isn't harmed. He has no moral compunction anymore, so if you want to save her, you better go now. And be careful. He stole a machete from the field."

"Where is he holding her?"

"The hiding place you showed me. The abandoned root cellar.

I told him where and how to find it. If he followed my directions right, he's holding her there."

"You told him where to hide her?" She gaped at him. "So you're part of this too!"

No answer. He turned into the wall as if to dismiss her.

She needed to think of the safety of her people. The protection of the sistership was paramount. As much as Shyla didn't deserve to come to harm, the threat this new stranger posed was far more sinister. If she delivered up their dwindled cache of Immunity-2 to him before more of its source was discovered or synthesized, she would place her people in harm's way when their immunity wore off. One epidemic could decimate the island's population.

She had to eliminate the threat. She had to stop that man from fleeing the island and bringing others back here. And if she failed to save Shyla in the process?

The needs of the many prevailed over the life of one expendable girl. She took a deep breath and left the room.

Ms. Eleanor stood in the reception area when she raced downstairs. "I couldn't find Miss Shyla, but I bet she's already at the dorm by now. We should go back."

"Zealand asked me to stay and help in the lab, seeing we have an inpatient." Kat hated lying to the elder, but it couldn't be helped.

"Very well. And change out of those wet clothes. Maybe it's safer for you to stay here tonight. I'll make sure we find your ward."

All she could manage was a nod. She watched Ms. Eleanor leave before she sprinted to the lab.

Twin fears compounded her worry for Shyla: not getting her hands on the extract or exposing herself as a thief if she did. This was her sole opportunity.

Bent over a microscope, Zealand barely acknowledged her.

"I've been told to work an extra half-shift, seeing you have pressing lab work." She stepped into the utility room to take off her wet clothes and empty her pockets, pulling on scrubs and a lab coat.

"Good stuff," the intern said. "Did he wake up and tell you what he did?"

"Marcus? No, what did he do?"

"Got his hands on some of our Assimil-Lixir stock and drank about a half-gallon of the shit. If Dr. Olivia hadn't forced him to puke most of it up, he'd have been toast for sure." He straightened up from his work. "Any clue why he'd do that?"

"Wow. No, not really." She buttoned her lab coat to hide her alarm. "Explains his grogginess, though."

"Would you please put those tubes soaking on the counter in the sterilizer? Then take the new specimens to the cooler until I can get to them."

"Sure." Hands clammy, she rubbed her palms on her hips. How would she get the drug with Zealand here? This isn't going to work! Shyla is doomed! She wanted to scream or hit someone.

A ploy popped into her head. She pulled on lab gloves, gathered the specimen tubes into a slotted tray and withdrew to the sterilization room off the lab. With shaking hands, she managed to fill the sterilizer with the tubes, switch it on, and go back to get the specimens.

She snatched up the specimen tray from the worktable at the precise second Zealand walked past her. Before she could change her mind, she released the tray from her hands and watched it fall to the floor. The glass tubes filled with Marcus's blood shattered on the tile. The splintering crash echoed through the laboratory and out through the hall.

"Damn it, girl! Look at this mess!" Spatters of blood speckled his white lab coat, trousers and his shoes. Tiny shards of smashed glass littered the blood-soaked floor. "Now I have to draw more samples from the patient. How could you be so clumsy?"

"I'm sorry—it slipped out of my hands! You go change and I'll get the janitor's supplies."

Swearing under his breath, Zealand fled to the washroom.

Kat wasted no time. She ran to the corner desk, yanked open the top drawer, and pawed around for the key to the medicine cabinet.

It wasn't there.

She pulled open the deep side drawer. Her pulse quickened. Atop a stack of file folders—a ring with three keys. She plunged her hand in and grabbed it. One of them had to fit.

She flew across the lab to the cabinet of controlled substances and jammed a key into the lock with jittery fingers. When it didn't work, she tried the next one on the ring. No luck. Damn it! The last one had to work.

Yes-s-s! The key released the lock and the door sprang open with ease. She read the label printed on a larger vial, grabbed it off the shelf, and slipped it into her pocket along with a fistful of syringes and needles. Trembling, she locked the cabinet and dashed back to the desk. She threw the ring of keys into the drawer, and before Zealand returned, she ducked out of the lab. When she reached the front door and flung it open, she stepped out into the pelting rain and took off in a dead run.

CHAPTER TWENTY-TWO

On the way to the root cellar, Kat made a quick detour to the storage shed behind the dormitory. She hauled the door open and secured it tightly behind her against the buffeting wind.

The first item she needed, a slicker, hung on the wall next to the door. She tugged it on over the clinic scrubs and tied up the hood. She grabbed a backpack, dropped the syringes, needles and vial of medicine inside, and swung it onto her back. She hurried to the opposite wall where hunting gear cluttered the rows of shelves. Standing on a stepladder, she stretched up to the highest shelf for the familiar leather hunting belt, complete with its sheathed survival knife. She buckled it around her waist and took a deep inhalation to calm her jangled nerves.

A huge part of her quaked at the thought of what she was about to attempt. The part that yearned to do nothing more than run to the shelter of her dorm or the safety of her elders, not face Shyla's captor. But what would Wren have done in her position? She wouldn't have chickened out.

She opened the shed door. The fierce gale smacked her in the face and threatened to tear her arm out of socket as she wrestled with the slippery handle. After a furious struggle with the rusted latch, she fastened the door behind her and ran out into the howling maw of the hurricane.

The storm had heightened significantly in mere moments. Ponderous, bruise-coloured clouds rolled down from the mountain peaks and raced overhead, eastward to the coast. Whirling winds had battered the cove into a riotous black bowl, churning and dotting its surface with whitecaps of spume and spindrift.

As she bent into the wind and bolted to the barrens south of Black Spruce Forest, she sent a prayer up into the universe she would find Shyla in the cellar, intact and unhurt. But what if Marcus's brother hadn't tracked down the cellar and had hidden her in another location? She cast her doubts and suppositions aside. She would rely on her tenacity and deal with any unforeseen developments as they occurred.

Fifteen minutes later, she made it to the marshy barrens. Her chest pounded from exertion. She stopped and leaned over, hands pressed to knees, gasping for breath.

The roaring gale tore the hood from her head and threatened to topple her over with every gust. Heavy rain slanted down on her in sheets. It soaked her hair and streamed into her eyes. Broken tree branches swirled past and giant fragments of brush cartwheeled across the sky. Shadows blended together as dusk fell, but she knew this area well enough to find the cellar blindfolded.

Almost there, Shyla. Hang on, girl.

When she made it to the incline at the edge of the barrens, she slid on her back down over the slick slope of land. Passing the wall of boulders that directed the way, she edged along the thicket of alders that hid the root cellar from view.

A movement caught her eye. Something large flapped wildly from a high alder branch—Marcus's red handkerchief. She passed the wet, windblown bushes to the cellar opening. The heap of deadwood she had used to conceal the miniature entrance was gone, most likely thrown aside and swept away by the storm. The low passageway to the inside yawned open in ominous invitation.

Before she entered, she found her voice. "Shyla?" she called out, clearing the cool rain from her face with her hands.

"Mm-mm-mm!" Her ward's voice, but as if gagged.

Kat pulled the knife from her belt. She crawled through the darkened entrance to the cellar's interior and straightened up.

"Well, well, well," a low, guttural voice greeted her. "Kat, is it? We've been expecting you."

The flat tone of the rogue's words penetrated her like a stab in the gut. Blind to the scene until her sight grew accustomed to the weak twilight that shone in, she answered. "Yes, Trent, Marcus told me you were here. Don't worry, Shyla. You're going to be alright."

The girl squeezed out a moan through her muted sobs. Kat could make out the two shapes inside, huddled by the rear dirt wall ten feet away: the hulking form of a man, and to his right, the slight form of her sister-ward.

With her sight now better adapted, she saw the man's arm around Shyla and the twisted strip of potato sack cloth tied across her mouth. She saw the whites of her enormous eyes, their sheen of naked panic, and the curve of a long, sickle-shaped blade held to the girl's throat—the farming machete Trent had stolen.

"Please let her go."

Kat's sack of moose jerky from the produce bin sat in his lap. He reached in for a strip. "All in good time." He chomped on the tough jerky. "You should know, your young friend here put up a brave front when I grabbed her. She fought me, wild as a wolverine, and can she ever cuss!"

"She's a child, you bloody fool."

He held up his left forearm to show four long scratches clawed into his skin, weeping blood. "See? Your little bitch did that! Even when I socked her in the gut and tied her up, she didn't shed a tear.

Did she learn her bravery from you? Ah, but she's a needy pup after all."

"I have the medicine with me, so we can do the trade. You'll have what you came for and you can leave us alone."

"A trade? Oh yes, a trade then, it will be. Not for the drug, though. Hand it over at once." The blade of the machete inched up under Shyla's chin. He flipped its flat edge to her jaw and pushed up, tilting her head back. "Unless you'd prefer to see this hole in the ground awash with her blood. I'll slit her from ear to ear. I don't want to hurt her but if I do, it will be on your head."

Kat had no cause to doubt his sincerity. She stepped toward them, pulled the backpack from her shoulder, and dropped it on the ground. "There it is. Should be enough to immunize thirty or forty people."

"The knife too, and your belt," he ordered in a gruff voice.

Having no other option, she stuck her knife back in its sheath. She undid the hunting belt and threw it down. "I've done what you asked. Now please, stick to the deal!"

He leaned forward, snatched the belt and backpack, and slung it behind him. "Not so fast. You see, I have another demand. A much more...personal one." He lowered the machete and fondled Shyla's long hair. "I've been alone for a long time, girlies. Far too long, with no one to love and...appreciate."

A thick silence filled the cellar before Kat could respond. "But I can take you to Marcus and you can both leave with the medicine. You have other family and friends back on the mainland waiting for a cure."

"We'll be leaving alright, but first things first. I've almost forgotten how it feels to be this close to a pretty girl. We have no children left, and the few women we did have in our hamlet, well, they've died too. Everyone and everything has been taken from me, but now the time has come for me to take—to take what *I* want. So you have a choice. You, or her?" He grabbed Shyla's jaw and yanked it close to his.

Kat cringed, noting that he'd also used strips of potato sack to bind her ward's ankles, and undoubtedly her wrists, obscured from view behind her. She watched in disgust as he glanced sidelong at her and dragged his tongue across the girl's tear-stained cheek.

Shyla fought against his grip and the gag. She let out a high-pitched whine. Her stricken eyes found Kat's, pleading.

"Leave her alone!"

He loosened the hold on his hostage. A look of pleasure danced in his eyes as his yellow teeth peeked through his beard. "Is that your decision? I'll let her go if you agree to take her place, and not put up a fight about it either. How old are you? Sixteen? Seventeen? You still a virgin?" The row of teeth grew wide.

Every molecule of her being longed to flee, escape, hide from him as fast as she could. The way he leered at her repulsed her. But she couldn't let him harm her ward.

"I'm eighteen." She choked out the words as she moved closer. "Take me instead."

"Smart girl," he said with a sly grin. "I thought you might see it my way, and I'm sure your friend won't mind switching places. Let her untie your legs, kid, and you can go. We'll be done and out of here by the time you tell the others."

Kat released her pent-up breath. At least Shyla would be alright. With quivering hands, she loosened the strip knotted around the girl's ankles. She reassured her no harm would come to her if they did what the man asked. When she started to untie her wrists, Trent barked at her.

"Don't bother with those, or the gag. She can run home for the rest. Come on, time's a-wasting."

Shyla stood but held back, fear mirrored in her eyes for her sister-guide.

"Go home!" Kat bawled at her. "I'll be alright. And go the way of the barrens, it's too dark through the woods. Go on, get out of here!" She pushed her hard toward the doorway and watched until she was certain the girl had fled. At the same time, Trent grabbed Kat roughly by the arm.

She turned and faced her captor. Her throat burned and her pulse hammered in her ears as she braced herself with grim resignation. "Are you going to kill me?" she whispered in the dimness of the cellar.

"What do you take me for, a monster?" A terse laugh. "I've got an idea. You should come with us."

"With you and Marcus?"

"Fucking right. We'll go home and you'll be my woman from now on. But hey," he said magnanimously, "we should let Marc have some of this honey too. I'm all for sharing with my brother, even if he is a wuss. That's me, generous to a fault."

Her mind raced. "But what about our island? What's stopping you both from staying and making a life here?"

"Girlie, let me tell you this. The last thing I wanted was to come here and burden my brother with bad news, but we need this medicine for ourselves and we couldn't afford to wait until he showed up. I was the best man for the job all along, not my brother. I can see life here is grand but taking care of the shit-show back home is priority number one. When illness is no longer a worry, we can all come back. There'll be plenty of men for you to contend with then."

The dull glint of his sneer sickened her.

"Where exactly is Marc?" he asked.

"He...he's at the clinic."

"Good, we'll go there shortly. This storm should provide an excellent distraction. How many others are at this clinic?"

She hesitated.

"Spit it out, bitch!"

"Two."

"Perfect. We'll catch them unawares and grab Marc."

Again, her body went rigid. Trent would terrify Zealand and Dr. Olivia and likely have no qualms about killing either of them if they got in his way. The galloping beat of her heart filled her throat as she tried to figure out her next move. A suffocating dizziness threatened and she fought against a strong urge to vomit.

Stooped under the low ceiling, he squeezed her arm hard. "Lie down." He placed the machete on the ground near his feet.

She cowered from the vulgar man, shaking from head to toe. His fetid breath hit her in the face. She recoiled.

Whack!!!

Stars bloomed in her vision as she wobbled backwards. Her hands flew up to shield herself as blood spurted from her nose. Biting back rising hysteria, she spun around and rushed to escape the cellar. But when she dove to her knees to slip through the hole, powerful hands caught her around her calves and dragged her back inside as if she were no more than a ragdoll.

He forced her over on her back and pinned her to the ground by the neck with the brute strength of one meaty hand. "Not a chance, my pet. Don't make me hurt you again. Lose the pants or I'll rip them off you."

Turning her face away from his, she spied the faint outline of the machete near his legs. In one last bid to dodge her fate, she felt the dirt floor with outstretched hands for an object to protect herself with. Her fingertips skimmed a large stone, a hair's breadth out of reach.

When he released her neck, she heard the metallic jingle of his belt buckle.

CHAPTER TWENTY-THREE

Kat remembered her self-defence training. The wild rage that had festered inside her begged for release. But she could use that rage to amplify her strength.

Before Trent had realized what she'd done, she jack-knifed her leg and kicked hard against his hip with her heel, knocking him off-balance. In a sudden burst, she twisted away from his clutches and leapt to her feet. Wheeling around him as he stood, she wrenched his arm behind him and yanked it up toward the back of his head.

He yelped in pain, but she acted too fast for him to attempt a counterstrike. She kicked hard at the back of his knees, driving him to the ground. She lunged to her right for the stone in the dirt. In one fluid motion, she raised it over his head and with all her power, bashed it against his skull. He pitched forward and fell face first into the dirt.

She'd tossed the stone away too soon. A sudden whimper told her he was still a threat. He tried to get up again, his bulk blocking the exit. Kat skittered away like a crab and crouched low against the side wall, beyond the last vestiges of pale dusk.

The side of her knee grazed the edge of something in the blackness. She felt for it. The bone knife she thought she'd lost weeks ago! Her hand closed around its narrow hilt.

Trent staggered to his feet, his hand to the back of his head. "You whore!" He weaved a few steps toward her and lunged for the machete.

She had to act fast—her only chance. She sprang at him before he could react or wield his weapon. She jumped on his back, clutched a fistful of his filthy hair, and lifted the makeshift knife. He bucked and thrashed. He tried to throw her off, waving the machete. It glanced and struck the low ceiling. A whoosh of air fanned her cheek. The curved blade missed her head by inches.

Kat's arm flew down in an arc at lightning speed. Her crude weapon found its mark. The narrow blade skimmed a rib and punctured him deep in his side. She gave it one last upward thrust.

He jerked and dropped the machete. His ear-splitting scream echoed out into the storm.

Kat withdrew her blade. She slid off his back as he fell to his knees and crumpled to the ground. Sweat stung her eyes as she kicked his bleeding, lifeless body.

"Damn right, you're a monster," she screamed, "but this is the last time you will ever hurt *anyone!*" On wobbly legs, she bent and placed two fingers on his neck. She found no pulse.

Her insides heaved. She leaned over and retched until there was nothing left. Shivering, she retrieved the backpack near the rear wall and put the knife belt back on. She pulled out a rag, wiped her mouth, and cleaned the gore from her weapon. In a daze, she rebuttoned her slicker. The bleeding from her nose had lessened, but the bones of her face throbbed from his blow. Her whole body hurt from the trauma and threat of his brutality.

Throwing the bone knife in next to the vial of medicine, she looped the backpack over her shoulders and turned to leave.

She paused to fumble in the pocket of her scrubs and pulled

out the rabbit's foot. Cursing on Marcus and his brother, she flung it at the corpse and crawled out into the swirling rain.

* * *

"...and that's where I left him."

"You're absolutely sure he's dead?" Ms. Jaleena asked, wringing her hands.

Kat dabbed at her swollen nose with the cool compress the elder had given her. "I'm sure."

Coming home to her dorm, she'd seen the light on in the common room. Before she entered, she'd rubbed her eyes in her sleeve, her lashes stiff with salty tears dried by the whipping wind. All four elders were there, along with Bryce and Caleb. Ms. Bee was dispatching the peons to rescue Kat when she stumbled in the door, rain dripping off her slicker, blood weeping from her nose.

The first time she'd seen him lose his temper since Wren's murder. She fell, limp, into the peon's arms. Caleb put his arm around her too and brushed muddy clots of cellar dirt from her hair. The commotion had brought her dorm mates from their bedroom down the hall.

"I wish you hadn't gone alone, though," Ms. Bee chided. "We didn't know what to think or what had become of you when the poor child burst in here, gagged and with her hands tied together!"

"I worried about losing valuable time if I came for help. If Marcus hadn't tipped me off, I can't imagine what might've happened to her."

"You acted alone and saved her, then eliminated the threat with no help from anyone." The old woman tut-tutted, but a flicker of a smile illuminated her face. "Bless your contrary heart, Miss Katrena."

"Let me get this straight," Ms. Naomi interrupted. "You killed the brother in self-defence, after he agreed to release the child in exchange for you?"

"I had to. He wasn't going to let me go. He intended to infiltrate the clinic to get Marcus and take us both back to the mainland with him. And I couldn't let him hurt any other people ..." Her voice cracked before going on, "...I cared about."

"You must've been terrified!" Falon said.

Harper, Ruby and Grace stared at Kat in awe.

Ms. Naomi studied her closely. "But suppose he had overpowered you? Are you sure it's only your face he hurt?"

"I'll be fine. Is Shyla gone to bed already?"

Shyla crept into the room, her hands wrapped around a mug. "You're alright!" she said, her voice ragged. As exhausted and traumatized as she must have felt, she put down her drink and stumbled into her mentor's open arms.

They hugged, and Kat stroked her feverish cheek. The teen's eyes were swollen from crying, her wrists and ankles red and chafed from the strips of hemp her kidnapper had used to restrain her.

"I knew you'd come to rescue me," she whispered.

Ms. Eleanor said they wouldn't let Shyla sleep in her own bed tonight, and perhaps not for a while. The girl had accepted the order without protest. "We gave her chamomile tea with a bit of St. John's wort to help her sleep. I'll brew another mug. By the looks of it, you could use some too." She bustled from the room without waiting for a reply.

"Bryce and Caleb," Ms. Bianca said, "tomorrow our girl will give you directions to that root cellar. You must collect the body and burn it."

"Please fill in the cellar too," Kat said. "I don't ever want to see it or go near it again." She wished she could erase the terror of the last few hours as easily.

"Will do," Bryce said. "Don't give it another thought."

"This will make one hell of a campfire story," Ms. Bee said, "and an exemplary new addition to our journals." She smiled at her with unvarnished pride. "I promise you'll be rewarded for your valour, Miss Katrena."

She swallowed around the hard lump in her throat. She didn't want to remember the cruel rogue's hands on her, let alone put the entire ordeal into words and relive it. She wished she could erase the horror of that night as if it never happened.

Kat should have rejected the trade he'd proposed. She should have restrained him with a martial arts move—immobilized him with a choke hold, for instance—at least long enough to flee intact with Shyla. But she'd been too afraid for the girl's sake to take the chance. The image of the machete at her tender throat flashed through her brain. She blanched, realizing how close she had come to losing her sister-ward, and possibly her own life in the bargain.

She still had to tell the elders what Marcus's brother had told her, about the others in his hamlet and their frantic need for medicine. How Marcus had kept his real mission on the island a secret. But she hated for anyone to find out she'd taken the Immunity-2. They wouldn't understand why she had jeopardized the health of their entire population. She should have told them why Marcus came to their island as soon as he'd confided in her. They might have given him a portion of medicine, sent him on his way, and none of this would have transpired.

Pangs of conscience tormented her, too, for hiding an outsider in the first place. Events may have turned out differently if she hadn't kept his arrival in September a secret, but it was too late to beat herself up over it now.

She didn't want to upset her ward any further tonight. One day's grace wouldn't matter. After a solid night's sleep at the elders' house and a day to recover from the initial shock of her capture, Shyla would hear about it with the rest of them tomorrow.

A nauseating headache thrummed at her temples. Every

muscle in her body ached with pain and fatigue. She dreaded morning. News of a second infiltrator would spread like wildfire to the other villages, and they would hail her as the heroine who'd saved her ward from her malicious captor and exterminated him.

She didn't need recognition for her purported heroism. She'd smuggle the vial of medicine back to the clinic at dawn tomorrow before the staff noticed its absence. Once she'd accomplished that, all she wanted was to forget.

She hugged Shyla once more, and the girl left with Eleanor and Jaleena. As she readied for bed herself, her bunkmates confronted her.

"What else is going on?" Harper asked. "We can tell something's up."

"Time to come clean," Ruby added.

"I'm dead tired." These girls were sharper than she'd given them credit for. "Please go to bed!"

Ruby pivoted on her heel. "Fine. Excuse us for trying to help!" She stormed from the room and crossed the hall to the washroom, slamming the door.

But her other bunkmates wouldn't back down. Falon moved closer, forehead puckered. "It's bad, isn't it?"

Kat fell on her bed and burrowed into her pillow. She told them to get the elders. Without delay, Harper slipped out of the bedroom while the others rallied around her. Kat dried her tears and tried to compose herself.

Her friend came back with Bianca and Naomi. "I managed to catch them before they left the dorm," she said.

The junior elder sat on the edge of the bed next to Grace. "What haven't you told us?"

Ms. Bee stood over them, her arms crossed. "Come on now. You've been through hell tonight, but if you know of something we all should know, speak."

She drew a shaky breath. "There are more of them. Marcus has people on the mainland waiting for him and his brother. If in due time they don't show, we have to acknowledge the possibility of those people... coming to search for them."

Falon gasped.

The senior elder's piercing stare bore into her. "The dead man told you this? Tell us every word the bastard said. It really shouldn't blindside us that there are more. Did he say how many?"

"No, Ms. Bee, but Marcus might know. His brother did say the survivors are male. Their women and children have all died."

"We'll get it out of him." She paced the floor. "At least now we can ready ourselves for them. We have time to alert the other villages and to prepare our shores for possible invaders."

"Our watchtowers and lighthouses should be manned around the clock, ASAP," Ms. Naomi put in.

Kat took another deep breath. "There's more. Earlier today, Marcus revealed to me that he had a woman—a wife, and a three-year-old son. Like most of his people, the woman died from an epidemic of some sort and then the boy contracted it. He came here for our Immunity-2 to save his son's life. But the boy died, and his brother came here to tell him."

"Marcus didn't reveal his true mission to us. Well, well, well. So the brother came for him and the drug?"

She nodded. "They don't have any meds to combat disease."

"It's quite likely the child had been too far gone to respond to meds anyway," Ms. Naomi said. "If we'd treated him sooner..."

"Maybe the others will sicken and die too," Harper interjected.

Ms. Bee glided forward to Kat's bed and placed her hand on her shoulder, the lines of her countenance etched with concern. "There are many unknowns, my dear. We haven't a clue how significant a threat these people pose. And Harper, if they are a threat, let's hope you're right. The disease they've contracted could be a major plus. Whatever the case, tomorrow we launch our new course of action." She swept toward the door and motioned for the young elder to follow. "Get some rest, sisters."

"Kat?" Falon whispered in the darkness when they were in their beds.
"What?"
"I don't know..."
"Say it, Falon."
She sniffled. "What will happen to us if more invaders land on our shores?"
Kat sighed. "Come on over."
The teen jumped from her own bed and climbed into hers. Pulling her close, Kat cradled her head to her chest until her whimpers diminished. Falon didn't realize Kat craved the comfort of a friend next to her, perhaps more than she did.
"We'll get through this," she soothed, stroking her hair. She held Falon until the girl's breathing evened out, giving way to soft snores in the darkness.
Though grateful her friend was able to sleep, Kat lay awake, motionless and hypervigilant. Her mind raced with flashbacks until the first wan light of daybreak glimmered through her dorm window.

* * *

The hurricane had not fully abated by the following night. Due to high winds, the elders held an impromptu assembly in the Gathering House instead of the usual Sundown Circle campfire. Even the elders and sisters from the three nearby villages braved the gale to attend, eager to catch a glimpse of their youthful new heroine.
They gaped in outrage at her facial injuries. Her nose remained

red and swollen from Trent's fist, and the bruises around her eyes had deepened to a dark violet since yesterday.

Though news of her bravery had already spread by word of mouth, Ms. Bee summarized her heroic deeds in glowing detail to her captivated audience. At the conclusion of her recap, Kat received a standing ovation.

While the thunderous applause still echoed in her ears, a throng of little sisters gathered around her, presenting her with tokens of their gratitude: small gifts from sea star collections to shell necklaces to dainty bouquets of autumn flowers. A few of the smiling girls gave her cookies they had made themselves earlier, and Ruby's ward June gifted her a suncatcher she'd made from an antique horseshoe and dangling beads of luminescent sea glass.

The little girls took turns hugging her. Yvonne, Nola and her bunkmates lined up next. Each of them embraced her and commended her for her courage. Harper's sister-ward, Alice, came forward at the end. She beckoned for Kat to bend down to her, but instead, she knelt by the short slip of a child.

"I'm sorry and sad the bad man hurt you." Ever so gently, she kissed Kat's cheek, careful to avoid her injuries. "Thank you for being a brave warrior and rescuing our friend Shyla."

Kat hugged her and told her she should be better soon.

When the excitement died down, their chief elder stepped to the podium and spoke again, her voice warmed by uncharacteristic tenderness. "Sisters and elders. Before we sing, I have something to say. Please bear with me.

"Working together with you to save our island from the devastation that has befallen much of our planet has been a labour of supreme love and commitment. Some of our citizenry might not believe it and may challenge my style of leadership, but rely on this: you are the sole reason I get up in the morning, why I wake each day with optimism and a clear sense of purpose. Our people and this little rock in the sea we call home are at the core of everything I say, and everything I do.

"Watching you grow into capable, intelligent individuals and realizing a vision that has come to life beyond our wildest expectations has confirmed we had the right idea from the inception of our governance. You should feel proud of yourselves too."

Her voice cracked with emotion, but she swiftly regained her poise. "But our work is far from over. Growth in our population and continued stewardship of our natural world is essential. And now with the likelihood of others living close to us on the mainland, we must step up tactical efforts to keep our coastlines better defended from outside threats. Work on the lighthouses and watchtowers is ongoing, with priority given to those on the north and west coasts. In the weeks to come, we'll reinforce our security by making use of more weaponry. We will collect all available artillery to better protect our shores. We will also accelerate self-defence classes for all our citizens and initiate them at a younger age, and to include our consorts in weapons training as we have always done with our sisters, elders and peons.

"Now it's time for a momentous announcement from our health coordinator," she said. "If you please, Ms. Eleanor?" The old woman retreated from the podium.

The elder acknowledged her colleague and stepped forward. "Good evening, my sisters. I promise I won't keep you long, but this is tremendous. I'm thrilled to be the bearer of exciting news. Our Labrador sister village of Eagle Inlet informed us recently that they've discovered ample growth of a new species of spiked sage orchid. This bog orchid grows among the coralroots in a previously unexplored fjord in the Mealy Mountains, and their horticultural experts are testing it for its efficacy as we speak.

"If trials are positive, they'll use plant tissue culture to micro-propagate the flower and to teach us how to cultivate our own. And because the northern Inuit people shared their discovery of the original orchid and development of its extract with us, we in turn will share our new find with them. This will ensure a new and abundant source of Immunity-2 extract for all our futures and for generations to come. To mark this discovery at our eleventh hour, let us sing in a celebration of hope for its success!"

The assembly burst into another spontaneous round of clapping and enthusiastic cheers. Kat drank in the joyful, shining faces, their happiness working as a balm. But her exhaustion from yesterday and her insomnia last night had taken a debilitating toll. She had no energy or inclination to join in the singing. She would turn in as soon as she checked on Shyla. She might not get much sleep, but she needed to block out the world, at least for a few hours.

"Thank you, sisters," the elder finished. "Please place your chairs in a circle and we'll begin." The women descended from the stage while everyone rearranged their chairs.

Ms. Naomi pulled Kat aside. "I need to speak to you in private. Come on back to my room."

Bone-weary but curious, Kat followed her outside into the gusty night. The pair crossed the windswept pasture to the elders' home.

With the house to themselves, Naomi showed her into the cozy sitting room and lit the vintage blue-glass lamps on either side of the overstuffed sofa. She picked up Jaleena's ukulele that leaned against the embroidered cushions and propped it in the corner behind her. She told Kat to make herself comfortable while she brewed a pot of herbal tea.

Sitting on the sofa, she wished this could have waited until the next day. The whole house shook and the window shutters rattled as the relentless gale howled. When the elder reappeared from the kitchen with an antique silver tea service, she set the tray on the coffee table, poured two cups from the teapot and sat beside her.

She searched Kat's battered face. "For starters, Miss Shyla told me you brought some Immunity-2 to that Trent character."

"She...she did?" When Kat had brought it back to the lab this morning, she'd thought herself in the clear. Her body tensed. "Who else knows?"

"No one, and your secret will not pass these lips, or Miss Shyla's either. I get why you did it. I'm fairly sure I would have done the same in your place. You've grown to love your ward, and at the time you couldn't see any other way to save her."

She stared down into her china cup. "I put our people in danger."

"But you persevered and won the battle with that rogue. You relinquished no drugs in the end. And now that we've found a whole new source, none of that matters anymore."

Kat let out a heavy breath. "Thank you for keeping it a secret."

"You're welcome. Now, I've plenty more to discuss with you. Bianca and I have talked it over with the other elders, and we are excusing you from the breeding program. Because of your remarkable heroism and your natural proclivities and talents with animals, we have re-evaluated your future. We release you of all duties and consent for you to pursue your passion. You will go to Western Path as a senior ranch apprentice later this fall and take up a permanent career there as originally planned."

Setting her cup and saucer down with a clatter, Kat threw her arms around Naomi and clung to her. For one elated instant, she forgot about her discomfort. "Oh, my stars—you don't know how much this means to me!"

The elder's eyes twinkled. "I have a fair idea."

"Thank you from the depths of my soul!" she cried, jubilant. "When do I leave?"

"Hold on," Naomi said with a chuckle. "We need you here for several weeks yet, for the Festival celebrations and following our year-end Elder Summit. Wild Cove has been awarded the honour of hosting the Summit this year, so we can use extra help to prepare for that too."

"That's quite alright by me. I'll be counting the days, though."

"We are filled with admiration for you, dear. How you saved your ward on that terrible night took exceptional courage." She placed a warm hand over hers. "Just as our dear Wren traded places with you that day, you did the same for Miss Shyla. I'm beyond relieved you didn't have to sacrifice yourself for your ward too."

No, she thought, she hadn't given up her life for Shyla, but she'd never taken a human life before either. Trent had forced her hand. He'd given her no other choice.

"I'm not as proud of myself as you are. I was no hero to Quinn, especially during that swimming lesson at the pond." Her face burned hot again and a suffocating deadweight filled her chest, remembering how the little girl had fought to keep her head above water. How she'd ignored the child's pleas for help. How she hadn't pulled her out until she'd gone under for the third time.

"Point taken. You completely overreacted to her childish demands and her shortcomings and took it out on her with your troubling actions. Or inaction, in this case."

"I was a total dick to her, Ms. Naomi. I criticized her when she was tardy or didn't do her chores properly, and I teased her when she couldn't keep up with me on our forages through the forest. On our way to her swimming lesson, she told me she hated me and wished Ruby was her mentor instead. It makes me sick and ashamed how I treated her for not being able to stay afloat, for not getting the hang of it as quickly as I expected. Thinking about it now, how I punished her by scaring her that way..." She blinked back tears. "But I would *never* have let her drown. You do believe me, don't you?"

"I believe you. I'm curious, though. Did she remind you too much of yourself at that age? Anyway, you're more mature now, it's behind you, and I hear Quinn is doing well. She's gotten over her fear of the water and is taking lessons again. And you've learned from this and you're a better person for it. I'm convinced you were in deep pain over Wren. You felt rejected by her and believed we did you wrong by sending her away, which is why I think you acted out the way you did."

"I was still a douche of the highest order."

"What's done is done. I have one more matter to discuss with you." The elder lay down her cup and rose from the couch. She walked across the threadbare rug, hands clasped behind her. "What I'm about to tell you is a well-guarded secret. I have not been given permission to reveal it, but I'm going to anyway. You must promise not to tell another soul."

"You have my word. You will keep my secret, and I will keep yours."

Naomi stood at the window and gazed out into the blustery night. "You know the breeding program has been in effect for many decades. It was the brainchild of our former matriarchal government as a way to repopulate more expeditiously, so the vast majority of our births since its inception has resulted from mating with consorts. After my twentieth birthday, naturally I too was expected to procreate. I conceived in my first month at an Origin Suite in my village of Eastern Arm. I had a successful pregnancy, though I was riddled with anxiety throughout all three trimesters."

Kat studied the smooth lines of her elder's profile. "Was the baby exchange in effect in those days too?"

She remained at the window. "An excellent question. I was part of the second generation to participate in the new exchange component of the program. Many of us were miserable about the new regulations of It Takes a Village, to say the least. To make matters worse, I had a long, harrowing delivery. The infant had been in a breech position, and I lost a lot of blood. But somehow, I survived."

"I'm so glad you recovered, but how awful! What about the baby?"

She came to sit by Kat again. "It was tiny and underweight but otherwise fine. But they couldn't stop the bleeding and had to take my uterus, so the baby I birthed would be my last. I fell into a deep sadness. And it felt nothing like a typical postpartum depression you may have heard about. The expectation to give up the only child I'd ever conceive killed me. It bucked against everything my maternal instinct told me. To this day I challenge the transfers and have lobbied with the elders, albeit unsuccessfully, to end them."

Kat leaned forward. "Back to your story. What happened next?"

"The elders took pity on me. They consented to let me apprentice as a junior teacher in the village where my baby had been transferred."

Kat's mouth dropped open. "Well, isn't that the crow's toes! You mean here in Wild Cove?"

"Yes, I taught as a junior for six years," she said, her voice tinged with pride. "Then I graduated to Senior Educator and Humanities teacher, and Ms. Lynn stepped into my old position. The following year I was inducted into the eldership."

"Yeah, I remember." Kat lowered her eyes. She'd always felt the junior elder softened the rigidities of their governance in ways the other leaders never could.

Ms. Naomi smiled. "Of course, the deal came with a catch. At no time could I reveal my identity to the child or to anyone beyond the elders. And I did agree to it..." She fidgeted with her hands in her lap. "Until now."

Kat froze, not sure she understood. "You don't mean..." She sprang to her feet. "Are you saying—"

"Yes, my dear Kat," Naomi said softly as their eyes met. "You are my daughter."

CHAPTER TWENTY-FOUR

It took two weeks for the overdose to clear Marcus's system. During those weeks, he remained at the clinic under intensive care and close supervision.

For the better part of the first week, he slept. His dreams were filled with Hudson and Ava as if they were still alive and together as a family.

In one dream, an older likeness of his son rambled on about the particulars of his day. He asked probing questions about the island and groaned at his father's corny jokes and puns. In another, the three of them fished together back at Minipi Lake, but this time, the waters teemed with abundant life. When they hiked home to their shack, they fried up their generous catch for supper and played Yahtzee and Crazy Eights afterwards. And in another dream, he and Ava told Hudson stories from the past, tales they'd heard from their grandparents about how the world had once been different. So wondrous and beautiful when they were children like him.

Each time he roused himself from sleep, he cried anew, crushed and alone.

One morning during his second week of hospitalization, Dr.

Olivia and Zealand came into their patient's room and closed the door. The doctor informed him of Kat's valiant rescue of her sister-ward from his brother. Zealand told him she had to stab Trent to save herself, and his brother hadn't survived.

When he'd recovered from the shock of it, Marcus understood the girl had had no choice. He wished Trent hadn't resorted to kidnapping and violence to fulfill his purpose. He wished he had done something to forestall him instead of giving him a hiding place. When he asked if his brother had hurt Kat or Shyla, they reassured him that beyond the emotional trauma and a few minor injuries, they believed both girls would be alright.

Thoughts of Kat had preyed on his mind throughout his recovery. Somehow, in some way, he resolved to make it up to her and Shyla for what he and Trent had put them through.

When they left him alone again, he wept for his brother and his wretched life. Whether he deserved any sympathy or not, Trent had been the last member of his family to die.

A few mornings later, as the blue-grey dawn filtered through the clinic room curtains, he experienced a dream so true-to-life he could have sworn he'd already woken up.

He is saying good-bye to the pint-sized boy he left behind. He kisses his cool cheek and hugs him close—not ready to surrender him, never ready to close that door, yet he knows he has no choice. At last, he lets his son go and watches as he reunites with his mother, running into her waiting, welcoming arms. He tells Ava he'll try to be brave in this new place. He will make both her and Hudson proud of him for staying the course. And he promises them, and himself, he will never become a sadistic thug like his brother.

At the end of the two weeks, a restless energy took hold and Marcus felt well enough to leave the clinic and pick up his life with the peons. Straightaway, he noticed a marked difference in the behaviour of the other men towards him. He knew they had no real comprehension of the pain and sorrow he'd lived through, but they seemed to share an unspoken spirit of camaraderie with him, the latest full-fledged peon among them.

He resumed his weight-training workouts, particularly targeting his upper body for his pending occupation as one of the island's newest water-taxi skippers. He threw himself into his chores and duties with dogged resolve, grateful for the exhaustion of mind and body to eclipse his thoughts and dreams when he fell in bed at night.

Sustained by the new healthy diet and standard minimal doses of Assimil-Lixir, he grew stronger with each passing day. He contemplated his life. Was his future a fait accompli, or something else? The tender beginnings of a different outlook were slowly taking root. Not yet contentment, and certainly not happiness, but more of a resigned acceptance.

It felt akin to hope.

CHAPTER TWENTY-FIVE

ONE MONTH LATER

The day of Shyla's departure from Wild Cove had arrived. Kat also had a deadline to meet today: to pen the journal entry she'd promised the elders before her own life took a new and unanticipated turn. Instead of using the deck of the Origin Suite she now shared with Harper, she chose to write her story overlooking the cove from the peaceful comfort of the elders' veranda.

She expected to have her writing completed by the time all the village citizens gathered at the harbour wharf to see Shyla off. That gave her three hours. Angling her table and chair to face the sea, she pulled a blank sheet from the sheaf of sun-bleached hemp paper. A cool breeze with a hint of damp salt air wafted in, fluttering the stack of pages. She placed her mug of peppermint tea on top to anchor them and wrapped her shawl more tightly around her shoulders.

Though no one else had landed on their shores since, Kat knew she needed to share her own cautionary tale to educate and warn other women of any future threats. Her story of Shyla's rescue would be added to the New World journals. She knew what to exclude from her account, as Naomi had ordered. To avoid any potential whiff of favoritism between them, no one would ever learn of their kinship, and the other elders would never know Naomi had revealed it to her. Though Kat had often pondered about her origins, she had harboured resentment at first for not knowing sooner. Living with the disclosure for a few weeks had softened her stance. It gave way to an understanding of why she had often felt a unique connection with the junior elder.

As for Naomi's opposition to the newborn transfers, she saw her point but hadn't yet decided how she felt about it. In her view, pros and cons existed on both sides.

She thought of her sister-ward. Shyla had celebrated her fourteenth birthday yesterday, and now stood three inches taller than her. They'd finally gone for a swim together at Timber Pond, joining in the fun with the other wards and guides on a warm fall afternoon. She'd watched Shyla excel in the Festival contests at Grand Lake in mid-October, and the teen's first-place victory in the 400-metre dash had filled her with bittersweet pride. To give the younger runners better odds, Kat herself had opted out of participating in the races this year.

She and her ward had grown closer over recent weeks while Shyla finished her fall semester and prepared to leave for her Western Path junior apprenticeship.

The girl's nightmares since the root cellar ordeal were less frequent now. The surprising news—of Kat's withdrawal from her ranch placement to allow Shyla to go in her stead—likely played an integral part in her ward's emotional recovery. When she announced her wish three weeks ago for Shyla to replace her, the elders had been astounded and puzzled. But they'd put their heads together and had come up with a novel proposal for Kat's future: formal training under Ms. Lynn as a junior teacher. In light of her recent show of courage and new maturity, Ms. Bee deemed her a worthy role model for their girls and had recommended the teaching career. Kat had thought about it, and the following day she accepted the proposal and got the go-ahead to tell Shyla the news herself.

They had made special treats for the horses that morning, cookie balls made of oats, maple syrup, carrot, and diced apple, and were feeding them the snacks when Kat told her. She remembered how the girl's face lit up at the news, promptly followed by her distress over her mentor forsaking her life's ambition.

"Not to worry," she'd said as she held out a third treat to Joy and stroked her warm, brown muzzle. "I believe it's possible you cherish horses even more than I do. And remember, you must wait until the end of October before you go."

"But are you sure?" Shyla had pressed again.

"Don't give it another thought, kiddo. Besides, Pippa is still here for me whenever I need my horsey fix. In fact, Ms. Bee has given up riding because of her arthritis and is letting me adopt her. Pippa herself is getting on in years, which means she won't help with farm work anymore."

"I know you'll make an excellent teacher, but I'm afraid you'll resent me one day for taking your position."

"Not exactly my position, as you'll train as a junior, not as a senior apprentice. But I promise I won't resent you or my decision. Oh, did you hear about the two alpacas being delivered next week? And a pair of goats? Soon there'll be plenty more animals around the cove to keep me content."

In private later, Ms. Eleanor had hinted to Kat of an eventual candidacy for junior eldership. The distinguished role would become available one day, as not many more years would pass before Ms. Bee retired from active leadership and Naomi advanced from junior to senior level. The general conjecture among the sistership predicted Eleanor as the front runner to fill the vacancy as Chief Elder.

Did Kat have what it took to guide a schoolhouse of girls? Even more, did she want to run for junior eldership when—or if—she achieved tenure status? The only way to know if she had teaching ability was to go for it, and she had plenty of time to decide on running for office within the eldership. In any case, she would pick up the reins of her new teaching career at the same time she picked up those of darling Pippa.

Her thoughts rambled back to Marcus. Zealand and the other clinic staff said he'd recovered from the worst of his grief and depression and was striving to put his hellish past behind him. Though Kat knew he still ached for his wife and son, he seemed to have reconciled himself to his fate and had adapted to life here. The elders proclaimed this unprecedented naturalization of a fully-matured outsider an unqualified success. He'd passed his examinations and was issued the standard grey peon clothing to replace his recruit green. His integration had ended with the ultimate test of his loyalty: a set-up where, to all appearances, he was given the opportunity to escape the island by boat with a stock of provisions and a limited quantity of Immunity-2.

He didn't take it. He'd told the elders if any of the people of his hamlet had survived, he suspected they were too sick or impoverished to pose a threat. He confided in Kat how he'd asked to take a crew of peons to Minipi Lake and to bring back anyone who remained. The elders had rejected his request.

Marcus had yet to learn of the new role intended for him. Simply put, the island needed more children. Yet another newborn had died last month, much to the mortification of the elders and the nursery staff. Consequently, substantial hope had been pinned to the success of the younger breeders turning the numbers around. Harper had announced she was pregnant a few days ago, and Ruby's period was late. So far, Falon had made no such announcement.

With the low birth rate as the rationale, Ms. Eleanor had

privately told the sistership Marcus would be the first man ever to transition from peon to peon-consort for entrance into the breeding program. This would happen sooner rather than later, to tap his gene pool and give their population a better chance to survive.

Kat remained in turmoil over Marcus and his previous duplicity. As much as she commiserated with his significant losses, the concealment of his true mission still festered. Despite her many efforts to help him, his silence, dishonesty and his lack of warning about Trent's arrival had put her, Shyla, and the rest of her people in great peril. His telling Trent about her root cellar had been the last straw for her. Passing his loyalty test had helped, but she remained light years away from trusting or befriending him again. She resolved to keep a close eye on him whenever and wherever possible.

Tumultuous waves crashed against the rugged shore, a by-product of yet another recent hurricane which had made landfall late last week. Would the storms worsen from year to year? Would the climate become as unbearable as it had in much of the rest of the world? Or would their island home remain a pole star, a mecca, and a target for more outsiders and invaders?

She smoothed a hand over the sheet of paper, still blank. With a resonant breath, she pulled her chair in closer to the table, dipped the nib of her pen in the inkwell, and began to write.

New World Anthology – Adult Memories Archives of Physical Assault
Volume 2: Acts of Violence Against the Sistership
Recorded: October 31, 2203

My Account of Physical Assault by an Outsider:

My name is Katrena, I am eighteen years old, and I live in the Western Newfoundland village of Wild Cove. I do hereby swear my story is entered as truthful and to the best of my ability...

ACKNOWLEDGMENTS

With much gratitude, I wish to thank my husband Paul for his enthusiastic and unwavering support in my writing endeavours. I couldn't imagine this adventure without him.

I warmly acknowledge my second readers, Denise Mills and Brian Eddy. I am indebted to them both for their feedback and never-ending encouragement. In addition, I thank my circle of blogging authors for their words of wisdom, guidance, and inspiration. And I will always be grateful to my family and friends for keeping me on track with their caring and generosity.

Special appreciation to my publisher, Running Wild Press, and my editor, Lisa Kastner, for her professionalism and attention to detail. Thank you for believing in my latest work and helping me bring it to life.

Last but not least, I thank you, the reader, for supporting my writing. Your interest in finding out "what happens next"—particularly in these trying times—is truly what this journey is all about.

ABOUT RUNNING WILD PRESS

Running Wild Press publishes stories that cross genres with great stories and writing. RIZE publishes great genre stories written by people of color and by authors who identify with other marginalized groups. Our team consists of:

Lisa Diane Kastner, Founder and Executive Editor
Joelle Mitchell, Licensing and Strategy Lead
Cody Sisco, Acquisition Editor, RIZE
Benjamin White, Acquisition Editor, Running Wild
Peter A. Wright, Acquisition Editor, Running Wild
Resa Alboher, Editor
Angela Andrews, Editor
Sandra Bush, Editor
Ashley Crantas, Editor
Rebecca Dimyan, Editor
Abigail Efird, Editor
Aimee Hardy, Editor
Henry L. Herz, Editor
Cecilia Kennedy, Editor

Barbara Lockwood, Editor
AE Williams, Editor
Scott Schultz, Editor
Rod Gilley, Editor

Evangeline Estropia, Product Manager
Kimberly Ligutan, Product Manager
Pulp Art Studios, Cover Design
Standout Books, Interior Design
Polgarus Studios, Interior Design

Learn more about us and our stories at www.runningwildpress.com

Loved these stories and want more? Follow us at runningwildpublishing.com, www.facebook.com/runningwild-press, on Twitter @lisadkastner @RunWildBooks